cb

SO-AXJ-522

**One agent is already missing,
and now the U.S. government's most
confidential secret is in danger of falling into
a power-hungry dictator's hands.**

**The top-secret agents of ARIES
are the world's only hope.**

Agent Jared Sullivan: The ex-search-and-rescue
specialist thought he'd left his high-risk world
behind, but when unexpectedly reunited with
a face from the past, he found himself wrapped
in a web of danger more perilous than he'd ever
imagined.

Samuel Hatch: The wise ARIES director knew
that only one man could bring his agent home
alive and solve the mystery of the stolen gems.
He would do whatever was necessary to convince
Jared Sullivan to take the mission. Even withhold
the truth...

Dr. Roman Orloff: Officially, the American-
educated neurologist had returned to Rebelia to
heal the countless wounded victims of General
DeBruzkya's brutality. But he was also part of
an intricate ARIES plan to save their agent—
and possibly the world.

and finally...

Dr. Alex Morrow: The missing operative has
finally been found, but what dangerous secret
is the good doctor hiding?

Dear Reader,

This month we have something really special in store for you. We open with *Letters to Kelly* by award-winning author Suzanne Brockmann. In it, a couple of young lovers, separated for years, are suddenly reunited. But she has no idea that he's spent many of their years apart in a Central American prison. And now that he's home again, he's determined to win back the girl whose memory kept him going all this time. What a wonderful treat from this bestselling author!

And the excitement doesn't stop there. In *The Impossible Alliance* by Candace Irvin, the last of our three FAMILY SECRETS prequels, the search for missing agent Dr. Alex Morrow is finally over. And coming next month in the FAMILY SECRETS series: *Broken Silence,* our anthology, which will lead directly to a 12-book stand-alone FAMILY SECRETS continuity, beginning in June. In Virginia Kantra's *All a Man Can Be*, TROUBLE IN EDEN continues as a rough-around-the-edges ex-military man inherits a surprise son—and seeks help in the daddy department from his beautiful boss. Ingrid Weaver continues her military miniseries, EAGLE SQUADRON, in *Seven Days to Forever*, in which an innocent schoolteacher seeks protection—for starters—from a handsome soldier when she mistakenly picks up a ransom on a school trip. In *Clint's Wild Ride* by Linda Winstead Jones, a female FBI agent going undercover in the rodeo relies on a sinfully sexy cowboy as her teacher. And in *The Quiet Storm* by RaeAnne Thayne, a beautiful speech-disabled heiress has to force herself to speak up to seek help from a devastatingly attractive detective in order to solve a murder.

So enjoy, and of course we hope to see you next month, when Silhouette Intimate Moments once again brings you six of the best and most exciting romance novels around.

Leslie J. Wainger
Executive Senior Editor

Please address questions and book requests to:
Silhouette Reader Service
U.S.: 3010 Walden Ave., P.O. Box 1325, Buffalo, NY 14269
Canadian: P.O. Box 609, Fort Erie, Ont. L2A 5X3

The Impossible Alliance

CANDACE IRVIN

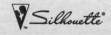

Published by Silhouette Books

America's Publisher of Contemporary Romance

Special thanks and acknowledgment are given to Candace Irvin for her contribution to the FAMILY SECRETS series.

For Sarah Ashley, my own little angel on Earth. Happy Birthday, honey!
Acknowledgments: As usual, I was out of my depth when I started this one.
My deepest gratitude to the following friends for lending me their expertise so that I could tread water long enough to write it:

Captain Norton A. Newcomb, U.S. Army Ret., Special Operations Intelligence
Dr. Lori Krupa, Ph.D., Brilliant Chemist & Rock Hound Extraordinaire
Dr. (Major) Michael J. Hoilien, U.S. Army, Special Operations Combat Medic Course Director
Priscilla Pittman, Alzheimer's Association, Central Arkansas Chapter

I'd also like to thank Melissa Endlich and Allison Lyons for their wonderful editorial insight and for encouraging me to take chances. Finally, as always, a huge thanks to my awesome critique partner, CJ Chase. CJ, writing wouldn't be nearly as much fun without you to share it with.

SILHOUETTE BOOKS

ISBN 0-373-27284-7

THE IMPOSSIBLE ALLIANCE

Copyright © 2003 by Harlequin Books S.A.

Visit Silhouette at www.eHarlequin.com

Printed in U.S.A.

Books by Candace Irvin

Silhouette Intimate Moments

CANDACE IRVIN

Being the daughter of a librarian and a sailor, it's no wonder Candace's two greatest loves are reading and the sea. After spending several exciting years as a U.S. naval officer sailing around the world, she decided it was time to put down roots and give her other love a chance. To her delight, she soon learned that writing romance was as much fun as reading it. A finalist for both the coveted RITA® Award and the Holt Medallion, as well as a two-time *Romantic Times* Reviewers' Choice Award nominee, Candace believes her luckiest moment was the day she married her own dashing hero, a former U.S. Army combat engineer with dimples to die for. The two now reside in the South, happily raising three future heroes and one adorable heroine—who won't be allowed to date until she's forty, at least.

Candace loves to hear from readers. You can e-mail her at candace@candaceirvin.com or snail mail her c/o Silhouette Books, 300 East 42nd Street, New York, NY 10017.

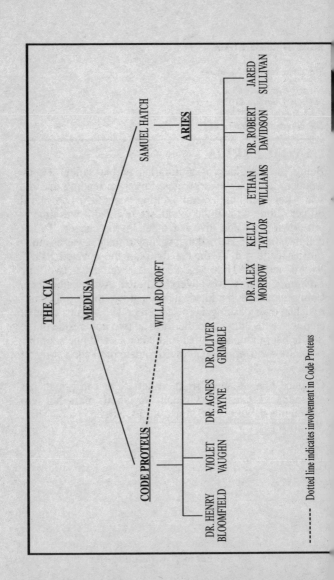

THE CIA

MEDUSA

SAMUEL HATCH

WILLARD CROFT

CODE PROTEUS

DR. HENRY
BLOOMFIELD

VIOLET
VAUGHN

DR. AGNES
PAYNE

DR OLIVER
GRIMBLE

ARIES

DR. ALEX
MORROW

KELLY
TAYLOR

ETHAN
WILLIAMS

DR. ROBERT
DAVIDSON

JARED
SULLIVAN

------ Dotted line indicates involvement in Code Proteus

Prologue

The thunder of an incoming chopper shattered the early-morning calm. Jared Sullivan eased up on his punishing stride and stared out over the rolling hills, instinctively searching the swath of red just beginning to bleed up into the distant sky. As he caught site of the chopper, apprehension locked in. Despite the fact that private aircraft occasionally drifted out of the designated flight lanes to and from Austin, he knew damned well this was no accidental flyby.

That bird was headed straight for the ranch.

Straight for him.

Not only was the growing silhouette a dead ringer for a UH-60, official U.S. military-black-ops paint job still intact, but today was Sunday. There was only one type of Company that came calling at the crack of dawn on the Lord's day—and only one man who'd dare to set foot on his ranch without an engraved invitation. And only one reason.

Resigned, Jared resumed his morning run, sprinting the final quarter mile of pasture separating the barbed-wire fence line from the granite steps of the three-story mausoleum he'd inherited by default. By the time the Black Hawk landed, eight miles of exhaustion had almost dissipated.

Jared tugged off his T-shirt and used the ratty gray fabric to soak up the sweat dripping from his face. He hooked the shirt behind his neck, clamping onto the ends, as the chopper's side doors slid open. Sure enough, he recognized five out of six members of the subdued but hypervigilant security detail that bailed out to fan out around the bird as the engine powered down. He exchanged a brief nod with two as he waited for the ARIES director's stocky frame to lumber forth. Seconds later it did, the trademark rumples of Samuel Hatch's suit already creased firmly in place despite the hour.

Due to the gravity of the situation, Jared suppressed his welcoming grin. Hatch had no such compunction as he clapped his palm into Jared's outstretched hand and hauled him close for a brief, bone-jarring hug that belied the man's years. "Great, son, you're home."

As if the man would have traveled all the way to Texas from his office at Langley without making damn sure he was. Jared's grin broke though. "Good to see you, sir."

"Damned good, son. *Damned* good. But I thought I told you to call me Sam last month."

He had. But then, they'd forged several agreements that day, hadn't they? The most significant of which was about to dissolve almost before the ink on his resignation had a chance to dry. Hoping to delay the inevitable, Jared gestured toward the main house. "Breakfast? The cook makes a mean skillet of *huevos rancheros.*"

The first rays of day glinted off Hatch's balding pate as he shook his head. "Wish I could, but I'm on a tight schedule. I'll just cut to the chase. I'm sure you know why I'm here."

Jared sighed. "At least come inside."

He'd be damned if he'd send Sam Hatch away with his hat in his hand in front of his own men. He had too much respect for his old mentor, as well as the men standing by, discreetly marking time. To his surprise, Hatch nodded.

This *was* bad.

Jared led the way to the house. He shoved the double doors wide and stepped inside the marble foyer, wincing as his former boss openly cased the place as they crossed the room. Damn, but he had to get a decorator in quick—before someone knocked over the succession of vases and transformed the precious Sullivan heirlooms into a pile of ceramic shards.

"Nice place."

He shrugged. "See something you like, take it with you." It would save him the trouble of hosting one hell of a garage sale.

Hatch shook his head. "I'll pass. Rita left me enough dust collectors as it is."

Jared reached the end of the hall and pushed open the door to the one room he'd decided not to change. He headed for the hand-carved walnut desk that dominated the center of the dimly lit room. His esteemed grandfather's desk and now his. But never his father's. He tossed his saturated T-shirt onto the leather blotter and nodded toward the matching armchairs.

"Seat? Coffee?"

"Neither."

Evidently conversation was out, too, because an uncharacteristically uncomfortable silence locked in. Out of respect, Jared waited.

The old man finally sighed. "Something's come up."

Jared hooked his thigh onto the corner of the desk, bringing his gaze down to his mentor's. "Figured as much." He drew a deep breath. "Sir, while I appreciate the courtesy—"

"Then at least hear me out."

Jared straightened instinctively. It wasn't the edge to the man's voice that gave him pause. He'd heard that plenty of times. It was something else. Something he'd never heard before. Desperation. He studied Hatch's carefully schooled gaze and nodded.

Hatch sighed. "Look, son, I don't want to be here, either. But I need you. This job's right up your alley." Hatch glanced at the armchairs, obviously reconsidering his initial refusal. He skimmed his hands over the cropped silver hair ringing his head as he sat, then dropped them into his lap. "An American geologist by the name of Alex Morrow disappeared while attending an environmental conference in Europe."

Jared stiffened slightly as the name registered, then forced himself to relax before Hatch picked up on it.

Distracted or not, the man would. Rumpled suits and normally laid-back manner notwithstanding, Sam Hatch hadn't made it to the position of director of ARIES without surpassing damned near all the agency's operatives in cold, clear and calculating intellect.

"Why me?"

After all, if someone the agency had flagged was missing, why waste time tracking down a former agent like him when there were any number of active and capable search-and-rescue operatives at the CIA's disposal—SAR operatives *he'd* helped Hatch train?

"Because this isn't your standard rescue op. Morrow's one of us. Disappeared while on assignment."

Regret seared through him. Hatch was right. That did change things. Unfortunately it didn't change enough.

Still, the irony of it.

That his mentor would show up on behalf of Alex Morrow, of all men. He wasn't surprised to discover Morrow was ARIES. The CIA often used scientists and businessmen to keep tabs on their respective communities. What better way to head off the transfer of potentially deadly information and valuable technology to the world's more heinous regimes? Hell, he should have made the connection when he crossed paths with Morrow three months before in Hatch's home—with Hatch out of town, no less. He would have, too, had he not been so rattled by that damned phone call.

For a split second, he wondered if Hatch knew.

He discarded the suspicion just as quickly. If Hatch knew he and Morrow had connected, however briefly, he'd have used it as leverage. As it was, Jared didn't need to hear more. He couldn't afford to. Not with the guilt already kicking in.

"Sir…I can't."

To his surprise, Hatch lurched to his feet. "The hell you can't. I'm here asking. You *can.* Dammit, I need a one-man insertion on this job and you're the best singleton I've got—or had." Before Jared had a chance to react, much less open his trap, Hatch spun on his heel and stalked across the study in a steady, clipped line to the still-shuttered eight-foot windows on the far wall. He stopped short at the first and twisted the wooden slats. The now full-blown sun-rise flooded in, chasing the dank shadows, as well as his grandfather's ghost, from the room. The stark light revealed the determination in Hatch's eyes as he turned. "Have you kept up since you left?"

Jared nodded.

"With General DeBruzkya?"

Again, he nodded. It didn't take a State Department stooge to keep abreast of Bruno DeBruzkya. The Rebelian dictator had led the nightly news since the day he'd murdered the entire Rebelian royal family five years earlier. Since then, the scourge of Eastern Europe had surpassed the world's current collection of ruling thugs in cunning and brutality.

To his surprise Hatch turned to the windows, stepping up to twist the second set of slats open. He stared out at the pasture and herd of Texas longhorns. "Before disappearing, Morrow received a message from a scientific colleague in Delmonico stating that DeBruzkya intended on spreading his tyranny and greed across the rest of Europe.

This colleague also swore the general had come up with a viable plan to accomplish his goals."

Jared shifted his weight against the desk, his interest piqued despite his better judgment. If DeBruzkya had a plan, it had better involve the Midas touch. As far as he knew, there wasn't a village left in the war-torn nation the general hadn't already plundered, pillaged or razed. Jared waited for his former boss to turn around.

He didn't.

Odd. What was Hatch hiding?

"Morrow was supposed to link up with a colleague under the guise of an environmental conference in neighboring Holzberg. We know they connected at least once. Morrow's initial communiqué revealed that for several months, DeBruzkya has been ordering his thugs to steal on his behalf. There isn't a continent or a country that hasn't been hit. Diamonds, emeralds, rubies—you name it, he's stolen it. When Morrow failed two successive comm checks, we sent in a recon agent." Hatch lifted the rod that controlled the blinds and snapped them shut, then flipped them open once more. "The agent discovered Morrow's colleague was dead. Murdered. Morrow had vanished."

"How long since last contact?"

"Twenty-one days, six hours, forty-five minutes."

Christ.

"I know what you're thinking. You're wrong." Hatch continued to face the window as he shut the blinds a third time, then opened them. "Five hours ago one of our operatives learned Morrow was still alive and is being held in DeBruzkya's private compound. A renovated castle located in the north of Rebelia. Heavily fortified and heavily forested. Mountains. This one won't be easy—even for you."

"Proof of life?"

Silence.

"You do have it?"

Again, silence.

"Sir—"

Hatch slammed the control rod against the window and spun around. Something Jared had never seen before flashed through his old mentor's eyes as the wooden slats continued to slap against the glass panes, and this time it wasn't desperation.

"Alex Morrow is *not* dead."

For the fourth time in ten minutes, silence locked in.

No matter what Sam Hatch claimed, this was more than some deep-cover agent trapped out in the cold, possibly for good. Jared waited until the blinds stilled, until the fire smoldering in Hatch's dark-brown eyes cooled. Despite the fact that he no longer worked for the man, he owed Hatch more than he could ever repay and they both knew it. For that reason alone, he chose his words with care. "You want to tell me what's really going on?"

"Can't. Not now." Hatch shrugged. "Later, perhaps."

Perhaps.

Hatch expected him to risk his hide, Morrow's, as well— *if* indeed it was still in one piece—on a flimsy 'perhaps'? Jared stared into that iron gaze once more and held it. He knew better than most how hard Hatch took the loss of an agent. But ten-to-one Morrow was already dead and they both knew it. As a military general, DeBruzkya had subscribed to the school of slaughter first, ask questions later. Since his graduation to dictator, the bastard had taken the motto to new heights—and even grislier horrors.

Dammit, Morrow was *dead*.

But what if he wasn't?

Despite Jared's efforts to slough off the insidious whisper, it continued to cling. The doubt refused to surrender. Another minute, and he could feel his resolve buckling beneath it. Christ, why not? A one-man op, Hatch had said. Screw the odds. He'd be in and out before DeBruzkya even knew he was there. If he did get caught, so what? It was a better way to go than the path the good Lord had already carved out for him. Besides, if he did succeed, he'd kill two birds with one stone. Repay two men. Sam Hatch *and* Alex Morrow.

The geologist had obviously kept his word. It was time for Jared to return the favor. While he still could.

His decision must have shown on his face, because Hatch launched into the mission brief before Jared so much as nodded. "Good. You'll leave with me. I've got a C-141 standing by at Lackland, secure comm link already on the plane. Decide on what you need in the air and call it in. It'll be waiting for you by the time you touch down in Germany. Once you extract Morrow, you'll need to hole up for a few weeks. Let things cool off before you risk executing part two of the mission."

"Part *two?*"

Hatch nodded. "You'll team up with Morrow and complete the original mission. We've added a few more pieces to the puzzle since Morrow's disappearance. At first we assumed DeBruzkya was stealing gems to boost his coffers. It turns out he's also obsessed with an ancient Rebelian legend regarding some mysterious "Gem of Power." You can memorize the file on the flight and fill Morrow in. If there's a kernel of truth behind this legend, I want you two to find it. And then I want you both to stop this bastard."

Just like that, Jared's decision reversed itself. "No."

Hatch stiffened. Blinked.

"I'm sorry, sir. I can't accept the—"

"Dammit, son, you just *did*. I could see it in your eyes."

That was before he knew this was more than a simple grab and bag, and the old man knew it. "You didn't let me finish. I'll do the snatch. But immediately after, I leave. I can't hang around."

"What if Morrow's injured?"

Crap. His gut had been clenched so tightly since the moment the chopper had set down, he hadn't considered that. See? He was already slipping. If Morrow was alive, the man was bound to be injured—beaten and tortured within an inch of his life. Why else was Hatch so desperate that *he* do the snatch?

"Well?"

"You can have another medic standing by."

"I want *you* standing by. I also want you to see the rest of this mission through." When he refused to answer, Hatch stalked back to the windows. "Dammit, son, what else have you got waiting for you? A bunch of goddamned cows? You've owned this ranch for eight years now, so don't rehash that half-assed line of garbage you dumped in my house about it being time to turn in your ARIES credentials and settle down. It stunk the first time."

Jared jerked up from the edge of the desk as the last punch landed square and low, deep inside his gut. "If you were so sure I was lying, why'd you let me go?"

The man just stared. Breathed.

That steel-gray brow finally arched.

Horror congealed along every square inch of Jared's body. A split second later, his stomach bottomed out as acid seared up his throat. Shame followed, hot and roiling. Hatch *knew.*

The man's slow nod confirmed it.

Jared sucked in his air. Swallowed the bile. "Then how the hell can you even ask?"

"Because I know you."

"Then you also know I'd do it if I could." Hell, he'd still do the snatch. But *not* the follow-on mission. A mission that had the potential to drag on for weeks, months...or longer. "Find someone else. Someone who can see the job through. *Please.*" He didn't care that he was begging. He couldn't afford to.

"I'm asking you. I *trust* you."

Jared slumped against the desk and clenched his fingers beneath the edge, dimly aware of the air ripping through his lungs as he worked to keep the tremors from racking his body. Of his heart hammering against the wall of his chest. Of the ice-cold void closing in as his remaining dignity died.

"I'm sorry, son. I know Janice shouldn't have called me, but she did. Even then, I'd hoped—"

"Yeah. Me, too."

Terse silence locked in once again. But this time, it was his. And this time, he was the one who finally broke it.

"All right. I'll do it."

Chapter 1

The world had gone dark again.

Silent.

No…it was her. She remembered now. Her eyes, they were closed. She tried opening them, but her lids refused to cooperate. She was still so very tired. She forced herself to fight the exhaustion deep within her bones and gather the dregs of her strength. It seemed to take forever, but she finally managed to pry her eyes open, to focus. The world wasn't dark. It was light.

White.

And it wasn't silent.

She could make out the constant hum and occasional clicks of machinery. The high-pitched, steady whine of electronics. A door opening and then closing somewhere in the distance. Voices. Muted and conversing in a clipped, guttural language she didn't recognize, but voices nonetheless.

Thank you, God.

She searched the white and finally realized she was staring at portable, floor-to-ceiling curtains. *That's right*. She remembered those, too. If she turned her head to the left, she'd be able to see the rest of the hospital room. Unfortunately moving her head took so much effort. So much energy. Energy she couldn't seem to muster.

Do it.

Somehow she did—and gasped softly. The man was still there, handcuffed to the safety rails on the bed beside hers. He'd been beaten. Viciously. He was unconscious to boot. Or was he sleeping? She hoped so. She opened her mouth to call to him, to find out, but nothing came out. She tried again. This time, she managed a hoarse rasp. Evidently she still couldn't speak. But at least someone had removed the oxygen and feeding tubes from her throat. She wet her lips, wincing as the saliva caused her flesh to sting. Her lips were as dry and raw as her throat. Cracked. Desperate to make contact with the man before she lost consciousness again, she tried whispering.

An explosion greeted her. Then another…and another.

In a *hospital?*

Sweet mercy, what was going on? Just where was she? And how long had she been here?

More importantly, why couldn't she remember?

She traced the intravenous line from the distended vein on the back of her left hand to the bag of clear fluid hanging upside down beside her bed. Disappointment swamped her as she realized she couldn't understand the handwriting on the label.

Another explosion rocked the room. The blast was so intense the resulting vibrations caused the steel frames of the curtained walls to separate and roll several inches apart. She forced her stare to the foot of her bed, horrified as the musty odor of bargain basement sanitation sealed her suspicions. The tangled roll of expended, bloody hospital gauze. The pile of soiled bed linens. Half a dozen bags of IV fluid, all empty. The nest of discarded needles and syringes.

This was not your typical hospital.

She shifted her right arm. Two inches later, it jerked to a stop. Bemused, she stared at the gleaming cuffs locking her own wrist to the rails on her bed. The heck with sanitation—this was not your typical hospital restraint. She flinched as another, louder, explosion reverberated through the walls of the room, hammering through her skull. The curtains parted another foot, affording her a partial view of a scarred slab of wood.

A door.

Where did it lead?

Before she could ponder the possibilities, much less gather the strength to find out, she heard the voices again, jangling keys scraping against the lock.

The other patient.

She swung her head to the left as another explosion rocked the room. The man's eyes were still closed, but he shifted, moaning softly as he twisted his battered body toward the side of the bed. Toward her. Her lips stung as she opened her mouth—but the door flew open, as well. She slammed her eyes shut instinctively. Dizziness swirled in along with the dark. She eased her lids up. Just a crack. It was enough. She watched as two men she didn't recognize shoved the hospital curtains aside. Two more men followed them through. All four wore camouflage fatigues.

Soldiers?

Perhaps. But not American.

Americans wouldn't be brandishing Romanian Kalashnikovs rifles. One of the thugs shouted something to his buddies as he raised the barrel of his AK-47. The thug then sighted the automatic rifle in on the battered head of the man in the opposite bed and shouted again. She had no idea what he'd said, but the dialect wasn't Romanian. The largest of the two thugs dragged the woozy man from his mattress, wrenching his arm behind his back as the smallest thug unlocked the steel cuffs. The man groaned in protest as his shoulder popped. He received a fresh bash to his skull in return. His glasses flew off, landing at the thugs' boots with a slap. A distinctive crunch followed.

Crude laughter filled the room.

Another thug shouted above the din as they dragged the now moaning man from the room. Yet another responded. As before, she had no idea what the men had said, but a split second before the door slammed shut and silence reigned within, she caught several mangled syllables she *did* recognize.

A name.

Alexander Morrow.

She stiffened, the implications of that memory alone giving her the strength to bring her free hand to her face. Dizziness and shock gave way to searing confusion as her fingers collided with the thick swaths binding her head.

That pile of expended, bloody gauze was *hers?*

Was that why she couldn't remember where she was, much less how she'd gotten here?

She searched the contours of her face, hoping for clues. Desperate for answers. But all she gained was another question. And this question burned more deeply than all the others combined. If the man those camouflaged thugs had just dragged from the room was Alexander Morrow—

Who the hell was she?

"Four minutes to the drop zone!"

Jared adjusted his oxygen mask and flashed a thumbs-up toward the plane's crew chief. He double-checked his parachute and gear one last time before latching on to the succession of safety straps dangling from the overhead as he worked his way down the belly of the CIA-modified C-130. Wind colder than a penguin's ass slammed into him as he reached the plane's yawning tail ramp, ripping through his pressure suit.

He ignored it.

This high up, he could take in ninety percent of the Rebelian countryside through the blanket of intermittent clouds, as well as all four major cities. Cities that were woefully dark despite the midnight hour. Hell, from here light pollution bleeding up from the destitute capital city of Rajalla put out less wattage than the subdued altimeter strapped to his wrist. Jared lowered the night-vision goggles from his helmet and locked them over his jump lenses. Seconds later the crew chief's voice flooded his earpiece.

"Two minutes!"

Jared flashed another thumbs-up. The second he bailed out of this bucket of bolts, the pilot would swing the plane's nose due west and hightail it back to Ramstein. By the time the droning C-130 reached German air space where he and Hatch had established a command post, he'd be knocking on DeBruzkya's door. Or rather, his DeBruzkya. Jared muscled his way into the icy crosswinds, stopping when the tips of his boots were flush with the lip of the plane's ramp. One predetermined electronic signal from the transmitter in his pocket and a well-timed blitzkrieg from the CIA team on the ground—artfully disguised as a renewed rebel offensive—would provide the necessary cover and concealment for the remainder of his objectives.

He hoped.

"One minute!"

Jared grabbed on to the familiar, heady adrenaline surging through his veins and harnessed it, using it to beat down the unexpected flash of panic. The doubt. Dammit, Hatch trusted him to see this through. Hatch also knew the situation, understood the risks. Mentor or not, surely the man would have tapped someone else—hell, anyone else—for Morrow's snatch if there was a chance of him screwing up, however unintentionally.

But there was a chance he might slip, wasn't there? The worst part was he'd never see it coming.

Or was that the best?

"Thirty seconds!"

Pull it together, Soldier.

The decade-old taunt worked. Two years with Army Spe-

cial Forces, five more in Delta Force, another eight with
ARIES. He hadn't botched a snatch yet. And he'd *never*
lost a package.

He wasn't about to start now.

"Go!"

Jared pressed his fingers to the gold medallion beneath
his pressure suit for luck and tipped his helmet toward the
crew chief, vaulting boots first into the icy void before the
sergeant could return his nod. Three breaths of canned oxygen later, he popped his chute. The dark-gray canopy bil-
lowed out, jerking his spine into perfect alignment as the
C-130 roared off into the night. A minute later there was
nothing but eerie silence and overly bright stars. Then the
chilling frost creeping across his goggles…and ten long
minutes to kill. Determined to banish the doubt from his
brain, he ran through the coming mission. He embraced the
hope.

Unfortunately, all three converged on one man.

Alexander Morrow.

Just let him be alive.

His trusty medic's bag would do the rest. Hell, ten seconds after he stabbed Morrow with the pre-filled amphet-
amine injector, *he'd* have trouble keeping up with the
nerdy, myopic geologist, bashed body and broken bones
notwithstanding. Jared studied the inky blackness as he
continued to float down. The feeble lights of Rajalla had
long since passed behind him. Even with night-vision goggles, the remaining flickering pinpricks were few and far
between. Though he couldn't yet make out the closing
mountainous terrain, he already knew the only hazards between his silk chute and DeBruzkya's private compound
were the thousand and one massive pines crowding the jagged crags.

Years of whizzing through the clouds warned him he'd
passed the halfway point, as did the gradually warming air.
A quick glance at his altimeter and his watch confirmed it.

Ten thousand feet, 2410 hours.

Time to lock and load.

He slipped his right hand inside his pressure suit and retrieved his MP-5, automatically flicking the safety off with his thumb as he reintroduced the submachine gun to the night air. He reached inside his suit again, this time punching the kickoff button with his left hand. A high-pitched tone followed.

One covert transmission sent.

His confirmation arrived five seconds later as the terrain below came to deafening—and blinding—life.

Minutes later, as fellow ARIES operative Marty Lyons and his band of masquerading marauders lobbed half the CIA's local arsenal at the northern facade of DeBruzkya's compound, Jared's own boots slammed onto the granite roof of the castle's southernmost tower. He rolled with the force, ignoring the shards of glass that ripped into his pressure suit. He severed the lines of his chute as he came to his feet. A quick snap of his wrists deflated the billowing silk. He expended precious seconds whipping the fabric into a tight ball, then raced across the roof, stopping to cram the chute into the first ventilation shaft he hit along the way.

Christ, Marty!

Jared hit the deck as the trail from a stray rocket lit up the night sky. The moment the explosion died out, he was up and running again. Marty and his men continued to pound at the northern facade of the castle as he tore into his rucksack and yanked out the waiting coils of rappelling rope. He dropped the bulk of the nylon to the roof and used one end to form his seat, threading the other through a makeshift pulley. Seconds later he scrambled over the granite ledge, his face and chest, as well as his submachine gun, front and center as he bounded down the wall Australian-style, face-first toward the now unguarded basement door at the base of the southern tower.

He left his ropes dangling in the breeze and tore into his ruck again, this time snagging a block of C-4. He molded the plastic explosive to the array of dead bolts, then played out enough time fuse and pre-rigged the caps. He ripped off his night-vision goggles and glanced at his watch as he sought cover in an identical recessed doorway ten feet away.

He jerked the ring on the fuse igniter.

Ten seconds later, the C-4 blew the locks off the door. Jared wrenched the metal slab open and scrambled down the stone steps. He was already halfway down the main corridor by the time the smoke cleared, night-vision goggles firmly in place as he compared the doors and secondary corridors he passed against the floor plan ARIES agent Robert Davidson had managed to obtain before he was forced to evacuate Rebelia. The hair on the back of Jared's neck snapped to attention as he passed the first door that didn't belong. And then the second.

He slammed the demons down as he swapped his goggles for the thermal imaging scope stashed in his ruck. A solitary heat source glowed within. It wasn't moving.

Morrow.

Though the scarred slab separating them was three doors away from the one Davidson's source had pegged, Jared's instincts locked in. They wouldn't budge. Unfortunately neither would the door.

If he blew this door, the resulting internal vibrations would announce his presence within the castle with all the finesse of a fragmentation grenade chewing through a sheet of rice paper. He double-checked his watch. What the hell—five minutes from now it wouldn't matter. He was almost out of time and definitely out of options. He grabbed another block of C-4 from his ruck, this time rigging half of it. Seconds later, the locks on the wooden door followed the explosive fate of the outer metal one. With them went his sole chance at culling enough time to execute a quick search for DeBruzkya's cache of purloined jewels before the exfiltration chopper arrived.

Jared vaulted into the room and shoved a set of portable

hospital curtains aside. Bypassing the empty bed, he leaned over the occupied one and peered through the darkness and still swirling smoke. The man's eyes were closed, but Jared recognized him instantly, despite the bandages and missing glasses. He leaned closer and checked the man's breathing. Prayed.

Razor-sharp steel kissed Jared's throat.

His estimation of Morrow shot up a notch. The man wasn't unconscious, after all. Not with those eyes wide open.

"Name's Jared Sullivan, ARIES. We met three months ago in a guest room in Director Hatch's house."

Recognition flooded brown eyes as the scalpel clattered to the floor. Morrow's relief was palpable. Humbling. Unlike many Jared had served with over the years, it wasn't the adrenaline or the toys that had kept him coming back for more.

It was that look. It made it all worthwhile.

It made this particular job worthwhile.

He saw Morrow's mouth open, heard the air rip past his lips. "Where?"

"Later. Can you stand?"

He caught the man's answering nod—and tore into his medic bag, anyway. Given the wobble punctuating the motion, Morrow needed the boost the amphetamines would provide. Jared scanned the makeshift hospital room as he snagged the syringe from his bag, biting back a curse as he recognized the array of machines and monitors. There was no way he could risk shooting Morrow up with speed now. He pitched the syringe, still capped, to the floor and leaned down to heft Morrow over his shoulder, clearing the still-smoldering doorway before the man could argue.

"W-wait! There may be someone else. A—"

"No time. Sorry."

He truly was. But he had his orders—and his package. He carried the former engraved in his brain, the latter locked over his shoulder as he headed for the basement's main corridor. DeBruzkya's goons would be arriving soon. Even the stash of gems estimated to rival the contents of the main vault at Fort Knox would have to wait for another day. Another opportunity.

Yesterday morning Morrow had clearly been Hatch's priority. Today the man was his.

Unfortunately Morrow opted to struggle. "Dammit, you've got to—"

Jared deliberately clipped the geologist's head into his shoulder to muffle the rest, relieved when the sudden motion also caused the man to pass out. Right now he didn't need the distraction. Especially when he rounded the basement corner and spied the two camouflaged goons examining the remains of the outer door he'd blown on his way in. He was about to receive distraction enough as it was. The first goon raised the barrel of his rifle.

That was as far as he got.

Two quick bursts from his own submachine gun knocked the men down and swept their AK-47s across the stone floor. Jared shouldered Morrow up the moldy basement steps and into the shadowy night, then dumped the geologist at the base of the ropes he'd left dangling down the wall. Thirty seconds later, he'd attached the risers and hefted Morrow again. The moment he locked his boots into the risers, the man's body jerked to life.

"*Goddammit,* you just can't leave the—"

A massive explosion rocked the castle walls.

Jared blessed Marty and his team once more as he used the rappelling ropes and risers to quickly scale the remaining thirty feet of granite separating him and his living package from the roof. That chopper had damned well better be waiting by the time they arrived. Halfway up, gunfire riddled the night air, along with the length of the castle wall.

Christ.

Someone must have discovered the bodies and sounded the alarm. Jared instinctively tightened his hold on Morrow with one hand as he jerked his other to his face, ripping his night-vision goggles off in the nick of time. Seconds later a hundred floodlights exploded around them, illuminating the castle, the grounds, the rooftops and the walls…illuminating them.

He and Morrow cursed and flinched together. Fortunately the thugs were in the same boat.

The soldiers recovered quickly, however, because a second spat of gunfire, this one more vicious and closer than the last, riddled the wall. Jared bit back another curse as fire ripped across his left hamstring. Fortunately it felt like a flesh wound, not a direct hit. He twisted his body, instinctively shielding Morrow's as another spray rent the air.

Jesus, Mary and Joseph! Another hit. This time, his right biceps. He glanced down to confirm it, spotting the dark stain rapidly spreading across the black fabric of his sleeve. Flesh wound or not, that one *stung*. He sucked in his breath and forced himself to move past the ache.

Hand over hand, Soldier.

Suddenly they were there. Six beautiful inches from the ledge of the roof. His already surging adrenaline must have kicked up another notch, because he no longer felt the pain in his arm or his leg. He could, however, hear the blessed pulsing of a chopper's blades in the distance. Their chopper.

Morrow protested as he braced his good arm against the wall to boost the geologist up first. Jared silenced the man with a terse glare as he locked his fingers to the man's suit belt, not bothering to question why Morrow hadn't been stripped and placed in a hospital gown. He was too busy blessing the leather strap and the anchor points it afforded. But as he shoved Morrow up, the buckle slipped, then parted altogether. Before Morrow's body followed, he shifted his grip and gave one last, all-out heave, barely noticing as his right hand slid squarely up between the man's legs, right smack into his groin.

Oddly enough, Morrow wasn't the one who stiffened.

He did.

Unless he was severely mistaken, half the world's diamonds, emeralds and rubies weren't the only gems that were acutely, inexplicably missing. The good doctor also lacked jewels. Those of the family variety. Either that or Alex Morrow wasn't a man.

But a woman.

Chapter 2

Of all the ways she'd imagined her cover being blown, this was not one of them. Alex dragged her gaze down to the man whose oversize paw was still locked to the most intimate part of her body, praying with every fiber of her being.

She needn't have bothered.

He knew.

The irony of Jared Sullivan discovering one of her most fiercely guarded secrets this way scorched the remaining fog from her brain. Ice-cold terror replaced it. Terror that now that he knew the truth, he'd be able to see straight through her and divine the rest. If Sam hadn't already told him.

No, Sam wouldn't have.

Would he?

A spray of gunfire ripped her thoughts back to the terror at hand. Bullets tore into the ledge beside her head. Either the thugs that had been chasing them had improved their aim, or they'd managed to close the distance. A swift glance down past Jared's boots confirmed the worst. One of the men had reached the base of the tower. If his AK-47 hadn't jammed, her brain would have been seeping through the sieve of her skull by now. The thug cursed his malfunctioning rifle and pitched it, opting to grab the end of the nylon rope and scurry up the wall before his buddies caught up enough to cover him.

It was a mistake.

Jared's hand—MP-5 submachine gun attached—snapped downward as he popped off the remainder of a thirty-round banana clip. She didn't need to understand the local language, much less catch the thug's shocked grunt to know Jared had scored a direct hit. She shot a round of thanks heavenward—until she spotted six more thugs bringing up the rear, all armed.

Jared heaved her frame over the ledge as the squad opened fire. Thankfully the spray was haphazard at best. She reached back over the wall, but from the terse shake of his head, it was clear that Jared didn't trust her strength. He hooked his right boot up on the ledge as the bullets continued to fly, the men rapidly closing the distance and, unfortunately, improving their accuracy. To her horror, the heel of Jared's boot hit a crevice in the rock and slipped. She reached over the ledge again, this time ignoring the man's fierce frown as she grabbed his forearm, pulling with all her might as his boot swung up again. His body cleared the ledge a split second before the next spray of bullets trimmed the granite down by inches.

"Thanks."

"Don't mention it." She jerked her chin toward the thundering chopper drawing closer and closer to the roof. With no less than three floodlights shining directly into her eyes, she had no idea what model the chopper was, much less which country it hailed from. All she knew was that each pulse of those blades drove a thousand daggers into her ear and straight through her brain. She'd forgive the pilot—as long as he was one of theirs. "Just tell me that bird is ours."

"It is."

Moments later a sentry on a parapet sixty yards away turned and spotted them. He opened fire as she and Jared hit the roof. Before Alex could draw her next breath, Jared had dumped the expended clip from his submachine gun, locked in a fresh magazine and rose slightly to spray the parapet with bullets.

The sentry pitched headfirst over the wall.

Its flight path clear, the chopper ate up the remaining distance. But the moment the bird moved in over the roof, the roar shot off the scale, damned near shattering her eardrum. The pain was so intense she didn't even notice Jared kneeling again until his kneecap slammed onto her hand.

"Christ. Sorry, I didn't—"

"Please. Just…get me…on that…" She couldn't finish, much less move.

It must have shown.

With no time to cut the rappelling ropes still dangling over the ledge, Jared hooked his arm around her waist and hauled her to her feet. He dragged her toward the chopper, probably chalking up her stumbles to her coma—at least, she hoped so. Five steps later she no longer cared. Just as long as he didn't let her go. If he did, she knew in her soul that she'd dive straight back down to that roof and this time she'd crawl beneath it.

Anything to get away from that goddamn *noise*.

She'd been ruthlessly pummeled by sound before, ambushed by the relentless depravity of a malfunctioning hearing aid—but never like this. Just when she thought she couldn't take another step—with or without support—a steel cable, complete with twin harnesses attached, spilled out from the chopper. Jared shoved her in front of him, sheltering her six-foot frame with his taller, more massive body as a vicious onslaught of lead chewed up the roof directly behind them.

The thugs had reached the ledge.

She felt Jared twist to return the spray. Seconds later several screams punctuated the rotor wash. Jared dragged her to the waiting cable as they died out, but it was too late. The sound waves were ricocheting directly off the flat roof now, their intensity magnified beyond endurance as they slammed back up into her ears. She couldn't help it; she cowered into Jared's shoulder, unable to control her body long enough to grab one of the suspended harnesses, much less hook her arms through.

"Dammit! I can't—"

He jerked the cable close and hooked both her arms inside a harness before she could finish, supporting her with one sinewy arm, then the other as he donned his own harness. He clipped the submachine gun with its expended magazine to his web gear and shoved his medical pouch aside as he hauled her against him, this time anchoring her entire body to his as the chopper swept them up into the air and off into the night. There was no escaping him.

Or the noise.

But at least that began to ebb as the chopper gained altitude. Desperate to ignore the thunder still hammering in her ear, Alex dragged her thoughts together and forced herself to concentrate on her other senses—on *any* other sense—finally latching on to the only one strong enough to sear through the pain. Touch. She focused on the iron arms banded about her chest, on the cords of taut muscle welded to her belly and her thighs. On the fiery heat smelting every embarrassing inch in between. Jared Sullivan's touch.

Jared Sullivan's heat.

Alex gathered her strength and her nerve and lifted her chin, pushing through the noise to stare into those dark amber eyes. Though she'd seen them in person but once before and not nearly this close, that unusual, simmering glow had already managed to work its way beneath her defenses. Since that fateful day, those eyes had managed to gain the power of night, slipping into the intimacy of her bedroom, stoking her illicit desires, setting fire to her resolve. Setting fire to her.

If only in her dreams.

So much so that when she'd risked opening her eyes in that damned makeshift hospital cell and found herself staring into this gaze, she was certain she was hallucinating—until he spoke.

Even now, with the icy wind slicing into the back of her tattered jacket and trousers, with that god-awful racket still reverberating through her skull, that steady amber gaze worked its magic, unnerving her to her very core. But this time, she welcomed it. It seared through the thunder and the cold until, gradually, she was able to notice the rest. This close, despite the camouflaged greasepaint he'd smeared into his face, she could make out the majority of Jared's striking features.

The rest she filled in from memory.

Those stark, dusky cheeks. The clipped lines of his square jaw. The thin scar that teased the center of his chin, puckering the flesh when he forgot he didn't smile. And those full, dangerously sensual lips. Even with Alex Morrow's male physique still firmly in place, her fingers itched to reach out and smooth the exertion beading above the upper curve. Startled that the man had affected her so deeply even now, she shoved her gaze up to the black knit cap Jared had donned for the mission. It rode low on his forehead, butting into and blending in with his thick, midnight brows. Brows that matched the long, inky hair he'd inherited from his Mexican mother.

Was it as soft and silky as it looked?

She shoved that forbidden fantasy aside as well, but not soon enough. Just like that, she could feel the blistering intimacy of the man's touch as he'd hefted her over the ledge of the castle roof. Still recall the shocking warmth of his hand tucked firmly between her legs. She made the mistake of glancing into those hot amber eyes once more and knew—so did he.

Damn him.

As if the dreams weren't bad enough. As if hanging here, trapped beneath some viciously bellowing bird in this man's arms wasn't worse, now she'd have that humiliating memory to torture her resolve when she least expected it. She sucked in her breath as the chopper pitched suddenly and swerved to the left, then swooped down fast and low. The memory disintegrated. The thunder slammed back. The pain.

She ripped her gaze through the icy night. As the chopper's altitude whittled down to a nauseating rotor's breath, she realized that she and Jared weren't racing over the tops of a few pine trees, but many.

A forest?

The chopper whipped their harnessed torsos and dangling legs between two, insanely close, sheer cliffs before swooping down to hug the rocky riverbed below. Shock punched the breath from her lungs as, once again, the pulsing thunder ricocheted directly off the hardened terrain before lashing back up, lashing into her. It was if some depraved construction worker had locked the steel bit of his massive jackhammer into her skull and slammed the machine into overdrive. Pulse after pulse splintered through her head. Her eyes began to water. She began to whimper. Any moment now she was going to drag her hands up through the filthy mop on her head and rip her ear off.

She didn't get the chance.

Before she could stop it, the darkness flooded in, the cold, the nauseating dizziness. Until suddenly, incredibly, the noise began to ebb. And then there was nothing.

Nothing but blissful silence.

His package had passed out.

At least, he hoped that was all that'd happened.

Jared leaned forward, automatically shielding Morrow's body from the freezing rotor wash. From the sudden shift in the chopper's flight plan, he knew DeBruzkya's radars had finally started pinging like a bat screaming straight out of hell—especially when the chopper plummeted precariously low, hugging the pitch-black Rebelian terrain in a last-ditch, all-out attempt to remain undetected. He readjusted his grip as the next rise and dip caused their nylon harnesses to shift, locking his arms around Morrow's now limp body. But as the pilot swerved to avoid another cliff, Jared also knew that despite his iron determination, he was losing his package.

Fast.

The next whiplashing turn sealed his fate—and Morrow's. He didn't give a rat's ass how much ground the chopper had been able to cover. He had to get the pilot to set them down. *Now*.

He kept his gaze fused to the shadowy terrain, hoping to anticipate the next swerve as he slid his right arm down to hook it around Morrow's waist. He locked his hand to the man's—no, make that *woman's*—belt before carefully releasing his left arm. The second he was sure his modified grip would hold, he snapped his free hand up and ripped the emergency strobe off his web gear. He popped off a succession of red flashes straight up into the yawning steel belly, then immediately lashed his left arm back down around Morrow. To his relief, the crew chief returned the emergency signal within moments.

There was nothing to do now but wait. And pray.

Had he put enough distance between them and the castle?

Unfortunately the same dense cloud cover that had aided his initial insertion into DeBruzkya's stronghold hampered him now. He wouldn't know where they were until they hit the ground and he got a reading from the handheld global-positioning unit. But that was the least of his worries. Right now he needed to find out why Morrow had lost consciousness. From the moment he'd spied the machinery clustered between the beds in that makeshift hospital cell, he knew he was dealing with his worst-case, live-package scenario. Something or some*one* had knocked Alex Morrow into a coma. Head trauma or drugs—given their current precarious position, he couldn't be sure which. Much less who had caused it. But he would. Just as soon as this bird landed.

The chopper veered sharply again.

This time he was relieved. The moment those pounding blades changed pitch, he knew they were headed even lower. A quick glance at the shadowy, rapidly closing terrain, confirmed it. The pilot had located a clearing large enough to set them down in—but not large enough to land the bird.

Moments later his boots slammed into loose rock.

He let go of Morrow and ripped off his harness, recapturing the woman's still-unconscious body moments before it hit the ground. He cut her harness loose and scooped her into his arms as the chopper's crew chief kicked out several extra ammo clips. His battered hamstring and bicep burned in concert as he leaned down to snag the banana clips. He ignored the seeping wounds and carried Morrow into the shelter of the trees. He'd seal the gashes later. Just as soon as he examined his package.

His army medic training kicked in to high as he tossed the fresh ammo onto a bed of pine needles before laying the geologist's body out at the base of a tree. Within seconds he'd pulled his rucksack from his shoulders and dumped it along with his weapon, plowing through the ABCs of first aid as he leaned over her and gently removed her old bandages. Airway—clear. He lowered his head until his right cheek grazed the sparse, formerly hidden mustache above Morrow's lips. Breathing—shallow but mostly regular. He moved on to circulation, automatically sliding his fingers up his patient's exposed neck to seal them to her carotid artery.

Damn. Much too slow. Bradycardic and thready.

Jared tore through the medic's pouch at his hips, grabbing his stethoscope with his left hand and hooking it around his neck as he pressed his right to Morrow's sternum.

Only…it wasn't there.

If his palm wasn't still smoking from that blisteringly intimate introduction at the castle's ledge, he'd have panicked. Instead, he thumped the barrier. Solid rubber. *Prosthetic.* No doubt designed to flesh out the disguise.

It would have to go.

He grabbed the collar of her shirt and jerked his hands down and apart. Buttons flew off, smacking into pine needles, the tree trunk and his own jaw as the once-white fabric gave all the way to Morrow's waist. An extremely convincing masculine chest lay beneath, meticulously crafted from broad shoulders and moderately muscled pectorals, right down to the sparse thatch of hair embedded within the shadowy, textured skin. A quick sweep of his fingers assured him it was definitely synthetic skin.

Thank God.

The disguise was so good that for a moment there, he'd wondered if he wasn't losing ground more quickly than he feared. For all Hatch's reassurances, where would he and Morrow be then?

Jared crammed the insidious doubts back into their box and locked the lid as he ran his fingers up the right side of the prosthetic chest, locating the row of hooks that sealed the edges of the molded rubber together, as well as the second set hidden along the ridge of her shoulder. He popped both rows almost as quickly as he'd popped the buttons on that grimy men's dress shirt, biting back an instinctive whistle as he cracked the false chest open and pushed the phony pecs to the side.

Any doubt he had left vanished at the sight.

What lay beneath was definitely all woman.

Generously so. Right down to the stiff nipples crowning the twin ivory swells. Swells that had captured the intermittent starlight filtering through the pines of the Rebelian forest to gleam softly amid the shifting shadows. He ig-

nored his body's sudden, inappropriate reaction to the sight
and leaned down to press the disk of his stethoscope into
the upper curve of the woman's left breast, blocking out
the nocturnal symphony around them as he focused on the
gradually strengthening heartbeat pulsing through his ears.

Relieved, he withdrew the scope.

He lifted the woman's shoulders and slipped the stethoscope between the rear of the prosthetic and her equally
bare back, timing the rise and fall of her lungs as he eval-
uated their capacity. Satisfied, he withdrew the scope and
hooked it around his neck. But as he settled that mop of
matted brown hair into the pillow of pine needles, his fingertips brushed across a row of tiny, tightly spaced bumps
tracking up the woman's scalp, mere millimeters inside the
hairline, just behind her right ear.

Stitches?

Possibly the cause of that coma? Before he could lean
down close enough to find out, the body beneath his shifted.
Stiffened.

"What the *hell* do you think you're doing?"

He stiffened. Unfortunately he also dropped his gaze.
Stared. And damned if he didn't flush. He ripped his gaze
from those taunting swells, hoping the darkness would conceal the damning tide rapidly spreading up his neck. The
moment he met the dark-brown fury leveled on him, he
knew it hadn't. He eased his chest up from the woman's
exposed breasts. "I beg your pardon. I was…examining
you."

"Really?"

Given the circumstance, her dry sarcasm shouldn't have
stung. But it did.

Why he even gave a damn what some nerdy, hermaph-
roditic geologist thought was beyond him. He'd saved the
man's hide, for Christ's sake. Jared shifted to his haunches
as that same geologist sat up and closed the prosthetic over
those firm, telling breasts. Okay, he'd saved the *woman's*

hide. Didn't that earn him at least one get-out-of-a-faux-pas free card?

Evidently not.

What it earned him was an unobstructed view of the woman's entire torso as she scrambled to her knees, the false chest swinging wide as she swayed suddenly. He reached out to steady her, but the fury cutting through the coke-bottle lenses that had somehow survived their harrowing flight stopped him cold. He anchored his hands to the ends of the stethoscope at his neck and settled back onto his haunches, ignoring his burning hamstring as he noted the raw edges of the intravenous needle site on the back of the woman's hand.

She hadn't been out of that coma for long. It was best not to push her. At least, not until she'd had a chance to regain her balance and her bearings.

The agent in her kicked in sooner than he'd expected, because the moment her balance steadied, she pushed herself.

He watched, ready to grab her if need be, as she peeled the filthy shirt off what turned out to be her own sinewy arms, not the prosthetic's. She removed the rubber chest and dumped it onto the pine needles, those distinctly feminine curves gleaming amid the shadows as she retrieved the shirt once more. She slid the dingy sleeves up her arms, finally pausing as she hooked her fingers to the shirt's edges—and the row of missing buttons.

The woman's muddy brows arched as she lifted her chin. "Been a while, has it, Soldier?"

Damned if the fire didn't return to his neck.

He thought about apologizing, but he didn't. There was no way in hell he was telling anyone just how long it had been, much less this woman. Still, her pointed brow succeeded in scoring its second point.

Despite her wobbly balance, he could have turned away.

Before he could answer, she knotted the trailing ends of the shirt around her waist, then brought her hands to her face, peeling off that sparse mustache, then those thick, muddy brows, leaving smoothly arched wisps behind. Dark blond, light brown, he couldn't quite make out the color. There were too many shadows between them.

Evidently there were still too many angles, as well.

The hard edges of her jaw melted away next as she tucked her fingers inside her mouth and removed a set of temporary dental implants that had obviously been designed to alter the shape of her face. Her cheeks stood out pale and high in the dim light. Without the implants squaring her chin or the fake mustache drawing attention from her mouth, her lips were now full, almost lush.

· Jared unhooked one of the canteens from his web belt and set it on the ground between them, knowing she'd be needing it soon enough, just as he knew why she'd decided to pull a Victor/Victoria out in the middle of the Rebelian forest. DeBruzkya and his goons would be tracking two men. She was turning them into one man and one woman.

Not bad.

In fact, damned clever.

That, combined with her increasing steadiness, told him she'd come out of that coma with the brilliant brain Hatch had raved about still intact. He reached into his rucksack and pulled out the pair of work boots. He'd learned years ago that more often than not, a package was imprisoned sans shoes to lower morale and prevent escape. Morrow was no exception. He dumped the boots at her feet and added a pair of black socks.

"Thanks."

"No problem. I need to get a fix on our position. As soon as I get back, I'll finish examining you. Then we need to talk." He waited for her nod, then stood to retrieve the handheld global positioning unit from his jumpsuit as he headed for the clearing. Now that he was reasonably confident she'd survive the night, it was time to focus on other pressing concerns. Like where the hell they were. And how much ground they had left to cover before they arrived at their designated safe house.

Jared fired up the GPS unit as he reached the clearing.

Five kilometers.

His breath eased out. The chopper had ferried them farther than he'd thought, but still not far enough. Morrow might be steady now, but her weakened state had already caused her to pass out once. With this much ground to cover, there was a good chance it would happen again before the night was over.

The original plan had been to have the chopper cleave to the riverbed as long as possible. Three-quarters of the way up the river, the bird was supposed to have slowed just long enough to cut them loose. Then it would have resumed its breakneck speed, eventually veering west to head straight for the Rebelian-Gastonian border, De-Bruzkya and his radar twidgets never knowing he and Morrow had been left behind.

All that'd changed the moment Morrow passed out.

Once the chopper was forced to hover, the stalled blip on the scope would have afforded even DeBruzkya's inept twidgets a chance to pinpoint their modified infiltration site. Jared flicked off the GPS and shoved the unit into his pocket, then lit up the dial on his watch. Twenty minutes had passed since they'd set down. Just about long enough for DeBruzkya to scramble one of his own choppers and send it after them. He had to act quickly.

Jared retrieved his flashlight and lit up the gash on his biceps first. The ragged edges of the wound appeared black beneath the red beam streaming from his mini Maglite. So did the blood clot already filling in the center of the furrow. Even better, there was no sign of the bullet. This one could wait.

He swept the beam down to his left hamstring.

Unfortunately that one couldn't.

He twisted his torso to get a better view as he lit up the wash of black spreading down his left leg. *Damn.* He lowered his hand, biting down on a second curse as he probed the gash. The wound was twice as long as the rip across his biceps, but again, no bullet. Nor did it require a tourniquet.

Yet.

He retrieved a dark-green cravat from the first-aid pouch on his hip and stuffed the fabric into the tear in his pressure suit. Satisfied the makeshift bandage would do for the moment, he headed back into the pines, determined to get a look at the bumps he'd discovered in Morrow's hairline. Not to mention a better grasp on her vitals. He snagged the stethoscope from his neck and raised the flashlight, illuminating her form as he reached her. She finished tying her second boot and stood.

Sweet Mother above. He managed to retain his hold on the flashlight, but the scope hit the forest floor. If his leg burned as he leaned down to retrieve it, he didn't notice.

Damned near all he could discern was *her*.

As he'd anticipated, she'd used the water from the canteen to drench that unruly mop of hair. But the slicked-back result drew attention to more than a high forehead and smooth cheeks. Much more. The sleek style combined with those missing dental implants to highlight the curve of her now heart-shaped chin, drawing his gaze straight down her unusually long, graceful neck. Straight into the gaping V in that tatty shirt. All the way down to the knotted tails resting a bare inch above the riveting navel crowning her sleek belly.

"Well? I'm fresh out of lipstick and mirrors. Will I do?"

He must have taken too long trying to come up with a suitable answer. The unexpected awkwardness that flashed through her eyes as she waited killed the sultry effect and—thankfully—his body's powerful reaction to it. Her tongue slid across her bottom lip as he lowered the Maglite. He recognized the motion for what it was. A nervous habit.

For a split second he was reminded of Morrow, the man. Carnal sex and awkward, nerdy innocence?

It didn't make sense. Then again, what part of the entire transformation did? Beyond a copious list of professional qualifications, Jared hadn't been able to glean much from the personnel file Hatch had provided. But he had discovered that Dr. *Alexander* Morrow had been connected to ARIES for the past six years. What kind of woman was willing to suppress the essence of her being this completely, for that long? And why?

Dammit, it was none of his business. *She* was none of his business. He had a patient to heal. An agent to return to active duty. A joint mission to complete. And despite what his mentor thought, he also had a ranch and a life to return to.

For a few years, anyway.

Hatch.

Jared stiffened as the stunning realization slammed into him from out of nowhere—and then from everywhere.

"What's wrong? Do I look that bad—or are we that far off position?"

He dropped his gaze to the fingers that had made their way to his forearm. Fingers that were long and tapered but also, now that he thought about it, noticeably feminine. He dragged his gaze up to those murky eyes and stared into them, ignoring the growing concern as he searched the shadows that were probably as phony as the rest of her, furious at their boss and furious with her. But most of all, furious with himself.

In the heat of their escape, he hadn't even noticed the most insidious deception of all.

The lie of omission.

"Why the hell didn't he tell me you were a woman?"

Chapter 3

He didn't know.

Alex sucked in her breath as the relief crashed through her, buffeting her tenuous hold on equilibrium. Desperate to maintain it, she closed her eyes. It was a mistake. The undertow snagged her balance and she went down—until his hands came snapping up to grab her arms and steady her.

"Easy."

If anything, the raw husk in Jared's voice caused the world to churn faster. She sealed her eyes shut and dug her fingers into his forearms, waiting for the dizziness to ebb before she dared to open them. Before she dared to face that piercing amber stare—and that dangerous question.

The world steadied and she opened her eyes. Relief swamped Alex again, but this time she held fast. Jared had dropped the flashlight to grab her. With the crimson glow at his feet, his dusky features were safely cloaked within the shadows, his black jumpsuit and knit hat helping him blend in with the forest and the reigning night.

Thank God.

Her brain was still rattling around in her skull after that fiasco of a chopper flight. While the faulty microphones hardwired to her hearing aid were still magnifying every nocturnal buzz, drone, trill and chirp within a two-mile radius with fanatical precision, she could at least hear herself think. Even so, she did not need to stare into this man's shrewd gaze. Not until she'd had a chance to regain her composure.

She released her fingers. "I'm fine now. You can let go."

He didn't.

"I swear, I won't faint on you."

He continued to hold her arms for several moments, silently assessing her before he, too, released his grip. She waited as he leaned down to retrieve the flashlight. But as he straightened, she caught the glimmer of metal in his hands, plastic tubing.

His stethoscope.

Apprehension crawled through her, elbowing out the relief. "I said, I'm fine."

"I'm sure you are. But I need to get a look at your scalp." He shifted the scope and flashlight to his right hand and reached out with his left. "I think you've got—"

She jerked her head out reach. "I know. I found the stitches earlier when I removed the gauze someone had smothered my head and face with. They're fine."

"They may also be connected to your coma. I'll need to examine them."

The hell he did. She didn't care if those stitches were knitted across a six-inch, seeping gash, that hand wasn't getting anywhere near her hearing aid. She took another step. "I just told you, I examined them. They're fine. I'm fine. The cut has already healed." She took a third step, stopping when the back of her shirt snagged against a tree, trapping her. "Shouldn't you be filling me in on the plan? When's the replacement chopper due?"

He stood there for several moments, then sighed. She eased her breath out as he finally hooked the stethoscope around his neck and switched off the flashlight. Evidently he'd decided not to push the issue—for the moment.

She grabbed the reprieve gratefully.

"There isn't one."

She blinked. "I beg your pardon?"

"Replacement chopper. There won't be one. Not for several weeks. Perhaps longer." He tipped the end of the darkened flashlight toward her ear. "Which goes back to why I really do need to examine you. There's been a change of plans, Agent Morrow. You have new orders. We both do."

She sucked in her breath, swallowed her curse. He might not have been briefed about her gender or the hearing aid, but he did know who she really was. Or rather, whom she worked for. Wait a minute. "*We* have new orders?" She clamped down on a fresh surge of dizziness as she waited for him to respond.

"We'll be working together on this one."

No bloody way.

"That's impossible. I signed on as a singleton. I always work alone. Always. Sam knows that. Dammit, he wouldn't—"

"Sam?"

The rasp might have been deceptively soft, fused with the barest hint of the Texas drawl of his youth, but it was also rife with speculation.

This time, she swallowed an entire string of curses.

And then she nodded.

She didn't have much of a choice. She knew what he was thinking. What any agent who knew Samuel Hatch as well as Jared Sullivan knew him would be thinking.

She was on a first-name basis with the director of ARIES. A director who'd just risked an international incident to free her from that damned makeshift hospital cell. A director who'd risked the life of another agent—an agent Sam loved and trusted more than he would his own son if he'd had one. But he obviously didn't trust that agent enough to tell him she was a woman. He had to suspect that she'd slept with the man. She didn't care.

It was better than the truth.

She sealed her fate with a single, telling shrug and damned herself to hell in the process. "Since Rita died, Sam and I have become…close." It was the truth. But she also knew Jared would misconstrue it. Especially when she felt his gaze drop to the yawning gap in her shirt and linger there.

He dragged it up. "I'll just bet you have." His shadowy shrug was pointed. Insolent. "Too bad *Sam* has chosen to ignore your desires—and passed you off to me."

Damn him.

Alex sucked up her pride as each of her forbidden fantasies about this man crumbled beneath reality. She should have caved in to temptation and engineered another meeting with Jared months ago, that one as herself. It would have saved her far too many sleepless nights. As it was, she still had to deal with *this* night. With him. The real Jared Sullivan and not some erotic figment of her imagination.

The silence between them thickened until it succeeded in deafening the constant nocturnal cacophony ringing through her ear. She should wait. Force him to break it.

To her astonishment, he did it on his own.

He reached up and pulled the knit cap from his head as he sighed. "Look, I was out of line. I have a lot of respect for Samuel Hatch. He's a good director. A good man. What he does on his down time is his own business. Let's just say I'm a little pissed to find out he sent me on a job without giving me all the facts. But I shouldn't have taken that out on you. It's not as if you knew I was coming."

But she had concealed that same damning fact from him, hadn't she? Not tonight, but three short months ago. Though she now knew this man would never, ever, bring up that brief, piercingly uncomfortable meeting, she could feel the accusation hanging between them—thrumming with betrayal.

With disappointment.

He might not know that she'd overheard half that call, but he did know she'd come out of that bathroom in time to discover tears trickling down the face of the Man of Stone himself, just before she'd dared to offer her own awkward sympathy. Never once mentioning that she was a woman.

Maybe it was the convoluted effects of that blasted coma. Maybe it was the escape. Maybe it was the constant, distracting racket in her ear. Hell, maybe deep down she was really just a coward at heart. Because she'd just discovered that she didn't have the nerve to address that night at Hatch's house out loud, either. Much less confess that she knew why he'd been so devastated. So she addressed the only part she could. "You're right. Sam is a good man." The best. But he was also more.

At least to her.

Unfortunately, if Sam hadn't confided their relationship to Jared, then it wasn't her place to share it, either. To do so would shatter the bargain she and her uncle had struck years before and, whether or not she believed Sam, would also risk both their careers, as well as her life. A life Sam had entrusted to the man waiting patiently to see if she'd accept his apology.

She should. Truth be known, she owed Jared an apology, as well, for her behavior when she'd regained consciousness in his arms. Behavior she still didn't understand. She knew full well the man hadn't been copping a feel. From the few but telling comments Sam had dropped regarding this particular operative through the years, Jared Sullivan was not a rutting stag. The opposite, in fact. Hadn't she overheard proof of that herself?

She sighed. "Look, Agent Sullivan—"

"Jared."

Alex stared into the dark, searched the shadows shrouding the man's imposing body, especially the ones obscuring the equally imposing planes of his face. She finally gave up. He was just too far away. What she'd have given to have superhuman sight to go along with her souped-up hearing. Or at the very least have the nerve to snag that flashlight and shine it on that razor-sharp gaze. To know for certain if those eyes were glowing from the extension of an honest-to-goodness olive branch—or gleaming with open speculation.

He'd offered his real first name. What was hers?

She reached for the branch—and ignored the guilt. She extended her hand. "Dr. *Alexandra* Morrow."

Even a detailed check into her background from someone at his level would support her claim. Whether or not he believed her, he extended his hand as well, the hard warmth engulfing hers. Heat slid up her arm. Her breath came out in rush.

He frowned. "You okay?"

"I'm fine." She tugged her hand from his grip as quickly as she dared and forced a smile. "Still a little woozy, I guess."

How long could she abuse that excuse?

His frown cleared as he nodded. "It's because of the coma. I'm surprised you've held up as well as you have. You're one for the medical books, you know that?"

She might. But he didn't know the half of it.

She returned his nod, anyway. "I admit there was a moment there when I didn't think I'd make it. If you hadn't slung me into that harness…" She trailed off, wincing in memory—and then in reality as the magnified screech of a hoot owl somewhere overhead ripped through her skull. Even so, that owl had nothing on that thundering iron bird. "You saved my life back there. I'd like to thank—"

He shook his head, cutting her off. "It's not necessary."

"Yes, it is." She risked the dizziness and captured his hands, squeezing them quickly. "Thank you." She breathed her relief as the roiling vertigo remained at bay—

until an unmistakably erotic pull replaced it as he squeezed back.

"You're welcome."

She swore she could feel the air between them warm. Thicken. She did not want to know if he felt it, too.

Leave it to her blasted hyperactive hearing aid to pick up the masked *whoosh* of his own breath. This time, it was his hand that executed a discreet retreat. His entire body withdrew several steps, too. He turned and dropped his stethoscope, flashlight and black knit hat beside the rucksack and machine gun he'd left at the base of a tree. He unhooked his web gear next, adding the nylon harness to the pile. His first-aid kit followed. Moments later his massive chest blocked her view as he hunkered down. It didn't matter. The vibrations from the zippers at the legs of his jumpsuit ripped across her eardrum as he released the rows of metal teeth just above his boots. They died out as he stood to peel the insulated coveralls down and off his boots, boots that until that moment she hadn't realized were more lumberjack than Airborne Ranger. A second later the jumpsuit joined the pile of gear. She watched, intrigued, as he tugged the rubber band from his hair. The shadows obscuring his features deepened as the thick silk slipped past his shoulders to settle around his face.

"Well?"

She nodded approvingly as he stepped in front of her. Evidently she wasn't the only quick-change artist around. With his hair flowing freely and that matching cable-knit turtleneck toning down his massive chest and arms, in addition to his dark jeans and nondescript jump boots, Agent Sullivan looked more like a local woodsman out for a midnight stroll than a finely honed ARIES operative on the prowl in the backwoods of...

"Where are we?"

He stilled. "You don't remember?"

Before she could answer, he turned back to the pile of

gear, leaning down to retrieve something. She stared at the disk of that gleaming scope as he returned.

Great.

She steeled herself as he moved in close, determined to ignore his scent and his warmth as he tucked the cool disk into the curve of her upper breast. "I don't have a blessed clue where we are. The last I remember, I was attending a conference in Holzberg. I'm not even sure how long I was out. I woke up a couple of days ago…I think. It's hard to say, since I kept falling back under. Twice I saw someone else. A man. He'd been beaten severely. I think he was a doctor or at least a nurse assigned to treat me."

He slipped the scope from the gap in her shirt and tucked it beneath her collar, sliding the disk far enough down her back to listen to her lungs. "Why?"

"He was wearing a white lab coat."

"I don't suppose—"

"No. I didn't see a name. I didn't hear one, either. Except for my own." She breathed easier as he withdrew the scope and hooked the tubing around his neck—until he lit up the face of his watch. The dial glowed softly as he captured her wrist and timed her pulse. She willed it to slow.

"Hmm."

Was that a good "hmm" or a bad "hmm"? She decided on the former, easing out her breath as he withdrew his fingers altogether, then headed for the pile of gear. He headed back, sans scope—but with a mini flashlight in his right hand.

Oh boy.

"The man spoke to you?"

Her panic revved as Jared turned on the flashlight.

"Alex?"

She dragged her gaze to his. She'd been right to worry earlier. Those amber eyes might be mesmerizing, but they were also much too shrewd for her peace of mind. She could almost feel her ear throb beneath them. He was waiting.

What had he asked her?

She shoved the panic down and cleared her throat. "Excuse me?"

"The man. You said you heard your name. Did he speak?"

"No—yes." She shook her head, shook off the panic. "No. He wasn't the one who called my name. But, yes, he did speak. The first time I came to, he was leaning over me, talking softly, as if he thought someone might be listening. At least I think so. At the time I was woozy, confused. I couldn't understand the language. It could have been Rebelian, but I can't be sure." She'd been pretty out of it. "Anyway, by the time he switched to English, I'd passed out. The next time I awoke, he was handcuffed to the bed beside mine. At first I thought he might be sleeping—or dead. But then a couple of armed thugs entered the room. He'd been beaten into unconsciousness. They dragged him out, probably for another round of torture." She fell silent as Jared sighed. The sound was heavy, rife with regret

"I'm sorry. I had my orders."

"I know." She also knew he truly hadn't had time to search for the man when they left. In the end, neither of them had. If Jared had bowed to her demands and gone back, all three of them would be dead by now.

"I'll put out the word. See what I can find out. Maybe we'll get lucky. Hell, maybe he did."

She flinched as Jared slid his fingers beneath her chin. He had to have noticed, but he didn't comment on it as he gently turned her head and tipped it slightly. She forced the panic down again, forced herself not to pull away as he bathed the side of her face with the red glow from his flashlight.

"The thugs, did they say anything?"

She didn't dare move, much less nod. "Yes. But again,

I can't be sure about the dialect. I do know they were carrying AK-47s. The rifles sported Romanian forward pistol grips.'' No surprise there. The Romanian black market had been thoughtfully arming the goons of Eastern Europe for years. She dug her fingertips into her palms as he probed the line of stitches behind her right ear.

Don't move. Keep him talking.

It just might keep him distracted enough.

"So…where exactly in Rebelia are we?"

It worked. He withdrew his fingers and switched off the flashlight before tucking it into the back pocket of his jeans. "Fifty-one kilometers inside the northeastern corner of the Hartz forest. Two days ago, another ARIES operative by the name of Robert Davidson and his fiancée Lily Scott discovered you were being held in General Bruno De-Bruzkya's stronghold, Veisweimar—a medieval castle that served as a makeshift prison in World War II. As you discovered for yourself, DeBruzkya has since turned the castle into a fortress. The information came from the general himself. He told Lily you were alive, but he never said you were unconscious. Hatch sent me in to pull you out."

It made sense. The last thing she knew, she was supposed to meet a colleague. To discuss DeBruzkya and his threats to— Nothing. The memory stopped there.

Again.

"What is it?"

"My head." More specifically, her memory. "It's just not there." She dug her fingers into her temples, but the impromptu massage didn't help now any more than the previous hundred desperate kneadings had. "No matter how hard I try, I just *can't* remember what happened."

Thanks to her hearing aid, the base curse he'd meant to keep beneath his breath reverberated through her ear.

"I'm sorry."

He sighed. "Don't be. It's not your fault. In fact, it's extremely common. Most coma patients don't remember

the events directly proceeding their trauma. It's called ret-
rograde amnesia.''

Just what she *didn't* need to hear.

Her curse echoed his.

"What do you remember? According to Hatch, the last
he heard you were about to meet with a Delmonican colleague. A man by the name of Karl—''

"Weiss.'' She nodded. "That much I do remember. I
also remember why we were supposed to meet. Karl and I
first met years ago, shortly after I joined ARIES. It took a
few years to develop him, but he's turned out to be one of
my more reliable sources. He'd contacted me a couple of
days before, asking me to meet him in Prague. But he was
nervous. Karl said he'd stumbled across something regarding General DeBruzkya, something I would find fascinating…and frightening. I asked him to meet me in Washing-
ton, D.C. since I was scheduled to deliver a paper before
the Congressional Subcommittee on Environment, Technology and Standards. Karl refused.''

"Why?''

She shrugged. "He didn't say. But I got the distinct impression he was afraid he was being followed. Terrified
even. And you have to know Karl—he's a big man.'' She
flicked her gaze to Jared's massive shoulders. "Almost as
big as you. Karl doesn't scare easily. But trust me, he was
then.''

"So you agreed to meet on his turf.''

She nodded. "The conference in Holzberg was perfect.
Karl's a physicist who spends much of his spare time devoted to regional environmental issues, and I—''

"Received dual doctoral degrees in environmental geology and chemistry. You graduated with honors.''

She blinked. "How did you know that?''

"I read your dossier on the flight.''

She could have sworn he flushed.

It must have been the shifting shadows, the sliver of
moonlight filtering through the slowly parting clouds. She

shrugged it off and sent out a silent thanks to her former ARIES mentor for pounding home the first rule of under-cover work six years before. *Stick to the truth, honey, when-ever and wherever possible. It'll save you from getting bit in the ass when you least expect it.* Good ol' Aiden Swift. No doubt about her memory there.

She wished she could say the same for Karl. "I remem-ber checking in to the hotel, but that's it."

"Nothing else at all? We know you arrived, because you sent an initial message. Try picturing yourself at the con-ference, seeing Karl, shaking his hand, sitting down to catch a lecture with him, even a meal. Try—"

"Dammit, I *told* you. I don't remember. It's like the whole conference was sucked into a black hole. There's nothing to picture because there's nothing there. I can't remember if we were supposed to meet in my room or in his. Hell, I don't even remember if we met at all." She pushed her fingers to her temples and growled. But again, it didn't help.

"Take it easy. It's okay. If the memory's not there, don't force it. You'll only lock yourself up more."

She lowered her hands and sighed. "Is it permanent?"

"Loss of the final traumatic event that caused the am-nesia can be. But given enough time and rest, you may be able to recall the memories leading up to it."

May? She was stuck in the middle of Rebelia with no idea of who'd smashed in the side of her skull and dragged her across the border, and all Jared could do was tell her she *may* eventually remember? She turned and stalked over to the pile of gear he'd left at the base of the next tree, resisting the sudden, almost overwhelming urge to kick his rucksack back to Holzberg. And when those damned hands settled over her shoulders, their calming warmth sparked the opposite effect than the one he'd obviously intended, ratcheting her anger up another level.

"Relax."

She spun around. "Relax? That's easy for you to say.

You're not the one with a great big blank where part of your life should be.''

He shrugged. "Like I said, it's normal."

"Normal." She snorted, unable to let go of the inexplicable fury despite his soothing voice, or maybe because of it. She crossed her arms and glared at him. "You're awfully calm for someone who just learned his partner has a hole in her brain."

Another one of those infuriating enigmatic shrugs.

She was a split second from exploding when her fury simply…evaporated. Stranger still, she wasn't as stunned by that as she was by the intense urge to weep that supplanted it.

Weep?

No way. She did not cry. Dammit, she'd cried a total of three measly times in the past fifteen years. The first when her father died. The second when her aunt Rita had passed away. The third pity-fest had taken place four months later, halfway through graduate school, the day she'd discovered just how much the love of her life wasn't in love with her. She hadn't cried since.

So why the devil was she blubbering now?

"It's the coma." He tipped her chin. To her utter humiliation, he reached up and smoothed the tears from her cheeks.

"I swear, I never—" She sealed her shame with a violent, shuddering hiccup.

"I know. I told you, it's the aftereffects of the coma." He pulled her close and guided her head to his shoulder, stroking his hands up and down her back as she continued to sob for all she was worth, drenching the inky strands of his hair along with the wool sweater beneath. "Shh. It's okay. The anger, the crying jags, the mood swings. They're normal, I promise. They'll pass."

Eventually they did. At least this one did. Unfortunately, by that time she managed to pull herself together, the shame had set in. She tried backing away, but his arms stopped her.

"Don't."

She flinched as he tucked her hair behind her ear. She was simply too raw to prevent it. "*Please.* Let me go."

"No." His fingers slipped beneath her chin. "Look at me."

Why? It was too dark.

Except it wasn't. Not this close. Not anymore. The blanket of clouds had thinned even more, spreading apart to leave a generous three-quarter moon and a broad swath of stars behind. The twinkling lights studded the canopy of the pine forest, allowing her to make out that tawny gaze with painful perfection. She didn't want to see it. To see him. And she certainly didn't want him seeing her. Not like this. She'd hadn't felt this exposed in her entire life. In less than two hours, under the obscuring cover of night, this man had managed to see far too much.

God only knew what he'd see in the harsh light of day.

"Are you okay now?"

Not by a long shot. "Yes. Will you please release me?"

He did.

They both breathed easier.

She stepped away from the pile of gear as he hunkered down, fully aware that she was affording herself room, rather than him. He dug through his ruck and pulled out a dark T-shirt. Before she could stop him, he'd stripped the sweater from his chest and he held it out.

"Put it on. We've got a decent hike ahead of us."

"No, you keep it. Since you've read my file, you know I did my grad work in Colorado. I doubt I'll even notice the cold."

"You've also been in a coma for three weeks. Trust me, you'll notice."

Three weeks? Just like that, the vertigo returned. She swallowed the nausea that came with it. "That long?"

He nodded…and held out the sweater.

This time she took it. Evidently he was right about the mood swings, because she couldn't muster the brazenness she'd ridden earlier as she'd stripped the prosthetic from her chest in front of him. She left the filthy shirt tied beneath her breasts and pulled the thick turtleneck on over it. His tantalizing scent swirled through her, suffocating her. Worse, the sweater still carried his heat.

Ignore it.

Somehow she managed—until she glanced up and caught the glimmer of moonlight slipping across that seriously sculpted, dangerously dusky chest. A moment later the rippling muscles disappeared beneath the T-shirt. Disappointment warred with relief as he tucked the hem into his jeans, then leaned down to repack his rucksack. But at least her lungs had kicked in. She breathed deeply as she pushed up the sweater's sleeves.

Shock yanked the air right back out.

Blood?

She raised her right arm and fingered the damp stitching again, the raw edges of the rip. She leaned closer, this time sniffing the knit fabric, and cursed.

"You were shot."

He nodded as leaned down to tuck his jumpsuit into the ruck. "Grazed."

"Let me take a look."

"I already did." Before she could argue, he reached into his first-aid kit and pulled out another cravat. He flipped the green fabric over itself and wrapped the resulting triangle around his right biceps as he stood. "But you can tie it off for me."

Alex retrieved the ends as he stepped in front of her, avoiding the man's steady gaze as she pulled the fabric snugly against the muscle bulging beneath the bandage. His subtle, smoky scent swirled through her. Dammit, he was fantasy fodder, nothing more. A figment of her dreams. She secured the knot quickly and stepped back. "How far?"

His dark brows rose as he glanced up.

"The hike," she clarified. "I assume we're headed to a safe house."

"We are. Four kilometers." He flipped his thumb over his right shoulder. "That way."

"And this new assignment? It has to do with Karl and Bruno DeBruzkya, doesn't it?"

Jared took a step back, as well. But he said nothing.

He was holding out on her. She could feel it. The air between them had changed. Grown cool, distant. Almost wary. Like him. For a man who'd been tasked with a mission, a mission he'd already told her she shared, he was suspiciously closemouthed. Why? All she'd done was ask about DeBruzkya and—

"Karl."

Jared reversed his direction, this time stepping toward her. Still guarded, still wary. If anything, even more so. His body language sealed it. Her memory might not have been functioning up to par, but her instincts were. She took a deep breath, sucked up the pain and regret and just said it. "He's dead, isn't he?"

Jared nodded slowly. "When ARIES lost contact with you, they went searching for Karl. He wasn't there. Not in your room or his. He didn't settle his hotel bill, nor did he attend his own lecture scheduled for the following day. He just vanished. Our recon team found traces of blood in his room. His type. A week later his body turned up on the outskirts of town. It wasn't pretty." He reached out and cupped his hands to her shoulders. "You okay?"

"No. He was a contact, but he was also my friend." She grimaced at the irony of it. At her pathetic self. Karl might have been her friend. But he hadn't even known she was a woman.

"H-how—" She swallowed the tears that threatened for the second time. She refused to give in to them. Nothing would be gained by it. Karl would be better served if she focused on finding the bastard who murdered him. She pictured her friend. His shaggy blond hair. His awkward, hulk-

ing body. That damned goofy grin. The passion that radi-
ated off him when he spoke about his true love, physics.

It worked.

The tears dried and the pain in her heart eased, if only
slightly. But at least she could think about Karl without
that stifling sense of suffocation that had clamped down
onto her lungs since she awoke. She could even see him at
the conference, in his hotel room— ''That's it!''

''You remember seeing him?''

''Yes. We were supposed to meet in his hotel room. We
did. I was furious, too.''

''Why?''

''Because he'd had me fly halfway around the world to
rehash some wild Rebelian legend about the Gem of
Power.''

''The Gem of—''

''Power.'' She nodded. ''I know. As wacky as it sounds,
it's true. It has to do with some ancient regional story about
a jewel that was supposed to give one man the power to
rule the world. Can you believe it? Karl Weiss was a con-
tender for the Nobel prize in physics three years ago, and
he's wasting my time on some pile of hokey drivel. I was
pissed as hell and I told him so.'' Poor, driven, didn't-get-
out-much, Karl.

Maybe that's why they'd hit it off.

''You're sure it's hokey?''

She blinked. Surely Jared wasn't referring to Karl's tale?
She studied his face in the moonlight.

Good Lord, he was.

''What did you say your degree was in?''

''I didn't.''

She waited.

''Well?''

''I dropped out before high school. Eighth grade. I have
a GED.'' Shame burned through her as he stepped away
and turned to busy himself with tucking the spare ammo
magazines into the side pockets on the rucksack. Except

for the prosthetic chest, the remnants of her disguise followed his gear into the main pouch.

He pulled the flap down and tugged it tight.

Way to go, Alex. Open mouth, insert foot. Chew.

He stood.

"I'm sorry."

"Why?" He shrugged. "I'm not."

She opened her mouth, but his gaze cut her off. A gaze that unfortunately, despite the two feet of forest between them, she could see quite clearly. Steel wasn't gray, it was amber.

Dark, cool amber.

He swung the ruck onto his shoulders, then grabbed the machine gun and prosthetic, effectively ending the conversation as he turned to take the lead position through the sparse but shadowy forest undergrowth. Maybe he was right. Maybe it was best to let it drop. At least for the moment.

She turned to follow him. Alex took exactly five steps—and stiffened.

Either Jared's hearing was as good as hers or his instincts were better, because he swung around. "What is it? Are you still feeling dizzy—"

She held up her hand.

He fell silent. Unfortunately the forest didn't. The sounds were faint, but they were definitely there. Snarling, yapping. Yelping. She definitely heard it. Heard them. An entire pack of them.

Dogs. Worse, she could make out the faint bellows of their handlers as well. Adrenaline surged through her.

"Run!" She lurched forward and grabbed Jared's arm, managing to drag his massive body a good eight feet before he jerked the both of them to a halt. "Move, dammit! I hear bloodhounds."

And they were racing *toward* them.

Chapter 4

Jared froze, blocking out the nocturnal noises of the forest, the shallow breathing of the woman locked to his arm. The woman was hearing things. She had to be.

"Alex, I don't hear—"

"I don't *care,* I do. Now let's go!"

He winced as her frenzied fingers bit into the wound on his biceps again as she attempted to drag him another eight feet. He was ready this time. He planted his six-foot-four-inch frame to the forest floor and refused to budge. "Dammit, Alex, DeBruzkya's castle is a good twenty minutes away by chopper, and I don't hear one of those, either."

Her fingers dug deeper. "I don't care if that castle is in South America. Maybe DeBruzkya has an outpost nearby. I don't know. But I do know I hear *dogs.* Now move!"

He closed his hand over hers and gently pried her fingers from his smarting arm. Maybe the coma had affected more than her memory. Maybe it had affected her hearing or her reasoning, too. He didn't know. But he did know she was serious.

She was also frantic. *"Please.* You've got to trust me."

He stared into her eyes and weighed the risks. If he allowed Alex to push herself physically before her body was ready, she could suffer a serious setback. But if he didn't, the perceived betrayal could bring on another, possibly violent personality shift, potentially damaging her brain and neural system, anyway. "All right. But I set the pace."

"Fine. Just make it a fast one."

He did, deliberately choosing the smoothest and most level route he could through the undergrowth. Five minutes later, he changed his assessment of her mental state. Her hearing, as well. Both were functioning perfectly—because he could now hear the occasional faint snarl and yap of hounds, too. He locked his right hand to her arm and picked up the pace. Fortunately Agent Morrow was a runner. Or she had been before the coma. She met his pounding stride easily, matching the focused pace of his breathing intake for intake. Five minutes later he had the sinking feeling that if they kept up the challenging clip much longer, he'd soon have trouble keeping up with her.

His leg was worse than he'd thought.

He could feel the blood trickling down his left hamstring, soaking his jeans down to his calf, causing the fabric to cling and ride up on his entire leg. The cloth pulled across his wound steadily, tearing the gash wider with each step. Another few minutes and the hounds would be following the ripe, steady scent of fresh blood.

He slowed their pace, then brought them to a halt as he shoved his free hand into his first-aid kit, air ripping in and out of their lungs as he rooted around for another cravat.

"Wh-what is it? What's wr—"

"I need a tourniquet."

He felt her gaze drop to his arm, but before she could swallow her exhaustion long enough to tell him his biceps didn't look that bad, he smelled it.

"Water."

He jerked his gaze to hers, startled because she'd said it

for him. She was staring directly over his shoulder. What the hell? "You hear ducks, too?"

She glared back. "Don't you?"

No, he smelled them. But now wasn't the time to get into that. He spun about until his back faced her. "Reach inside the outer pouch, at the bottom. You'll feel a vial. Grab it."

He felt her release the strap. "What's in it?"

"Deer urine."

"Thank God." The rucksack shifted as she rooted through the pouch. "Got it."

He waited until she tugged the strap home before he spun around to sprinkle a liquid more precious than gold between their boots and the closing hounds. If he'd doused their trail properly, one whiff and those dogs would lock on to a new target—an imaginary female deer—with a vengeance. There wasn't a damned thing the hounds' handlers would be able to do about it.

Alex grinned as she grabbed the empty vial from his hands when he finished and stuffed it into her pocket. "It's almost worth it to stick around to see their faces."

He grinned back. "Yeah."

Almost. It was time to take care of the handlers. He tore through his medic's pouch, retrieving the cravat he'd originally stopped for. He wasted precious seconds wrapping it around his thigh and knotting it before they took off again, this time ninety degrees out from their original route.

Two minutes later they were there.

Relief burned into his lungs, supplanting air, as he caught sight of the lake. The water stretched a good mile. He skimmed the map he'd memorized the night before, verifying the global positioning unit's earlier results as he pinpointed their location in his head. His leg gave way slightly as he stepped forward.

This time she caught him.

"Thanks." He glanced down at his leg and cursed. The

tourniquet had loosened during their sprint. He was losing blood and a lot of it.

The snarling hounds grew louder, closer.

Alex waded into the water and leaned down to study the thatch of plants floating at the surface. "The water's healthy." They both knew it wouldn't have mattered. They didn't have a choice but to cross. She turned back, her hand outstretched as she reached the rocky bank. "Give me your flashlight."

He reversed his earlier assessment. The coma had to have affected the woman's reasoning, after all. Why else did she intend to offer those bellowing men a visual?

"Dammit, Jared, I'm not nuts. Give me the Mag."

He dug the flashlight out of his pocket and passed it over. What the hell. If he had to go, might as well be on the job. But by the time she'd unscrewed the base of the Maglite and started in on the flared head, he knew she wasn't nuts. He also knew why Samuel Hatch had been dragged far enough out of his grief to notice the woman. Not only was Alex stunning, she was truly brilliant. Most people he'd met who were that sharp didn't have more than two common-sense brain cells to rub together. She had billons. And she'd just used them to buy them time.

Air.

She shoved the discarded ends of the Mag, as well as the batteries and spring, into her trouser pocket and gripped the empty black steel tube as she latched on to his arm once more. They leaned on each other as they waded out into the lake, stopping when the water reached chest level. From the stats he'd skimmed, it wouldn't get much deeper. Not soon enough to do them any good. He kept the ruck on his back and slung the rifle on top. The gear's weight would help keep them down.

He glanced back. "This is far enough." Besides, the snarling hounds were just over the rise. He could hear them. Feel them. It was now or never. "Ready?"

She nodded firmly.

"Then let's do it." He sucked in one last breath along with her as he knitted the fingers of his left hand firmly into her right, pulled her close and dragged her under.

He settled the ruck into the rocky lake bottom, settling her body beside his in the murky water. Ten seconds later he refused first pass at the Mag's tube with a squeeze of his hand. He raised his arm slowly, guiding her toward the surface, instead. The squeeze she sent back told him she'd reached it, had emptied and refilled her lungs, and was ready to come back down. He pulled her to the lake bottom, holding her there as he accepted the tube with his right and pushed off with his boots. A silent exhale, a fresh store of air, and he was headed down. They repeated the drill for close to a hundred breaths apiece before he felt comfortable enough to let his gaze skim the water.

Dogs.

Half a dozen, near as he could tell. Twice that many handlers. Though the deer urine had destroyed the hounds' single-minded resolve, it hadn't put a dent in the handlers'. The camouflaged men were still milling about the perimeter of the lake, determined to pick up the trail.

Crap.

Jared slipped beneath the surface once more. The moment he settled on the bottom and prepared to nudge Alex to the surface, he realized he had more to worry about than DeBruzkya's goons. Morrow's hand was locked to his, her fingers tense. Shaking. He pulled her close when she completed her breath, skipping his turn to seal her torso, hips and legs to his side. Damn. Her entire body was trembling. A three-mile sprint on top of a coma? He didn't care how in shape she'd been. If those soldiers didn't leave soon, her battered body was headed straight into shock. Her grip tightened as he claimed his next breath, the shaking in her limbs increasing as he settled back.

He forced himself not to panic.

She was fine. They'd be fine.

Just as long as she didn't pass out.

The world was dark again. Silent. And she was damned near *frozen*.

Alex clamped down on every major instinct in her body. The ones screaming at her to shoot to the surface, to stand and kick her legs into motion, to run as far away from this dark, suffocatingly wet coffin as she could get. If it wasn't for the steady hand still locked to hers, guiding her toward the surface of the lake for what had to be the thousandth time, she would have. A wave of almost violent chills ripped through her body as she sank back down to the bottom and passed the steel tube to Jared. She locked her jaw against them, willed herself not to take in water. If she did, she'd be done for. If she didn't go insane first. Though she hadn't wanted for air since she and Jared had settled in, the pressure on her chest was slowly but surely driving her over the brink. The next wave of chills didn't help.

And then, suddenly, it was over.

She hadn't even realized Jared had broken the surface of the water until he reached down and used both hands to drag her to her feet. Water streamed down their faces and bodies, as well as the machine gun and rucksack on Jared's shoulders. He wrapped his arm around her waist and led her to the bank. She stopped when they reached the shore, instinctively straining her ear against the night, sifting through the nocturnal sounds of the forest.

There.

She could still hear the hounds, as well as their handlers, but they were faint and growing fainter by the second. She breathed her relief—until her hearing aid sparked.

"—kay?"

A lifetime of electrical interference, low batteries and the occasional downright shorting out allowed her to nod.

"I'm fine." But if she didn't get him on her left side soon, that could change. A moment later, her hearing aid cut out, then back in again. She heard Jared's deep, steady breathing as he, like her, worked to convince his lungs their air supply was no longer being rationed. She forced herself to relax as he helped her over the bank. But the second they re-entered the forest, the tension returned.

She winced as a high-pitched electronic whine sliced through her ear—and then there was nothing but silence. She reached up as discreetly as she could and cupped her right ear, tucking the tip of her index finger inside to tap the center of her concha. Again, nothing. The hearing aid was dead.

She was completely deaf on her right side.

The vertigo returned and not because of the coma.

Or him.

"—ur yo— —kay?"

Hell, no. She nodded, anyway, taking advantage of Jared's distraction as he stopped to adjust the ruck, and slipped around to his right side, affording him her left ear. The only hearing ear she had left. "I can take a turn with the ruck."

His gaze snapped to hers. With the clouds nearly gone, moon and starlight bled across the sky, glinting off the disbelief in his gaze. "You're still shaking."

So she was. She'd gotten so used to the chills she hadn't noticed. "I'll live. You, however, may not. I should look at that leg for you, too."

"My leg is fine—the tourniquet should hold. We'll just need to stop every ten minutes so I can release the pressure." He reached under his arm and pulled the water-logged GPS unit from the side pocket of his ruck. Unlike her hearing aid, the unit appeared to have survived their dunking unscathed. He switched off the GPS and tucked it home before reaching down to draw her hands into his. The chills struck again as he plucked the Mag tubing from her hands. "This, by the way, was brilliant."

Yeah, right. That was why she was half-deaf and almost frozen solid. He tucked the tubing into his pocket and rubbed his hands up and down the arms of her soggy sweater. They both knew his efforts were futile. The brisk

Rebelian spring breeze of just twenty minutes ago now resembled an arctic chill, at least to her.

She swayed as the next wave hit.

He grabbed her before she hit the forest floor and hauled her close, pressing her good ear into his shoulder. Despite the companionable truce that settled in while they were trapped at the bottom of the lake, she stiffened.

"Dammit, Jared, I'm n-nowhere near fainting a-g-gain."

He pulled away, but only by inches. "The hell you aren't." He pressed his hand into the curve of her neck, then slid his palm beneath the collar of her sweater. "Your body temperature is practically nonexistent."

He was right.

Not to mention that the goose bumps and chills appeared to have set in for the count. But that was one more reason why they should get moving, regardless of who carried the ruck. Before her chattering teeth chattered right out of her mouth. "I n-n-need t-t-to m-move." To her relief, he didn't argue.

But he did slide his arm around her shoulders as he turned and pointed them in the right direction. "Take it easy. Slow and steady."

His warm breath washed her ear as they cleared a fallen tree stump together. She must be worse than she thought, because even that didn't heat her. Neither did the steady gaze he shot her. Five minutes later she knew she was in trouble. They both were. Not only was she beginning to doubt she could make it on her own, but given the blood staining the entire leg of Jared's jeans as they pressed on, she knew he wouldn't get far if he had to carry her, either.

Dammit, keep moving. Don't give up. Never give up. But the chills were getting worse. So was the annoying chattering. Another minute and neither mattered. Neither did her determination. Regardless of what she'd said back at that lake, she was going to pass out again and it was going to happen—

Now.

She was naked.

Alex remained absolutely motionless as the realization splintered through the fog still clogging her brain. She had no idea why she was naked, much less how she'd gotten that way. But she was definitely nude. Except…it didn't make sense.

She never slept in the raw.

Reduced to depending on her normal ear—the ear she was currently lying on—she concentrated on other senses to pick up the slack. *Soft*. Whatever she was lying on, was soft.

No, it was hard. At least part of it was.

Warm.

And her breath, that was warm, too. But for some reason, her slow exhalation seemed to be wafting back to her own cheeks, mingled with the musky scent of…someone else?

She stiffened.

An excruciating second later, she realized that something else had stiffened, too. And that *thing* was now pressing directly, blisteringly, into her equally bare thigh.

Jared.

Good Lord, she was naked. And so was he.

What the devil had happened?

The floodgates in her brain slammed open as the memories came roiling back, jumbled together as they ripped though the fog. The castle, the chopper, the rescue, her hearing aid. His wound! She jerked her eyes open and forced her gaze to focus as she shot up right on the bed. She tore the thermal blanket and sheet from their bodies and grabbed the muscular arm that'd fallen from her waist to her hips, hauling the man's forearm to her chest as she leaned over his injured thigh, terrified she'd find the mattress beneath soaked with blood.

But…there wasn't any.

In fact, except for a spattering of dried, brown flecks, the bleached sheet beneath was completely devoid of blood. So was he. She stared at the six-inch diagonal cut slicing across his hamstring, well down into his inner thigh, thoroughly bemused. Not because the wound had already been sealed, but at how it had been sealed. She couldn't spot a single stitch. It was as if someone had pulled the raw, puckered edges together and sealed the gash with a massive squirt of superglue. Better yet, it looked a lot like—

"Dermabond."

She froze. Blinked. A split second later she realized exactly where his hand was, exactly where she'd shoved it in her panic, and flushed. He was awake. Idiot! Of course the man was awake. She'd just ripped the covers off his body, exposing his entire length to what appeared to be midmorning rays of sunlight burning in through the cabin's partially shuttered windows.

Just as she'd exposed hers.

The fire scorching her cheeks and neck spread down to her breasts, increasing her humiliation and, unfortunately, the intensity of her blush. She tugged her gaze up just in time to watch that amber glow follow her flush lower—until it settled on his hand. Her blush deepened as the amber simmered and darkened, as the ridge pushing against her thigh grew harder.

He released her breast.

But then he just waited. For what she had no idea. Nor did she have a clue about how to extricate herself tactfully.

As it was, her head was still swimming, her thoughts still churning and her hold on her equilibrium once again tenuous from sitting up too fast. She swallowed firmly as she worked to regain balance, determined to ignore the scorchingly intimate ridge between them, as well as the strands of inky silk that hung past the man's shoulders, slipping down to shadow the thick muscles of his chest and arms. She ignored the masculine nipples beneath, as well as the answering pucker the sight caused in her own. Most of all, she ignored that toe-curling, smoky scent.

She focused on the gold chain around his neck, instead.

On the matching medallion nestled in the dusky crevice between his pecs. Until she felt his gaze on her face.

This time *she* waited.

The irony of waking in this man's arms twice in a row, much less the reversal of her leaning over his body, wasn't lost on her. At least this time, she'd realized almost immediately that he had to have been motivated by medicine. She finally dragged her gaze to his.

His brow lifted.

"I was, ah, checking out your...leg."

He nodded. So solemnly she couldn't be sure if he'd caught the gaffe. "I apologize if my...leg...has embarrassed you."

He had. The rat.

She straightened her spine and stared directly into his eyes. "No embarrassment. I'm sure the lingering stiffness is normal, given the circumstances." She frowned slightly, feigning concern as she dared to let her gaze drift low, but not too low. "Though it does appear painful."

The hint of a smile ghosted across his lips as she returned to his face. "Touché."

She awarded the next point to him as the man calmly pushed the edges of the thermal blanket and sheet into her hands and sat up, oblivious to his birthday suit as he swung his legs to the floor. He hooked his right hand to the bunk bed above them and stood. She tugged the covers over her breasts and bit down on her bottom lip as that sinewy rear end sauntered across the wooden slats that formed the one-room cabin's floor. She studied the gash beneath as Jared reached the pine crates stacked in the corner, three feet from a cold, potbellied stove. She held her breath as he hunkered down, exhaling only when she was convinced the Dermabond would hold.

She was impressed in more ways than one when it did. So much so, she didn't bother averting her eyes as he pulled a fresh pair of jeans from the uppermost crate and donned them. She actually missed not being able to hear the telling zip—until he turned. She swallowed a groan.

That blasted stethoscope.

Hadn't she already suffered through this?

"You know what, Jared? I feel great this morning."

He nodded as he padded barefoot across the slats, back to the bed. "That's good. But I need to check your vitals, anyway."

It wasn't the vitals she had a problem with. It was the check that would follow. Her stitches. Her ear.

Stunned that she'd been so captivated by the man's body she hadn't even thought to double-check her own while his back was turned, she threaded her fingers into her hair. She ran her fingers down the line of stitches before discreetly probing the anatomy around them. She sucked in her breath as Jared took advantage of her distraction to slip the scope's disk beneath the thermal blanket and sheet.

She stiffened as his fingers brushed her breast. Gooseflesh rippled down her neck and lower. Humiliation followed.

"Cold?"

Not by a long shot. And after their suggestive tit-for-tat, he darn well knew it. She lied, anyway. "Yes."

He pulled the disk from her flesh and palmed it briskly. He returned the scope to her breast…along with his dusky fingers. "Better?"

Worse. "Uh…yeah."

He removed the scope again. Seconds later his entire arm scorched into her side and back as he slipped his hand around her naked torso to settle the disk over her ribs. She stared blindly past his shoulder as he leaned closer to close his eyes and listen intently to her lungs. His eyes reopened and, mercifully, he straightened.

He snagged her wrist.

She resisted the urge to close her own eyes, cursing her racing heart, instead, as he timed the pulse beneath his fingers.

"Hmm."

"What?"

"A bit fast."

You don't say. "That's me. Fast."

She winced. She knew what he was thinking. What they both were thinking. Sam. Just as she could tell from the way Jared's gaze shuttered that, like her, he'd been too groggy this morning to remember she was supposed to be his mentor's girlfriend. He remembered now.

Guilt bit into her.

Relief supplanted it as he released her wrist and stood— until his entire body swayed. Jared reached out, but missed the edge of the upper bunk as he fell. She shot up a split second later, her own head connecting with the bunk as she grabbed his arms. But at least she caught him as his knees hit the floor.

"Careful!"

She held on tight, supporting him as he closed his eyes and waited for the dizziness to pass. By the time he reopened them, his gaze had focused. But his cheeks and forehead were still tinged with gray. "I'm fine now."

"You sure?"

He nodded. His color was improving. His cheeks were dusky once again.

She released his arms.

"Thank you." The color returned to his lips as they quirked. "I seem to have lost more blood than I thought."

"Obviously." She returned the quirk as she flicked her gaze to the stethoscope. "Maybe I should be listening to your chest."

His gaze dropped. Flared.

His color deepened.

She was still so rattled it took a moment for her to realize why. The blanket and sheet. She'd dropped them to grab him. They were pooled at her waist and, once again, that gaze was fused to her chest. A chest that had, unfortunately, already responded to the chilly temperature permeating the room.

Again, she knew exactly what he was thinking. Sam.

This time humiliation stained Jared's cheeks, and this time shame escorted the guilt to her own. She'd spun quite a few stories over the years. Woven them into covers so tight no one had ever thought to call her on them. But this one wasn't right. She stared at the Dermabond-sealed gash marring Jared's right biceps. The man had taken not one, but two bullets for her. And then he'd brought her out alive. Her uncle would just have to understand.

She retrieved the sheet and sighed. "I've never slept with him. Sam and I are just friends. Very good friends."

It was still a lie.

But at least this one would damn only her.

From the relief that swept though Jared's gaze as he met hers, she knew it was the right thing to do, the right thing to say. No matter how many questions the correction might lead to.

To her surprise, it didn't lead to any.

He stood, instead. Slowly this time, cautiously, then headed back to the crates. He tucked the stethoscope into the first-aid pouch, still stained with his dried blood, and set the dark-green bag at the foot of the crates before reaching into the uppermost box. He pulled out another pair of jeans and a sweater similar to the one they'd shared the night before, this one gray. He added a pair of socks and carried the pile to the bed.

"Put these on."

My, my. They did make quite the team, didn't they? She arched her brow, pointedly waiting for his misplaced manners to show up and slap him in the face.

"Please."

She lowered her brow and held out her hand, inhaling softly as their fingers brushed. Sparks flickered up her arm as she settled the clothes on the bed. She swore he'd felt the rippling charge, too. But from the way he masked his reaction just before he turned and stepped away, he seemed determined not to acknowledge their attraction—to her or himself.

Why?

He wasn't married. In fact, after that phone call in her uncle's guest room, she knew better than most that he probably wasn't even involved. Not only that, Jared now knew Sam wasn't standing between them.

So what was?

She pondered the question as she pulled on the sweater, grateful for the thick cotton weave, since it appeared she'd be going braless for the next few days at least. She swung her legs off the bed to slide into the jeans.

"Done."

It wasn't her imagination. The denial was still there when Jared turned around. It was there when he leaned down at the foot of the bed to scoop up the clothes she'd worn hours before. He carried the damp pile to the table beneath the window and dumped them on one of the matching wooden chairs. The denial continued to linger as he headed back to the crates, shifted the uppermost box and began unloading food supplies into the squat cupboard beside the cabin door.

Why, dammit?

She had no intention of acting on their attraction, either, but at least she was willing to acknowledge it. If only to herself. Or was that it? Was *she* it? Surely the distance he'd carefully placed between them didn't stem from that brainless comment she'd made in the forest. Except, now that she thought about it, he had seemed preoccupied with her doctoral degrees.

But she definitely remembered how quickly he'd cut off her subsequent apology. She'd hit a sore spot.

Was that it? Did he honestly think his GED mattered to her?

Well, it didn't. Jared Sullivan might not have a diploma tacked up on his office wall, but he was not a stupid man. She might not have much personal knowledge of that, but she had plenty through her uncle. Sam was sharp. He'd set out years ago to surround himself with operatives who were even sharper. And according to Sam, Jared was as sharp as they came. The thought gave her pause. Enough to reconsider her own position concerning the discussion that had led up to his confession in the first place.

"Jared?"

He slid the final can of food onto the cupboard shelf and closed the double doors. "Yes?"

"Last night when I told you about my meeting with Karl and what he said about this…Gem of Power legend, I got the distinct impression you thought there might be something to it."

He stood beside the cupboard, silent for a good ten seconds as he held her gaze, searching it. And then, "Perhaps."

Coming from Karl, the assessment had made her laugh. Coming from this man, especially after what they'd been through? It made her shiver.

He shrugged. "The same American exposé reporter that discovered your location at Veisweimar also uncovered DeBruzkya's obsession with the same legend. Like I told you last night, Lily is engaged to an ARIES operative by the name of Robert Davidson. According to the debrief I skimmed, Lily and Robert both feel there may be something to it."

"I asked what you thought."

"I'm withholding judgment—for the moment. I do know that while you were missing, two other ARIES operatives tied a series of jewel heists together. All threads led back to DeBruzkya."

Now *that* was interesting.

"What's his preference? Diamonds, emeralds, rubies?"

"Judging from the thefts, all the above. Plus sapphires and a few others." He turned to the crates, shifting the empty one to the floor so he could use the crowbar she'd noticed on the table to pry open the next. This crate held

their electronic gear. He pulled out a laptop, a radio transmitter and several battery packs, stopping to tip his head
as if he'd made a connection. "DeBruzkya didn't seem
interested in pearls, however."

"That doesn't narrow the list by much."

Jared shrugged as he set the laptop on the table. "You're
the geologist. That's where you come in."

Great. Her, with her memory currently resembling a po-
rous chunk of volcanic basalt. "Did the thefts reveal any
pattern at all? Other than the fact that he's got a preference
for crystals?"

"Not one Agents Williams and Taylor could discern."
He dropped his gaze to the laptop. "I've got their reports
stored in there. As soon as you eat, I'll fire it up and pull
up the file. You can review Davidson's and his fiancée's
notes, as well. Maybe you'll find a connection I over-
looked."

She doubted it. She had the feeling there wasn't much
those sharp eyes missed. She leaned back on the bunk until
her back hit the cabin wall. A wall that would be closing
in on her before long if she couldn't get her mind to release
those last moments with Karl. It was as if the mere thought
of the man had turned into a huge steel lock. On her brain.

"Give it time."

"Time." Last night she would have been surprised to
discover Jared could read her thoughts. Not today. She
raised her head, nodding curtly as she met that infuriatingly
steady gaze. "Okay, I'll give it time. But what the devil
am I supposed to do to amuse myself in the interim?"

"You don't. You rest. Recuperate. We both do. Last
night we used up the element of surprise. We'll have to lie
low for a few days at least, perhaps longer, to recover it.
If we're lucky, our local sources will have discovered the
identity of the man we left behind at Veisweimar by then.
If he was trying to help you, he may have friends who may
also be willing to help us."

Jared was right. But there was something else she wanted

from that elusive man's friends. Something they desperately needed. Information. If DeBruzkya had been willing to murder Karl, why had he worked so damned hard to keep *her* alive?

Chapter 5

Sam was wrong. He was losing his edge. Jared glanced up from his laptop and the file he'd downloaded from the ARIES central computer twenty minutes earlier and sighed. He'd hoped he'd be able to snatch Alex Morrow from that castle and complete the remainder of their mission before his symptoms locked in. It was too late. He'd already succumbed to the worst one.

Poor judgment.

Damned if he didn't succumb yet again as his gaze snuck across the cabin, straight at the bottom bunk for the fifth time in five minutes, lured by the captivating rays of late-afternoon light dancing across the woman's cheeks. Hell. It wasn't the light that had captivated his attention and he knew it. It was the woman. No matter how many times he looked, he still couldn't believe how completely the layers of illusion had been peeled away. Where an awkward, myopic man had once stood, a strikingly beautiful, innately sensual woman now lay. If anything, the faded jeans and drab gray sweater Alex had donned that morning enhanced her curves. Or maybe it was him. Maybe it was the fact that he knew firsthand what lay beneath. From the top of her freshly washed hair, courtesy of an impromptu bath in the pond out back two hours earlier, all the way down to her slender feet and every satiny inch in between. Especially those pale, full breasts. The dark nipples that crowned the peaks.

The way they'd stiffened beneath his greedy gaze.

Jared purged the sight from his mind, and fast. That was one memory he did not need to hang on to. He inhaled deeply, willing his body to forget, as well.

As if it could.

They'd played a dangerous game in that bed this morning. Hell, he still wasn't sure why he'd pushed it. The blood loss must have affected his brain. Why else had he decided to crawl onto that mattress after he'd sealed his wounds to try to use his body heat to quell the violent chills still racking her? Unfortunately, from the moment Alex's naked body curled into his, the only inferno he'd ignited had been his own. His flesh was still singed.

Apparently unlike hers.

Alex's flinch when he'd touched her told him that. In a way, he wished the woman *was* sleeping with Sam Hatch, or that she'd at least not opted to tell him she wasn't. It would have made his own insidious attraction easier to fight. Alex didn't know how right she'd been that moment she'd awoken in the forest. It had been a long time since he'd had a woman. Too long. But even if he wanted to cave in to temptation—even if *she* wanted to—there wasn't a damned thing he could do about it.

A year ago, he might have. Six months ago, even.

But not after that call.

The night she'd walked out of the connecting bathroom in Hatch's guest room, he'd suspected she'd overhead it. He knew now she hadn't. One look into Alex's sea-green eyes without those mud-brown contacts obscuring his view, proved it.

Relief seared into him once again as his gaze slipped over the honey-colored curls that framed Alex's face. From the mesmerizing curls, as well as the dark gold lashes that fanned out above her high cheeks, he stopped and lingered on lips that were much too full and smooth and much, much, too flushed for his peace of mind.

Dammit, man, take the gift and move *on*. Get back to the file, back to the mission.

So they could both get back to their separate lives.

He jerked his gaze from that distracting face and fused it to the laptop on his thighs, deliberately kicking up the pace of the scroll key, forcing his mind to keep up with the deluge of information that passed before his eyes. Three minutes later he stopped. Reread that last sentence—

And smiled.

"What is it?"

He swallowed a curse. How long had she been awake?

Worse, how long had she been watching?

He carefully shifted the computer from his lap to the wooden table. He turned to meet the unspoken question swimming within that sea of green and swallowed a second curse. She'd been watching long enough. He answered the question she'd actually voiced. "I think I've located your doctor."

"This soon?" She scrambled upright on the thermal blanket, tucking her feet beneath her as she hooked her hands on the edge of the upper bunk. "Who is it?"

"Roman Orloff. He's the chief of staff at the main hospital in Rajalla." The only hospital the city had left. The capital of Rebelia had once supported three hospitals and five outpatient clinics. As of yesterday Rajalla was down to one of each, with piles of rubble where the others had been.

"Orloff? Isn't that the doctor mentioned in Davidson's report? The one who'd helped hide his son?"

He nodded. "According to the report I received while you were napping, he disappeared shortly afterward. If Orloff was the same man you saw, knowing Debruzkya he was probably beaten to see if he knew anything about Davidson's assault on the castles.''

"Report?" This time she scrambled off the bed completely, padding across the tiny cabin in her socks to stand beside the remaining chair. "Do you mind?"

He punched up the file and turned the laptop toward her, waiting as she sat down to scroll through the document. By the time she lifted her gaze, the speculation had returned.

"You've already read all this?"

"I skimmed it." Why not? He owed her a fib or two.

He caught her soft curse as the screen went blank. "Great. I killed the file." She slid her finger across the touch pad, deftly retrieving the file through the laptop's "Documents Recently Viewed" icon. Scrolling through the ninety-six page report from the beginning would take too long. She sighed. "Do you remember where it is?"

"Page sixty-two, paragraph five."

"Thanks." She jumped to the correct page. "It says Orloff was born in the southern province of—"

He shook his head. "Skip the first six lines."

"Roman Orloff received his undergrad—"

"I said six, not four." Impatient, he nudged her gaze directly to the connection that intrigued him and said, " 'Dr. Orloff completed his residency at San Diego General in November of 1984. Orloff returned to Rajalla for three years' hiatus, rotating though several of the capital city's then free outpatient clinics before returning to the U.S. in 1987 to specialize in—' " He broke off when he realized Alex was no longer staring at the computer, but at him. Christ. It probably would have helped if he'd remembered to glance at the screen once or twice. The blunder was moot now.

"You have a photographic memory."

He held her gaze. "It's not as uncommon as you'd think."

But it was.

At least, ones like his were. He was four when he'd discovered that. Kindergarten orientation, as a matter of fact. He'd learned firsthand that not everyone could recall every sentence they read word-for-precise-word the way his mother could—or the way he could.

Weirdo. Show-off. Smart-ass.

He'd heard them all by the end of the school year. A couple of times from teachers, too.

Alex was still staring. She glanced down at the laptop. "How long did it take you to read this?"

Oh, no. He had no intention of answering that one.

Unfortunately she had a watch. She used it, comparing the dial to the time stamp the computer had inserted on the file's initial opening. She gasped as she gaped up at him. How many times had he seen that look?

He forced a shrug. "Welcome to the freak show."

Alex shook her head. "What happened?"

"Nothing happened." An outright lie.

She crossed her arms over her chest. "Try again."

"Look, Dr. Mor—"

"Don't 'doctor' me, mister. You could've gotten fifty degrees if you'd wanted to. All I want is a simple answer. How does a kid with a brain that probably rivals Albert Einstein's drop out of the eighth grade? *Why?*"

"That's two questions."

"Pick one."

The hell he would. What he did was stand up. Move. He paced his way to the bunk beds before he turned back, every inch of the floor's twenty feet between them as he pointed to the computer. "Page sixty-two, paragraph five, line eight. Finish it." The double-edged curse already exposed, he began reciting, "'Orloff returned to Rajalla for three years' hiatus, rotating through the capital city's then free outpatient clinics before returning the U.S. in 1987—'" To his relief, she took the hint and severed her gaze, dropping it the screen to pick up where he left off.

"'—to specialize in…neurology'?"

He nodded as her eyes widened. "Keep going. Scroll down the next page. Paragraph five, line four. 'Orloff is rumored to have taken multiple, unexplained trips during the past month. Each trip averaging three hours.'"

"Let me guess, plenty of time to drive from Rajalla to Veisweimar castle, examine a patient and return."

He nodded.

"Do you have a photo?"

"I was finishing the medical backgrounder when you woke up. I haven't had a chance to check our e-mail. Knowing Jerry, he's already anticipated the request."

She logged on to their encrypted account. Fifteen seconds later they had access, but the message wasn't there.

"Nothing." She tapped out a quick message and hit "send."

The tension returned as they waited.

Fortunately Jerry broke it a minute and a half later. Alex opened the e-mail and studied the electronic photograph the ARIES database tech had pasted within.

She nodded. "That's him."

Jared stared at the color photo. The man appeared as tall as both of them were, with hair close in color and texture to the mop Alex had sported two hours before. Brown eyes, graying temples and a matching mustache completed an angular but otherwise nondescript face.

"You're sure?"

She tipped her chin to meet his eyes, her own warm with gratitude and certainty. "Trust me, you don't forget the face of the man who saved your life."

The second surge of heat was meant for him.

He cleared his throat. "You're certain Orloff saved it?"

"He could have exposed my gender. He didn't. Not to mention, when I first awoke, my head resembled a mummy's. There's no way a three-inch track of stitches required that much gauze. I'm betting the man wrapped my face to hide a mustache and beard that wouldn't grow."

It was possible. Probable even. "So why didn't he re-move the stitches?"

She shrugged. "Maybe he never had the chance. Maybe he was afraid someone would come in. I don't know. I do know I should risk contacting him."

"No."

"Dammit, Jared. We're supposed to be a team. That means we both provide input, we both execute our respec-tive parts of the job. As former Delta Force, I'd think you'd be familiar with the concept."

He'd never told her he served with Delta.

He watched the color bleed from her cheeks. A moment later she pushed forth another shrug. "Sam's mentioned you once or twice."

"Odd. Until two days ago, Director *Hatch* never men-tioned you. In fact, six out of the seven ARIES agents I contacted on the flight to Ramstein never heard of your existence at all."

This time, her color remained steady. "Who was the sev-enth?"

"Aiden Swift."

Her gaze widened. "Aiden's retired."

He nodded. "He's also a friend."

Again, no color loss. But when she turned to exit the backgrounder file on the laptop, the slight tremble in her index finger as it glanced off the touchpad gave her away. What the devil was she afraid of?

"So…what did Aiden have to say about me?"

Nothing and but he'd give a hell of a lot to know what his friend had been withholding. "He said you were the best he trained. That I should hurry my ass up and get you the hell out of here."

A soft smile curved her lips. "Sounds like Aiden."

He swore she was still waiting. But for what? "Did Ai-den forget to mention something?"

Another smile, this one not quite real as she powered down the computer. "He helped construct my persona."

Her disguise.

Jared reached down and snapped the lid of the laptop shut for her. "That must be why he seemed particularly concerned. You concealing your gender and all."

"Must be."

She was lying. He couldn't put his finger on how he knew, or why. But she was definitely lying. The worse part was, it hurt. Jared hooked a boot under the bottom rung of his chair and reclaimed it, staring directly into those cool eyes as he settled back.

Why did he find her so damned fascinating?

She ran her fingers through her curls, then lowered her hands to drum her short nails against the table. "Now what?"

He crossed his arms. "We wait."

"Even though I think we should contact Orloff?"

He shook his head. "I never said we wouldn't contact him. Just not you alone and just not yet."

"You want to put a surveillance team on him first?"

He nodded. "We have the time. You need to recuperate. If he checks out, we can head into Rajalla when you're ready. In the meantime, I'll work on constructing a new cover that will let us into his world."

To his surprise, she shook her head. "We already have one. All it needs is a little tweaking."

"Yours?"

"Why not? Aiden always said to keep it simple, stupid and as close to the truth as possible. I'll tell Orloff I chose to be a man in the scientific world due to stereotyping. Since I've been frequenting the Eastern European, as well as Asian, environmental conferences for several years for ARIES, he'll believe me."

"And me?"

Her wide smile startled him even more. "You're my fiancé."

He blinked.

"Think about it. It's ready-made. You're U.S. Army.

Ranger, Special Forces, Delta—it doesn't matter. What matters is that you've been searching for me since I disappeared from the conference. With your connections, you managed to locate me and get me out of that dank dungeon DeBruzkya stashed me in. But when I passed out, you were forced to order the chopper to set us down.'' She shrugged. ''We didn't make it across the border. Everyone knows that ever since the day DeBruzkya came to power, the borders have been locked down tighter than a Soviet-era ruble exchange. Only medical and relief personnel are allowed through, and then only if they're carrying the proper documentation. Naturally we thought that Orloff—''

''—as hospital chief-of-staff, could provide it.'' Jared nodded. Like the Maglite tube, it was brilliant. Close enough to the truth to be believable, yet still deceptively simple. Aiden Swift would have been impressed to see his protégé now.

He knew *he* certainly was.

''It just might work.'' He leaned forward and tapped the lid to the laptop. ''Page sixty-seven of that backgrounder is even more fascinating. For two years our local boys have suspected the good doctor of providing medical relief on the side—relief to DeBruzkya's enemies. No one has been able to tie Orloff directly or even indirectly to the rebels, but that doesn't mean much. The man may simply be that good. The aid and concealment Orloff provided Robert Davidson and his fiancée is enough to warrant a cautious benefit of the doubt.''

''I agree.''

That was it, then.

Damned if Hatch wasn't right, after all. They made a surprisingly decent team. The thought stunned him. Anxious to cover it, he changed the subject to familiar, professional ground. ''Have you remembered anything more about—''

''No.'' She flushed. ''Sorry.''

So was he. Of all people, he should have known better.

It just went to show how much this woman had managed to affect him in so short a time. He leaned forward and closed his hand over hers. "It's okay. It'll come back."

"How can you be so sure?"

That whisper. The pain simmering within it sliced deeper than both his gashes before he'd injected the painkillers. There was no way he could tell her the truth. He squeezed her hand, instead.

It was a mistake.

Much as he hated admitting it, it was yet another example of that telling symptom. If waking up in this woman's arms hadn't confirmed it, the heat searing his fingers did. Touching Alex Morrow without a stethoscope in his hands qualified as extremely poor judgment. Especially when the air between them seemed to warm and shift, as well, magnifying the early-evening shadows that were beginning to steal into the cabin, enhancing the shadow of desire that had slipped into her eyes.

He watched the pulse at the base of her neck pick up its tempo until it matched the thudding of his heart.

He released her hand slowly, carefully, deliberately ignoring the questions that crowded into her eyes as he backed away. "How far did you get?"

She blinked.

He jerked his chin toward the laptop on the makeshift nightstand across the cabin before she could misconstrue his question. "Your own reading. How far did you get?"

Her gaze cleared. Her lips twisted sheepishly. "Not as far as you."

He actually laughed. "At least you won't dream it."

"You do?"

Perhaps because the question seemed motivated by genuine curiosity, he answered it. "Yeah."

"You're kidding?"

"I wish I was. Just last week I fell asleep to the first Dear John letter I ever got. I was twelve. She broke it off because I didn't know how to French kiss.'' He grinned. ''Still stings.''

She laughed. ''I'll bet.''

But moments later she grew silent, almost pensive. He might have drawn her out, but the rest of the week's dream fodder had already begun scrolling past his memory's still-eagle eye. Words filled his brain. Words he'd give almost anything to forget. Reports, tests, medical charts, updates. His mother's death certificate. *The cause.*

He closed his eyes and rubbed them.

It didn't help.

Her hand touched his arm, scorching into the skin left exposed by the sleeves he'd shoved up while reading.

''Are you—''

He stood. ''I'm fine.''

It was time to make sure she was, too. He headed for the first-aid kit he'd left on top of the food cupboard, retrieving his scope and a suture kit. Several of the kit's supplies would work in reverse. The warmth fled from her gaze as he returned. Carefully masked apprehension replaced it.

''What are you doing with that?''

He sighed. He'd waited all day, given her plenty of time to adjust. He'd even let her bathe and wash the temporary dye from her hair first. While he wasn't a neurologist, as far as he could tell Alex had made remarkable progress in the past twenty-four hours. Almost all the lingering effects of the coma seemed to have worked themselves out. Except two. Her missing memory…and this strange fixation she had regarding the stitches in her scalp. He set his scope on the table and withdrew a pair of scissors and tweezers from the suture kit before setting the kit down, as well. He pointed the instruments toward the side of her head. ''Alex, you need to get those sutures out. They're three weeks old. It may sting a bit since the skin's grown over in places, but it shouldn't smart too much.'' He forced a slight smile, aiming for reassurance and not exasperation. He laid the scissors and tweezers down beside the scope, hoping their absence would calm her.

It didn't. She tensed as he touched her jaw.

"Relax, I'll just take a look first. That's all."

Before he could turn her head to gain a better view of the ancient sutures, she stood. "I need to visit the outhouse."

Two seconds later he was staring at his empty hands.

He heard the cabin door open, then slam shut. He stared at the slab of scarred wood. What the hell was *that* about? Two days ago he'd have sworn he'd experienced it all with his mother. But in a way, Alex Morrow fleeing a simple pair of tweezers stunned him more than walking into his living room with his girlfriend on his sixteenth birthday all those years ago, only to discover his mother stretched out on the coffee table, snoring loudly—and completely nude. Gene Roddenberry was wrong. Space wasn't the final frontier. The brain was.

Alex slumped her head against the rough-hewn planks of the outhouse wall and closed her eyes, purging the remaining panic along with the air from her lungs. She forced herself to wait until her legs had stopped shaking before she raised her hand, seeking out the hearing aid. It had been a part of her for so long she couldn't remember what it felt like to be without it. She tested the hold. Despite the way she'd torn herself from Jared's seeking fingers, the hearing aid had stayed put.

Thank God.

Unfortunately, the microphone array was still as dead as the amplifier tucked neatly and discreetly all the way down her right ear canal. Partially deaf, but not exposed.

At the moment she'd take it.

But sooner or later—preferably very soon—she was going to have to figure out how to replace the damned thing. Easy enough while in the States. Not so easy while actively on the job. Especially this job. Even if the entire Rebelian countryside hadn't been gutted and looted, compliments of DeBruzkya and his goons years before, she wouldn't have been able to walk into a medical-supply store and buy another one. Not one with the hypersensitive capabilities she was used to. And certainly not without arousing Jared's suspicions.

Dammit, she should have let him remove the stitches. At least then, it would have been over with.

Don't.

Hindsight might be cheap, but it wasn't always a bargain. Without mirrors in that cabin, she'd been playing blind man's bluff all day. There were only so many times a woman could fool with her hair and not get noticed. Especially with a man whose gaze was as sharp as Jared's. Since the moment she'd looked into those eyes, she'd had the distinct feeling that dark amber stare caught everything and promptly memorized it.

She didn't know how right she was.

Jared didn't have just a photographic memory. His brain was like a computer. No wonder Sam had once said Jared was the smartest man he'd ever known. She also knew he was the most humble.

But there was something else.

What, she couldn't quite put her finger on. Whatever it was, he was consumed by it. Still.

Janice?

Months ago, when she'd stopped by her uncle's house two days early to pick up the latest model of her now malfunctioning hearing aid, she hadn't expected to run into anyone, let alone Jared. She'd blindly walked out of that bathroom only to stumble onto ARIES's top search-and-rescue agent slipping into the guest room to complete an extremely personal call. She'd been so stunned she'd almost dropped the vial. She still couldn't believe a woman would actually dump him.

But it was true.

Unlike Karl, she could recall with eerie perfection the shock in Jared's voice as he slumped down to the bed.

"You're sure?" A heavy pause. *"Then I guess that's it."*

His resigned sigh followed. She'd known then he hadn't intended on arguing. Maybe they already had.

"No, Janice, there's nothing else to say. No reason for us to see each other again. It's already over. Goodbye."

She'd never forget the thick swallow that had punctuated the silence that followed as he'd dropped his hands to his lap and bowed his head, cradling the cell phone as if it was a lifeline that just might ring if he stared at it long enough, prayed hard enough. But it hadn't. And then, moments later, Jared had stiffened as he realized someone else was in the room.

Her—but as a him.

He'd shot to his feet, scrubbing the tears from his dusky cheeks as he gruffly asked how long she'd been standing there. Too long. And not nearly long enough. As God was her witness, she'd never come so close to blowing her cover in her career as she had that day, staring across that tense, silent room, wanting so damned badly to cross it, to reach out and comfort him. To hold him while he poured out the pain. She'd been about to.

Until the humiliation set in.

His humiliation.

One look into Jared's eyes and she'd known exactly how he felt. She'd known in her soul that he would have given his for her to have been as deaf as she'd once prayed another man could be blind. Maybe that was why she'd done it. Maybe that was why she'd sucked up her compassion, picked up his pride and flat out *lied*.

Only now she was beginning to think she shouldn't have. She might have been able to help. True, she might not have known true love. But she had one hell of a handle on rejection.

Chapter 6

Where the devil was he?

Alex lifted her hand and rapped on the door to Karl's room, more loudly this time.

Silence.

Odd. She dug into her trouser pocket, automatically reaching for the remote control for her hearing aid. It wasn't there. She'd left it in her hotel room.

Great. She could have used it to kick up the intensity of the sound waves behind that door. She already knew Karl wasn't in the shower, since she didn't hear water running, but that didn't mean the man wasn't snoring quietly on his bed—unless he'd opted to stand her up, instead. She wouldn't put it past him. Not after that crazy story over breakfast, followed by his almost frantic insistence at the conference this afternoon that she meet him for dinner so he could provide proof. She ran her fingers across her mustache and readjusted her glasses, then rapped on the door one last time.

Maybe the man didn't snore.

Well, if Karl wasn't here, the proof wasn't, either. If it existed at all. She turned to leave—only to stop in midstep as muffled footfalls approached the opposite side of the door.

It opened.

She swung around. *"It's about time."*

"I know, Alexi, I know. I fell asleep." Karl's shoulders hunched sheepishly as he ran a paw through his already shaggy pile of straw, snarling it even more. She studied the whites of his eyes as he ushered her into the room. They were red, puffy.

Enough for her to believe him.

She skirted the rumpled double bed that couldn't possibly accommodate Karl's massive frame comfortably and stared at the table beside the window. There was plenty of light shining up from the capital of Holzberg below, but no food. *"Where's dinner?"*

"I have yet to order."

"Don't bother. I'm just here to see if you can put your money where your mouth is."

"My money? I don't—"

"The proof, Karl. The proof." She sighed as he walked toward the window, leaving her beside the bed. He turned to face her, his hips resting on the ledge. *"You do have it, don't you?"*

A second later, she caught a soft swish, followed by a muffled thump in the bathroom. *If Karl had been sleeping alone, who the hell was in there?* Alex spun around, but it was too late.

"Greetings, Dr. Morrow. It's a pleasure to finally meet you." The Makarov 9 mm, its meticulously polished, seven-inch silencer already attached, detracted from the sincerity of the salutation, as did the pockmarked face leering two feet above. *Hell, so did the identically armed goon hulking behind him. One against three, plus two pistols.*

Stall.

"Who are you? How do you know my name?"

*The pockmarked man passed his weapon to his goon—
and retrieved something that truly put the fear of God into
her.*

A syringe.

It was full.

*She stepped back, swung her gaze to Karl's, hoping
against hope that he was as baffled as she was.*

He wasn't.

*"I'm sorry, Alexi. I was forced. I have… How do you
Americans say it? Ja—divided loyalties. I could not—"*

"Halt die schnauze!" Mr. Pockman yelled.

*She stepped forward. "Why? Who are you to force Karl
to shut up?"*

Bad move.

*Ugly smile. "I am the other loyalty." The grin that fol-
lowed was even uglier. The syringe came up.*

It was now or never.

She chose now.

*Alex swung around, cleanly clipping across the jaw the
one man who didn't expect her attack. The back of Karl's
head bounced off the window frame with a solid thud, daz-
ing him as he fell forward. She hooked her shoulder into
his ribs and hauled his body around to slam it straight into
Pockman and his sidekick.*

The former lost his syringe, the latter lost his gun.

*She vaulted over Karl's body a second before he scram-
bled to his feet, only to freeze as the goon grabbed his
pistol. But the goon leveled his Makarov at Karl, not her—
and fired. The silenced thwack slammed into her eardrum
and ricocheted down her rib cage to rip straight though
her heart.*

"No!"

*But it was too late. Karl fell forward again and this time,
he didn't get up.*

*A moment later she felt something cold and hard slam
into the right side of her skull directly behind her ear,
bringing her to her knees less than a foot from her old*

friend. She tried turning her head as she pitched forward, but ended up with her hearing aid smashed into the thick carpet. Maybe that was why she saw Karl's lips move, but couldn't hear what he said.

His lips moved again.

Whatever Karl had said, it must have been important, because Pockman leaned over and grabbed that pile of shaggy straw. He ripped it up, exposing the thick, bobbing knot at the center of Karl's neck—just before he slit Karl's throat from ear to ear.

Karl opened his mouth one last time.

But all that trickled out was blood.

Alex screamed, putting everything she had into one last punch as the tip of that gleaming syringe shot toward her—

"Jesus, lady!"

She stiffened. "J-Jared?"

"I'm here, Alex."

Please, Lord, let her be dreaming. Her heart still pounding, her mind still racing, the blood still thundering through her veins, she forced her lids open and stared up into those deep amber pools. Not Pockman's eyes. She glanced at the black silky hair spilling over her neck. Not Pockman's hair. She studied the large hands locked to both her wrists, the solid forearms and generous biceps—one still healing—above them. She dragged her gaze across the sculpted muscles of that massive chest. Every inch was smooth, dusky. Naked.

Definitely not Pockman's.

Neither was the scarlet splotch staining the edge of that hard, morning-whiskered jaw. The same whiskered jaw she'd been staring at or, rather, trying *not* to stare at, from the moment she'd returned from that outhouse three nights ago. Two long, excruciatingly tense days had passed since, during which they'd both retreated by tacit agreement to separate corners of the cabin to study their mission's back-grounder files and heal.

She knew he'd chalked up her continued avoidance of

those damned stitches to her coma. She didn't care. It was better than the truth. Definitely easier.

Or so she'd thought.

After falling asleep after yet another evening of terse silence, she wasn't so sure. She did know she'd picked a hell of a way to break it. She dragged her gaze back to that scarlet splotch, any hope she'd had that she hadn't caused it vanishing as it continued to darken before her eyes, and cleared her throat.

"Sorry for…hitting you."

"S'okay."

When he didn't move, much less release her wrists, she cleared her throat again. "You, ah…want to let me go?"

"Depends."

She swallowed firmly. "On what?"

"You." His brow rose. "You done swinging?"

"Yes."

"Then I'm done holding."

But he wasn't. He did release her hands, but he didn't move. Not far, anyway. And not off her bunk. His hips were still pressing down into hers, his sweats-encased thighs still tangled with her own. His elbows still levered that dusky chest twelve inches above the mattress—mere inches above her. She stared at the medallion dangling between them. At the profile of some man she didn't recognize etched in relief on the small gold coin. At the color that reminded her of someone she did.

Karl.

The rest of the dream came flooding back, nearly swamping her. Only it wasn't a dream, was it? She bit down on her lip as the tears threatened.

"You okay?"

She nodded.

"You sure?"

She managed another nod. This one came out jerkier.

"You saw Karl die, didn't you?"

She swung her gaze to his. "How did you—"

Compassion filled the amber. "You shouted his name."

Despite her attempts to hold it in, her breath came out in a ragged rush. "He betrayed me." She would have given anything to be able to hate him, but she couldn't. Poor Karl. His double-crossing her would have led to his death in the end, anyway. From what she now clearly remembered, Pockman did not seem the type to leave witnesses. She stiffened as the rest locked in.

"What?"

"It wasn't an accident. I wasn't kidnapped because I stumbled across something, or discovered something I shouldn't have. I was the intended target all the time. Karl lured me there. There were two other guys in the bathroom." But the output on her hearing aid had been fluctuating all day. She hadn't heard the men until it was too late. "They were armed and one had a syringe. I managed to get the drop on Karl, but the shorter thug got the drop on me. Then he injected something into my neck. I passed out. But not before—" She broke off.

She couldn't finish. It was too painful.

For all his flaws, Karl had been the closest thing to a friend she'd had in years.

"You passed out, but not before they slit his throat."

"You could have told me." Even as she whispered the accusation, she knew it wasn't fair. Jared was right not to tell her. Now they knew the memory was real—and hers. She just wished to God it wasn't. She dropped her gaze to the medallion. "They shot him first. But he tried to tell me something before he died. That's why they slit his throat. To shut him up."

"Can you—"

She shook her head. "No. I can see his lips moving, but something's blocking the rest. Maybe it's me. Maybe some part of my brain is still fighting it. Or maybe it just wasn't audible." But that was impossible and she knew it. Her hearing aid had been acting up, but she'd been less than a foot away from those terse, moving lips. She'd still had one good ear. That close, she should have heard *something*.

She closed her eyes and pushed her fingers into her temples. She deliberately pictured Karl again, on that floor. The shock in his eyes, the regret. His lips moving.

She strained her ears, her memory.

Nothing.

Dammit. What had Karl gone to his death trying to tell her?

"Relax. We've got more than we had."

She jerked her hands down. "What? Exactly what have we got? Confirmation he was shot? That his throat was slit, too? A first-year medical student could have given you that. We need more. Answers. According to Agents Taylor and Williams, DeBruzkya has been snatching up gems all over the world for almost a year. But if DeBruzkya tried to kidnap me, then Lily Scott and Robert Davidson were wrong, and Karl was right. There has to be more to this Gem of Power than a dictator intent on using some ancient hokey legend to cow his subjects and keep them in line. Still, why me? I may be into lapidary, but it's strictly a scientific hobby. My interest in gems has never involved polishing up diamonds and rubies and plunking them into chunks of gold so some woman can hang them from her blasted ears!"

"Re—"

"I swear to God, Jared. If you tell me to relax one more time, I'll slug you again and this time it'll hurt."

He closed his mouth.

A moment later, the left end bumped up. The lopsided smile spread across his lips.

"What?"

"It hurt the first time."

"Oh." She flushed. Why? She'd apologized. She certainly hadn't invited the man to crawl into her bed to try to wake her from that nightmare. And she certainly hadn't asked him to stay.

He finally seemed to realize that, too.

She was certain when he shifted.

Unfortunately the bunk wasn't designed for one body of their size, let alone two. The mattress dipped beneath them, pushing him closer, shoving his groin directly into the flat of her belly. He froze as the same independently minded *leg* that had reacted several mornings before stiffened again. But instead of buffering the contact, the soft fleece of their sweats did the opposite, enhancing the ridge, as well as the heat. The awareness.

He flushed.

She watched, mesmerized by the tide as it spread up his neck, slowly merging with the splotch still riding the edge of his jaw. She reached up and smoothed her index finger over the slight bruise that had formed beneath the whiskers.

His jaw tensed. So did his…leg.

She ignored the klaxon blaring in her head, openly defying it as she slipped her fingertip up over his morning shadow until she reached his lips. Those smooth, dangerously sensual lips. For three days she'd awoken to this face and these lips. And for three days she'd somehow managed to turn her back on them, gather up her bar of soap and her towel and head out to that godawful freezing pond where she'd punished herself for the very desires that were pulsing through her now.

Well, not today.

Today, she was caving in to temptation.

She captured his gaze and held it, daring him to look away as she teased her fingertip across his bottom lip. His slow, deep exhale washed her hand, warming her hand as she reached the corner of his mouth. She stopped, reversed direction and traced her fingertip back across the upper curve. Gooseflesh rippled down her arm as he finally inhaled, sharply.

She paused at the center. Stared.

His gaze flared and grew hotter, until the amber glowed. He was going to kiss her.

He *wanted* to kiss her.

She could feel it in her belly and she could feel it in her soul. And God help her, she wanted to kiss him, too. For once she wanted to give in to the fantasy—in reality. She felt the slight, almost infinitesimal pressure as he leaned forward ever so slowly, but then he stopped. A moment later he pulled back. No more than a fraction of an inch. It felt like a mile.

He'd changed his mind.

Janice? Was that it? Was he still hung up on the woman who'd dumped him three months before? It was the only explanation that made sense. More than some hang-up about a dusty academic title and a couple letters tacked on after her name. Especially since she now knew he could have racked up the entire alphabet and strung it after his if he'd wanted to.

And then it hit her. No, it *slugged* her.

What was she thinking, much less doing? She should be thanking him, not whining. What if he had kissed her? What if he'd plowed his fingers into her hair and hauled her close as he had in her dreams? What if he'd covered her still-thrumming body with his and delved deeply between her lips? And what if those sultry dreams then turned into her worst nightmare—as he discovered the rest? The real her.

What then?

She dropped her hand and then her gaze as the reality of her life locked back in. She stared at the medallion, this time really looking at it. It wasn't new. Several fine scratches marred the surface. Had it been a gift from *her?* Was that why he still wore it? Driven by curiosity and its unexpected stepsister, jealousy, she reached out and slipped her finger beneath the coin.

"Who is this guy?"

He dropped his gaze. For a moment she didn't think he was going to tell her. But then he sighed. "Saint Nicholas."

She waited for him to elaborate.

He didn't.

"Saint Nicholas? As in…red suit, eight reindeer, North Pole? That St. Nick?"

The side of his mouth quirked. "No."

Again she waited.

But again…nothing.

This time she sighed. Loudly. "You know, for an ARIES agent who professes to be my partner, not to mention someone who's been actively digging through my brain for three days combing for memories, you're pretty tight-lipped. You keep up this deluge of mindless chatter and I just might get the idea you don't like me."

Silence.

It might be her bed, but what the hell. She could take a hint. She dug her elbows into the mattress and pushed up, stopping only when she met a wall of hard muscle.

"Do you mind?"

He pulled himself off her and swung his legs to the floor. But he didn't stand. He sat there, his broad shoulders and naked back to her as he stared across the cabin at the morning rays of sunlight beginning to stream in through the shutters. "He's a patron saint. Catholic. It was a gift from my father to my mother. He hoped it would protect her and me until he saw her again."

Again? "They were separated?"

He still didn't turn, but he nodded. "Vietnam. He was drafted. He came from money, but he felt it was his duty to go. They planned to marry upon his return, hoped his family would come around while he was gone—you know, accept the ignorant wetback and all. But when she wrote to tell him she was pregnant, he panicked. He was afraid he'd never see her again." Jared's right hand slipped around to his front. "He sent this.

"You said patron saint. Like Christopher?"

Another nod. "Christopher is the patron saint of travelers. He looks after them. Intercedes on their behalf."

"So this Nicholas looks out for…?"

"Infants, children. And the dying." He pushed his hand through his hair, shoving the bulk of it behind his shoulders. "He should have kept it. He ended up needing it more than she did."

"He was killed in action?"

Yet another nod. But the iron set to his shoulders told her he'd shared more with her just now than he'd shared with almost everyone else in his life combined.

Did she dare push it?

Ignorant wetback. An ugly word for an even uglier, ignorant prejudice. "And your mom? Did they ever accept her?"

"No." He laughed softly, curtly. "Kind of ironic when you think about it." He finally turned his head and stared into her eyes. "I got the memory from her." With that, he stood.

He stared down at her for several tense moments.

She swore he was on the verge of adding something else, but then, like the kiss that wasn't, he changed his mind.

"Breakfast?"

She blinked. That was it? He tossed out the first real insight into his inner self, waited until it landed in her lap and then wanted to just eat?

"Uh, sure."

"Good. I'm starved."

He should have kept his mouth shut.

Jared glowered at the empty bunk across the cabin. Sam Hatch was right not to trust him completely.

He truly was losing it.

Why else had he dumped so much of his life into Alex Morrow's hands? He couldn't even be sure that was the woman's real name. And there he was, pouring out his childhood, inviting her to examine it, judge it. He'd told himself she was right. That if they were going to function as a team, he needed to reveal something of himself. So why had he chosen that?

What had he really hoped to gain? Her pity?

It was the best he could hope for, anyway. Especially if she ever heard the rest of the sorry-assed story. Well, she wouldn't. Not from him. Heck, all he had to do was hang around long enough and even *he* wouldn't be able to re-member it. Maybe there were benefits in hell after all. He already knew there weren't any left here on earth. Not for him.

Just torture.

The past three days had been bad enough. The past two hours had almost killed him. He could still feel her fingertip tracing his lips. Just as he could still feel the urge to wrap his tongue around it and pull it into his mouth so he could taste it. So he could taste *her*. He would never know how he managed to turn his back on the invitation in those sea-green eyes, on that lush, exotic mouth. On what he knew in his soul would have been the hottest, most erotic kiss of his life.

Breakfast?

Ha! He hadn't been able to take a single bite. Neither had she. Not with that not-quite kiss hanging between them. They'd spent the meal dancing around each other, instead, the cabin's very air ripe with unspoken questions, deceptive answers and a damned-near-smoldering, inescapable desire.

It was time to face facts.

He was going stir-crazy—and so was she.

He tore his attention away from that empty, rumpled bunk and fused it to his computer. He had a reprieve, dam-mit. He didn't care if he read every file in the ARIES data-base before it expired, he was not going to waste the time speculating on how Alex's morning bath was progressing.

Jared dragged the laptop to the edge of the table, but as he settled back in his chair to decide on his next file, the computer's alarm sounded. He straightened. They had mail. Urgent mail. Finally, something new to read, however brief. If he was really lucky, he might actually have something to do. He tapped his finger onto the touchpad with more force than necessary. The flash message was from their local ARIES operative.

Even better.

He tapped the touchpad again as the cabin door opened, intrigued enough with the subject line to resist the temptation to look up as the door closed.

"What is it?"

"E-mail. It's from Marty."

"It's about time." Several water droplets splattered across the screen, as well as the back of his hand, as she dropped her towel on the table beside the computer. "What's the verdict?"

"It's a go."

"Fantastic." The bar of soap and shampoo hit the towel. "When do we leave?"

Here it came. He finished the final details of the message and pushed the laptop away, forcing himself to ignore the slicked-back hair and water droplets that clung to her cheeks as he faced her. Instead, he focused on the shapeless men's sweats she'd donned. "I'd like to go alone."

Those soft, green eyes widened for a split second, then narrowed. Hardened. "No."

He sighed. "Alex—"

"I don't think you heard me, *partner.* I said no."

Oh, he'd heard her. She just hadn't been listening to him. He'd pulled her out of that makeshift hospital bed three days ago. She'd been awake off and on for maybe two before that.

"You're not ready."

That only earned him a snort. "This from the man who shot lidocaine in his ass an hour ago."

He bit his tongue at the sarcasm. Nor did he bother offering her a crash course in anatomy. His hamstring was below his ass, not in it. "The injections are for the residual pain, and you know it. If I had to, I could go without. In fact, I'll be off the lidocaine by tomorrow. But that's not the point. The fluid volume in my bloodstream is back to normal.''

"So am I.''

"You can't know that for sure. Neither can I. Yes, your vitals are fine, but you still haven't been able to recall whatever it was that Karl Weiss tried to tell you. Nor have you let me close enough in the light of day to examine that scar on your scalp, much less take those blasted stitches out.''

"Fine, take them out. Either way, I'm going.''

He stared at her, stunned by the determination in her eyes. *Now* she was willing? After he'd just gotten e-mail from Marty telling him that not only did Roman Orloff check out, but they had to leave immediately.

"I can't.''

She stiffened. "You can't what?''

"Take them out. Not now. I don't have time.''

She crossed her arms and waited.

Christ. He might have known this woman only for a handful of days, but he was already well acquainted with that look. She was not about to give in. Nor would she wave him off and wait patiently behind. He sighed. "*We* don't have time. Especially if you're coming. I'll have to take them out tonight. Marty's managed to arrange transport with a local rebel fighter. But we'll have to really hoof it to make that truck. The main road is thirty minutes due north.''

"How long do we have?''

"Thirty minutes.''

He stood there, stunned, as she scooped the toiletries and towel from the table and headed for her bunk. She tossed them into one of the crates doubling as her dresser and proceeded to strip the sweats off her body without even waiting to see if he'd turned away. By the time he'd grabbed their handheld GPS unit, she'd donned a sweater, fresh jeans and her work boots. She jerked her gaze toward him as she reached the door.

"Come on, Jared. Let's *go*.''

Maybe it was her decision to finally let him at those stitches. Maybe it was the speed with which she'd changed. Maybe it was the barely restrained impatience burning within those eyes. He couldn't be sure. But as he locked the cabin door behind them, he had the distinct feeling that Alex Morrow had her own reasons for wanting to reach Rajalla, her own agenda. An agenda that had nothing to do with their mission.

They'd been standing in line for six hours.

Alex ignored the generously muscled arm looped gently but possessively over her shoulders, as well as the distracting thumb that grazed the side of her neck. Instead, she studied the trio of bullet holes in the tinted glass of Rajalla's main hospital doors. According to one of the files her doting "fiancé" had recently memorized, they'd been put there a week ago.

A moment later the double doors opened.

A camouflaged forearm shot out just far enough to wave the next woman and her daughter through. The door slammed shut behind them, leaving the endless line of silent, stoic patients behind. Heck, even the infants and toddlers around them seemed reluctant to voice more than a cough and a whimper. It was as if they somehow knew that crying wouldn't do any good.

Alex caved in to curiosity and counted the bodies still separating her and Jared from the front doors. Thirteen. God only knew how many women, children and the occasional grandfather had already made it inside. By the time they'd arrived at ten this morning, the line had already stretched around the front of the hospital and all the way down the side of the block. She was afraid to turn around and see how far the line stretched now, lest she be tempted to move to the back.

The thumb grazed her neck again, this time soothingly, as if its owner had read her mind.

She breathed out as she worked to loosen the ever-tightening threads of desire those warm, steady fingers had been knotting inside her belly all day. As long as the man kept his mouth shut and that subtle, toe-curling Texas drawl to himself, she'd be fine. Unfortunately that same owner compounded the caress when he leaned close, his breath stirring the curls against the side of her face, to murmur huskily into her ear.

"Relax. We've got another thirty minutes till we hit those doors, maybe forty-five."

She closed her eyes, wishing for the thousandth time since they'd arrived that she was deaf in her left ear and not her right. Anything to escape that subtle drawl. "Wanna bet?" Jared knew as well as she did that the entire line would step back to make way the moment the next gunshot victim showed up.

His sigh washed her ear.

She braced herself against the murmur that was sure to follow—then downright stiffened as the opening syllables were drowned out by squealing tires a good two blocks away.

They spun about together, eyes and ears straining as both their heights afforded them an advantage over the shorter Rebelian natives who made up the rest of the now palpably apprehensive crowd. Moments later a rusted black-and-white cab screamed into view. The human line lurched backward as the cab's right wheels ripped up and over the cobbled curb before shrieking to a halt. Metal ground against metal, chewing up gears as the elderly cabbie wrenched the car's stick shift into neutral. The man didn't even bother killing the engine as he leaped out, words spewing from his mouth in an incoherent torrent of Rebelian, German and Russian.

Unfortunately there was more Rebelian and Russian than German in the mix. She'd barely had time to translate *boy* and *blood* when Jared grabbed her arm, dragging her with him as he vaulted forward. He pushed his way through the crowd converging on the cab, not stopping until they'd reached the rear passenger door. She caught sight of a gaunt, keening, elderly woman, tears streaming down her cheeks as she clutched a boy, no more than four or five, cradling his dark head close as she rocked him against her chest. Alex lost sight of the woman and child as Jared gently but firmly shoved the still-babbling cabbie out of the way.

She nearly threw up as he yanked the car door open.

"Jesus H. Chri—"

"Grab his leg!"

She didn't have to ask which one. There was only one.

The poor tyke was missing a hand, too, leaving mutilated, seeping stumps where his right wrist and knee had been. She lifted the child's bare left foot and tugged it toward her so Jared could grasp the boy beneath his limp shoulders and waist.

Land mine.

The boy had probably stumbled across the Russian "butterfly" version. As she wrapped one hand about the boy's bloody calf, the other around his mangled wrist, Alex was painfully aware of the brutal irony of the butterfly's success. Unlike the American "Bouncing Betty," Russian mines weren't designed to kill, but to maim, thereby removing the injured soldier from the battlefield, along with the second soldier assigned to haul the first man to safety.

Rebelia might qualify as a battlefield, but the boy she and Jared shouldered though the crowd and inside the heavy glass doors was *not* a soldier. He was an innocent child, dammit!

She was dimly aware of Jared barking orders in German as they reached the hospital's sardine-packed main hall. Unfortunately, for all his brilliant memorization skills, the man's accent truly stank. She pulled herself together and repeated his butchered requests for a doctor and a bed as the crowd parted. The pair of armed guards who met them took one look at the child and promptly waved them forward, paving the way into a large open bay with twenty steel cots crammed along both ends. All but the last two were filled. Jared commandeered the closest empty cot as three more men raced into the room, their no-longer-white coats and stethoscopes flying.

A battered-and-bruised doctor led the fray.

Roman Orloff.

To her surprise, he took one look at the boy and cursed. Orloff shouted something over his shoulder and one of the men behind him peeled off to swing around and grab the boy's grandmother. The man pulled the sobbing woman close and led her from the room. Alex kept her hands clamped about the child's mangled limbs, desperately attempting to keep the kid's remaining blood from seeping into the bleached sailcloth and bed linens as Orloff and the remaining physician reached the cot. Jared peeled the flannel shirt from his back as Orloff hooked his stethoscope to his ears and closed his still-bruised eyes so he could concentrate on listening to the kid's heart. By the time Orloff pulled the scope from his ears, Jared had torn two strips of flannel from his shirt.

He shoved the first strip at Orloff, keeping the second for himself. Together the two fashioned dual tourniquets about the boy's seeping forearm and lower thigh. The Asian doctor hovered behind Orloff, responding to Jared's demand for blood typing in halting German.

This time, *she* cursed.

Jared snapped his gaze to hers as Orloff added his own spate of German before shouting for an amputation kit. Since they already knew the Rebelian neurosurgeon had been trained in the States, she assumed he'd stuck to German for his assistant's benefit. Unfortunately, from the confusion on Jared's face, his own translation skills were worse than his accent.

He turned to her. "What's wrong?"

"The boy's name is Mikhail. They've treated him before." She glanced down instinctively at the dark-red stains still spreading across the cot despite the tourniquets. Even she could tell the child desperately needed a transfusion. But that wasn't the worst of it. "Mikhail's blood type is B negative."

Rare enough in the States. But in a city where two out of three hospitals, as well as damned near all free clinics, had already been destroyed it was an impossibility. Alex jerked her chin toward Orloff as he retrieved what had to be the amputation kit and began to lay the instruments out on the empty cot. She swallowed firmly at the sight of the jagged saw and jerked her gaze back to Jared's. "Orloff says he used their last bag of B negative six days ago. Their last bag of O negative went into another patient two days before that. They drained the last of their doctors and able-bodied staff this morning."

Jared's curse matched hers.

She leaned close to him. "I can call my brother. See what he can…arrange."

That sharp, tawny gaze met hers. They both knew she was referring to ARIES. They both also knew that by the time Marty Lyons and his local contacts found a donor, the kid would be dead.

She wasn't surprised when Jared shook his head, but she was ready to argue.

He stunned her by turning to Orloff, not even attempting German as he settled on clear, crisp, carefully enunciated English. "I'm a U.S. Army medic. I have B negative blood. Get me an IV line and two needles. I'll donate it myself now."

Relief flooded Orloff's dark eyes. The purple welt on his right cheek stood out as he barked a series of orders to his assistant, as well as the physician who'd finally returned from escorting the boy's wailing grandmother to another room.

Alex recaptured Jared's stare, undaunted by the determination blazing within. What the hell was he thinking? The man might have been sucking down a steady supply of water for the past three days to replenish the fluid volume in his blood, but he was still a pint or more low on red blood cells himself. The child would need another two—at least.

"You can't—"

His terse glare cut her off.

She didn't care. "I mean it, you can't—"

"The *hell* I can't."

She waited until Orloff jackknifed up to head for a cabinet of supplies near the center of the room. She grabbed Jared's hand, keeping her hiss low in case any of the patients that appeared to be hanging onto their every word actually understood English. "You do this and you could end up dead."

"It's not your decision."

"It is. If you won't think of yourself, consider our job."

"Dammit, it doesn't—"

"No."

He twisted his hand until his fingers were locked to hers. He squeezed hard. "It *doesn't* matter. *I* don't matter. Accept it." His grip loosened. Her blood rushed back into her fingers as he sighed heavily. "I have."

What the devil was that supposed to mean?

Before she could demand an explanation, Orloff returned, intravenous line and an obscenely large-bore IV needle in hand. A needle that would soon be used to drain Jared's blood. She dragged her gaze to the boy, and prayed. Her own original petty needs and goals for the day faded beneath that tiny cherubic face. A face that was growing paler by the second. Her gaze slipped down the boy's limp body. As Orloff's assistants took over the surgical repair of the boy's viciously amputated limbs, Jared's dusky fingers moved over the child's remaining good, if deathly white, arm. Jared secured a rubber tourniquet to the kid's nonexistent biceps before swiping that slender inner elbow with alcohol, then waited patiently as Orloff did the same. A swift pierce of the smaller needle into the kid's vein, followed by an equally swift stab by Orloff into an artery running down the underside of Jared's right forearm, and the biological connection was complete. Alex watched as gravity aided the morbid transfer, slowly but surely draining the scarlet blood from Jared's body into the child's as he pumped his fist over and over to force it to drain even faster.

She closed her eyes, inexplicably terrified by the sight. She told herself she was worried about their case. Worried about the agent who'd saved her life. Hell, even anxious to keep the man alive so her nocturnal fantasy life could remain intact.

She was lying. She was worried about *him*.

"Are you okay?"

She opened her eyes, grateful the question had come from Orloff—now reduced to playing waiting assistant himself—and not Jared. She couldn't face him. She couldn't face that slender tubing of dark-red blood. She damned sure couldn't sit here and watch it drain out of him. Watch the life drain out of him. But neither could she turn her back on him. She stunned them both by threading the fingers of her left hand blindly into his, clamping onto the solid, reassuring warmth of Jared's larger hand as she raised her gaze to stare into Orloff's eyes.

"H-how long?"

Those deep-brown, compassionate pools shifted to the scarlet tubing, then to the steady, simmering amber of Jared's eyes.

She continued to avoid both.

The doctor shrugged, openly studying the recent gash on Jared's exposed biceps. "Twenty, thirty minutes. Your friend appears healthy. It may take as little as fifteen."

The gash in Jared's hamstring, flashed before her eyes. The way he'd nearly passed out in the cabin three mornings before. The way his strength had begun to flag toward the end of their half-hour, all-out sprint this morning as they struggled to meet the truck and rebel driver Marty Lyons had arranged. It wouldn't take fifteen minutes to drain Jared's next pint of blood. It would take forty, at least.

She couldn't sit here that long.

She drew a deep breath and latched on to the one reprieve she had left and offered it up. "As you've already discovered, my fiancé is a medic in the U.S. Army. His name is Jeff. Jeff Coleman. As for me, we've already met, Dr. Orloff." She extended her free hand beneath that dark, widening gaze. "Alice Marko. I believe you stitched up my scalp following an unfortunate accident several weeks ago?"

The man took her hand. Again, he stared, but not at her face. Rather, he studied her right ear. That was when she knew for certain.

He *knew.*

Orloff's thick brows rose pointedly as he squeezed her right hand, his solid, welcoming grip telling her so much more than the carefully masked expression in his eyes. "It's a pleasure to meet you again…Alice. A true pleasure."

She allowed her lips to mirror the soft twist in his. "Thank you, Doctor. For the stitches. And the rest."

He inclined his head.

She might be meeting the man for the first time while completely conscious, but she knew in her bones that unlike Karl, Roman Orloff would never betray her—or them. Though she had to confess she was relieved when she felt the tension ebb from Jared's fingers, as well, not to mention the matching, steady trust that replaced it.

Orloff glanced past the team of doctors still working in rapid, efficient concert to seal the raw edges of Mikhail's tiny limbs and tipped his head toward the door beyond.

"Alice, would you care to join me in my office?"

Chapter 7

His ass hurt like a son of a bitch.

Jared ignored the terse silence to his right, as well as his own bitter anatomy lesson, as he leaned back against the threadbare seat, clamping down on a groan as the taxi hit its thirtieth pothole in five minutes. His left hamstring, his right leg, his ass, his lower back— There was no way around it, his entire body hurt. Unfortunately, short of shooting up in the back seat of a rusted cab in the middle of a darkened, bombed-out back alley of Rajalla, there wasn't a blessed thing he could do about it. Not until they reached Orloff's house and the beckoning relief of the capped syringe of Demerol the good doctor had slipped Alex on their way out.

The dizziness returned as the cab turned onto the city's main drag, slamming into the thirty-first pothole. He shifted his gaze to the row of shot-out antique street lamps that had once added to Rajalla's Old World charm as the taxi bucked again. The jolt succeeded in ripping half the air from his lungs, purging it through his teeth on a full-blown, ragged groan.

"I told you we should have left after they finished draining your blood."

He waited for his lungs to restart, the light-headedness to pass, before he shifted his stare across the back seat of the cab. "Thank you, *Doctor* Morrow. I'll keep that medical advice in mind…tomorrow." He might not be able to see light in those blackened street lamps, but he could make out the fire in those green eyes.

"Tomorrow you rest."

Like hell he would. Not with Orloff and his meager staff still in that overcrowded triage bay, frantically treating everything from dysentery and pneumonia to land-mine and gunshot wounds. Come dawn, he'd be headed back to Rajalla's sole surviving hospital, back to that triage room, setting bones, patching gaping holes and rigging IV lines into what was left of some barely out-of-diapers kid who'd happened upon a hunk of metal that looked a lot like a makeshift Frisbee with wings…but was a whole lot deadlier.

"I've never felt so damned *useless.*"

"I know." His sigh followed hers, both filling the dark.

How many mines had been left on the battlefields of the world? Battlefields that had then become some unsuspecting kid's deadly playground?

He now knew firsthand that one was too many.

Alex was right. They had to take better care of the world. It might be too late for him, but it wasn't for that poor kid. Or the next.

The cab turned another corner, jolting again as the beam from its sole headlight swept a burned-out hovel twenty feet beyond the edge of the pocked road. A once white, now scorched two-story building stood beside it. It wasn't until the car stopped that Jared realized they must have arrived. He double-checked the shadowy number welded to the rusting wrought-iron gate.

The house was Orloff's.

Alex bailed out as he held up several eurodollars to cover the fare plus another fifty miles.

The cabbie shook his scuffed jaw. "I cannot. Not for friend of Roman Orloff. Not for doctor, also."

He was about to argue the point, until he caught the fierce pride in the old man's eyes. It looked a hell of a lot like the gleam he'd seen staring back at him from his bathroom mirror when he was seventeen. Jared stood back and waited for the cabbie to pull away, then tossed the bills neatly through the window. He ignored the vile curse hanging on the night as he turned back to Alex. It hadn't been meant for him anyway.

"You insulted him."

He snagged her elbow. "He's too poor to be insulted."

She shook her head. "I don't think that's possible."

"Trust me, it is."

He should have kept his mouth shut.

Maybe it was the light-headedness he hadn't quite been able to shake since the moment he'd finished draining off another pint of blood. Maybe it was the body aches that had settled in during the four-hour gunshot surgery he'd ended up assisting Orloff with as soon as his own IV needle had cleared his arm. Hell, maybe it was the trio of muscle cramps that had taken up residence along the length of his remaining good leg an hour before—and hadn't loosened yet. He didn't know. All he knew was that he'd already revealed far too much about himself during that conversation he and Alexhad shared that morning in the cabin. He should have kept his mouth shut then, too.

But he hadn't.

And now it was too late.

The pity had already locked into that exhausted green gaze, softening it further. He ignored it, snagging her elbow abruptly as he retrieved Orloff's house key from his pocket. Unfortunately her two good legs reached the iron gate first. She dropped her hand onto the rusting latch—and kept it there. "Is that why you joined the Army? Because you were poor?"

He waited.

The gate remained closed.

He sighed. "I joined because my mom needed the medical coverage." A split second later, he realized he could have lied. Then again, maybe not. That ever-eroding good judgment again.

So this was how it started. Husky words whispered in the dark, couched in compassionate conversation. Dangerous confessions offered in a futile attempt to unburden the heart, to share the load. Maybe even ease the soul. *Right.* What it was—what *this* was—was a mistake. But at least it was one that would correct itself eventually. Because these whispered words, this particular confession, wouldn't be hanging around forever. Not for him.

What do you know. An honest-to-God blessing in disguise.

She kept that blasted sympathetic stare fused to his, despite his stony silence, her hand on the gate. "I don't understand. My dad was Navy. While I don't really remember him—he died when I was two—I do remember receiving medical coverage until I graduated from college. My mom still has it."

What the hell. "Your folks were married."

"So…your mom became your dependent?"

The damned gate stayed shut.

"Yup."

Idiot. The acid was already eating a path up his throat.

"That's pretty rare, isn't it? Getting a government agency to accept a parent as a dependent? I know because Sam did it for someone, but it almost didn't go through and, well, the guy's situation was pretty dire. I mean—" She must have realized how bald that sounded because she swallowed the rest.

He swallowed the acid—until she started up again, this time softly.

"What was wrong with your m—"

"You gonna open that gate sometime tonight? Or are we gonna be standing here come dawn?"

The gate swung open.

He stalked through. Or, rather, tried to. "Thanks."

He forced himself to keep moving. To keep from hearing her response, true. But also to keep his leg from buckling under him. Nor did he want her catching sight of the iron clamp he'd placed on his jaw, especially as he cleared the three steps that led up to the front door. He shoved Orloff's spare key into the lock and pushed the door open before her hand could fuse to that handle, too, then stepped into the house, hitting the wall switch with more force than necessary.

Light flooded the small foyer.

"Thank you."

He glanced at the hardwood stairs on their right as their vision adjusted. The steps, like the house, had seen better days. But also like the house, the freshly waxed stairs and buffed banister had been meticulously maintained. Given Orloff's grueling schedule, not by him. Must be the maid Marty's background investigation had noted when the man had checked the house for wiretaps, bugs and booby traps earlier in the day. Unfortunately he and Alex didn't have a report on the woman. Yet.

"Orloff mentioned he has daytime help. The guest bed's supposed to be made up, though." He pointed to the stairs. "Up there. Middle door." When Alex didn't move, he nudged her toward the stairs, closing in behind her before she could argue. From the way her feet had been dragging all the way out of the hospital tonight, she was as tired as he was.

By the time they reached the top step, his legs were damned near begging for rest. Alex reached the door first and pushed it open. He slipped his arm around her torso, flicking the light switch on as he nudged her forward again. He immediately wished he hadn't. The room was half the size of their cabin, but that wasn't the problem. Nor was the armoire or the equally modest desk, chair crowding the tiny room. It was the bed. The only bed in the room.

The mattress was a full.

He was six-four, she was six even, and they were going to have to crawl beneath that bleached bedspread and curl up on that tiny mattress together? One small shift or outright turn from either of them and they'd end up twisted into some damned lovers' knot. An extremely tight and painfully close-knit knot. With all the tension and *none* of the release.

She exhaled softly. "I'm not really tired."

"Me, neither." He hauled his gaze from the bed and dragged it to hers. "But you should take a nap, anyway."

"Me? I'm not the one who's limping."

"I'm not—"

"You're right. You'd have to be putting weight on that leg to limp. You've got all your weight on your right."

That was about to change. Just as soon as she rooted through that leather sack-turned-purse Marty had managed to scrounge up on short notice and located his syringe.

She read his mind.

No great feat at the moment, granted. But he appreciated it nonetheless as she opened the knapsack. "Fine. Drop 'em."

He blinked.

"You heard me. Drop your jeans."

"I heard you. It's just not necessary. I can inject it myself."

The capped syringe cleared the bag, glinting beneath the sole overhead bulb. "You want it? Earn it. Now drop them."

"Dammit, Alex, this isn't a game. Give me the—"

She jerked the syringe out of his reach. Her gaze was steady, serious. Not in the least teasing. "You're right again. This isn't a game. I've had a pretty good idea all night that that leg is worse than you're letting on. Now quit hiding behind that damned army-medic's bag and let me take a look at it before you faint on me.''

Hiding? Now that was rich. There was also no way he could resist not cashing in. Not after spending all night stewing. He raised his brow. ''*I'm* the one who's hiding something?''

Her gaze widened, reflected pure innocence. She had the nerve to tack on a wide-eyed blink.

He must be tired, because he called her on it. ''No way, lady. Don't bat those lashes at me. You've been holding out on me for days. I may not know what or why, but I know something's there.''

''I have no idea what you're—''

''You think you're the only one who can read a watch? Fifty-eight minutes, Alex. That's how long Roman Orloff took to examine you while I was chained to that stained cot and that sorry kid. While that mile-long line of patients behind that kid grew even longer. You were up in that office for almost an hour with the man. Alone. What took so blasted long?'' He winced. He hadn't meant to sound quite so affronted.

At least, not personally.

And, dammit, she picked up on it. Those smooth, brows shot up while his leg continued to throb right along with his suspicions. His pride.

''Jealous?''

''Like hell.''

Liar. He'd seen the way Orloff had stared at her after the crisis had passed. As if the man couldn't quite wrap his mind around the stunning transformation from neighborhood nerd to pinup potential. He knew the feeling. Just as he could feel the frank male appreciation radiating off Orloff whenever the man's stare had lingered during the remainder of the night.

And it had lingered—far too often.

He knew that feeling, too. What red-blooded male

wouldn't? He'd have to be less a man than she'd once been not to be attracted to this Alex Morrow.

Hell, his marbles were cracked, not his b—

"Cat got your tongue?"

A bit lower, sweetheart.

He shrugged and stared at the syringe. "You gonna hang on to that as long as you did the gate?"

"Depends."

What the hell, he bit. "On?"

"You hanging on to those pants?"

Screw the Demerol. Screw her. He spun around and headed for the door. He didn't need the injection that badly. Not as much as he needed an answer to—

He stopped.

Turned back. Cocked his brow. "How 'bout a trade? My jeans for that syringe—and an answer."

It was her turn to blink. "That's two for one. Quite the bargain. For you."

"Take it or leave it." He shrugged. "I can always rig a compress." And curse beneath his breath all damned night.

The moment the guilt slipped into the mist, he knew he had her. Her resigned sigh followed. "What's the question?"

"What were you and Orloff doing for fifty-eight minutes?"

Her lips quirked. "The whole fifty-eight?"

"The entire time, honey."

He already knew she and Orloff hadn't been swapping case notes, because Orloff hadn't had anything to offer. He and Alex might not have been able to cull more than a couple of private moments from the night, but she'd managed to relay that. Orloff had no idea why DeBruzkya needed her brought out of her coma, just that the general had been desperate for it to happen. He had overheard the general discussing gems, even the old Rebelian Gem of Power legend Lily Scott and Karl Weiss had uncovered separately. But again, also like Lily and Karl, Orloff had no idea if DeBruzkya had managed to locate the Gem. The only fresh information Orloff had been able to offer was the reason behind his own beatings. Rotten timing.

Bruno DeBruzkya was brutal, not stupid. He was also calculating and methodical. In a world of encrypted cell phones and spy satellites, the master of thugs had outsmarted them all. Other than adding a moat and a set of luxury suites for his personal use, DeBruzkya hadn't touched the outside of the medieval castle. Until Davidson arrived at the otherwise crumbling compound and then left in a hail of bullets with Lily and his son in tow, only a handful of DeBruzkya's advisers knew the general could be found inside those stone walls. And, of course, Orloff. From the damage still marring the good doctor's face, it had taken a while for DeBruzkya to believe the innocence in Orloff's eyes at least about Davidson's castle assault.

Well, it would take answers before *he* believed in *hers*.

Jared nudged his brow a notch higher as he stared at her. "Well?"

Alex sighed. "After he removed my stitches, we ordered supplies."

They what?

She nodded. "Medical supplies. You saw how desperate they are." She shrugged. "I had Roman write out a dream list. Drugs, surgical supplies, diagnostic equipment. I happen to have access to them, or at least, I have a good friend from college who does. I called in a marker. And now we have another hook into Orloff. They should begin arriving by a global courier in the morning."

It was simple, stupid—and bloody brilliant. Aiden Swift would be proud.

So why wasn't he?

More importantly, why didn't he believe her? Jared stared into those light green eyes for what felt like hours. Days. He sifted through the mist, picked through the lingering shadows. Try as he might, he couldn't find so much as a hint of subterfuge. So why was his gut telling him she was lying? At the very least, withholding something.

She finally sighed. "Red blood cells."

He stiffened. Surely she hadn't—

But she nodded. "I also arranged to have 250 units of packed red blood cells flown in. Eight are B negative."

He sucked in his breath against the inexplicable shaft that stabbed his chest, his heart. Just as it had that afternoon. For a brief moment beside that kid's cot, he could have sworn she'd been concerned about more than just their mission, that she'd been concerned—deeply concerned—about him. While that had been alarming enough, what had terrified him even more was the realization that he actually wanted her to care.

But he shouldn't.

Dammit, he *didn't*. If anything, he should feel relief.

He'd nearly convinced himself he did when her fingers snagged his forearm. "Promise me—"

He jerked his gaze up as she swallowed softly.

"Promise me you'll take the first unit."

The stark whisper hung between them.

He didn't know what to say, let alone what to think. When was the last time a woman—hell, when was the last time anyone—had been truly and solely concerned for him?

He knew the answer. He was just afraid to voice it. To her. Much less himself. The warmth in her fingers spread up his arm until it damned near ignited the air between them. She had to have noticed it, too, because she stepped forward at the precise moment he jerked back.

He clamped down on his tongue as the hurt entered the soft mist of her eyes, cooling it rapidly. He refused to respond to it. Dammit, he couldn't. It was for her own good, even more than for his.

The mist finally cleared, and he breathed easier.

So did she. "Well?"

He blinked.

She held out her hand again. The empty one. "Strip."

He thought about holding out for the syringe, then decided against it. His leg had been locked into place for so long he no longer cared who stabbed that needle into his backside, so long as one of them did. He tucked his hands beneath the sweater Orloff lent him and grabbed the brass stud on his jeans.

"Boots first. I intend to see the entire man."

He tipped his head. "Yes, ma'am."

She flushed.

Knowing he'd pushed it further than he should have lest he risk her invading his dreams again, he turned. He scraped his boots heel to booted toe, then heel to sock as he doffed first the right, then the left. His switchblade thumped out onto the braided area rug. His favorite throwing knife followed, as well as the two spares he'd brought along for the occasion. He was in no shape to retrieve them. Fortunately his ankle holster had the decency to remain attached to his leg along with his backup piece.

Her gaze scanned the rug. "Nice cutlery collection."

He shrugged. "It comes in handy."

"I'll bet. Remind me never to challenge you to darts."

He ignored the dry twist to her lips and what they did to his gut as he tucked his fingers beneath his sweater, locating the stud on his jeans again as she moved around behind him. This time he released it, praying silently as he pushed his pants down to his calves. If he was lucky, either his leg wasn't as bad as he thought or her knowledge of chemistry didn't extend to the organic kind. At least, not far enough for her to diagnose it.

"Sweet Jesus."

Evidently it was. He frowned.

"How long has your leg been infected?"

Long enough.

"Well?"

He was about to bend down to retrieve his pants. He stiffened, instead, as her slender fingers brushed the angry skin surrounding his gash, cooling the fire in his leg but at the same time, stoking another in his groin. *Sweet Jesus* was right. He closed his eyes, and not against the ache. Not the one she was worried about.

"Are you taking something for this?"

He shook his head, breathing easier as her fingers left his gash to tear open the alcohol wipe. The cold swipe followed. He'd have missed the needle altogether had he not been waiting for it. She capped the syringe and tossed it onto the desk.

"I don't understand. Surely you've got antibiotics in that bag at the cabin."

He nodded. "But they were meant for you. Ciprofloxin's the best broad-based antibiotic out there. But I'm allergic to it."

"What about Orloff?"

"I warned him when you two returned from his office. Had to, otherwise the kid would be at risk. He's got the boy on Cipro now. He'll cull something else from the hospital's supply and bring it home for me."

"That could be hours yet."

"I'll live."

His leg might not. Either of them. The muscles in his right leg were tired of compensating for his left during the impromptu surgery he and Orloff had spent fishing out lead swimming in some soldier's riddled gut. His good leg had completely locked up. At the gate, he'd noted two charley horses. He could now pinpoint three.

He sucked in his breath as Alex pushed his jeans down to his ankles to work the one in his upper right calf.

"That's not neces—"

"Stand still."

He didn't have a choice. He stood there, silently grinding down on his molars as she worked the knot with her fingers.

A minute later his pique began to ebb.

The woman had good hands. Strong fingers. Nor was she afraid to use them. Still, it took another minute before he could feel the muscle loosening, the pain easing. He bit down again, this time trapping his groan. He didn't care how good her hands were. She was not getting those fingers near the knot in his right quad, much less the one in his ass.

He inched away as she finished. "Thanks."

"Don't thank me yet, I'm not done." She jackknifed up and swung around to his front before he could lean down to grab his jeans. "Lie down on the bed."

"You've done enough."

Pink stained her high cheeks as she folded her arms over her drab, gray sweater. "Look, buster. I got the message in the cabin, not to mention a couple of minutes ago. You're not interested. Guess what? I'll get over it. But if you don't stretch that leg out, it will cramp up so tight you'll take one step and you'll be lying flat on your face—on the floor. Then where will we be? Where will our cover be?"

He refused to answer. Much less admit how truly interested he was—in her.

She sighed. "Dammit, Jared. When was the last time you admitted you needed help, much less accepted it?"

He frowned as another face snapped into view. Another conversation. Another dare.

How long had it been? Six years.

Six years since a private investigator by the name of Kurt Miller had shown up at Fort Bragg to deliver the startling news. He'd won the biological lottery. The same loving grandfather who'd denied his right to bear the hallowed Sullivan name before kicking him out on his ass had taken his precious legitimate progeny sailing on his fancy yacht. Unfortunately his grandfather hadn't listened to the weekend weather report any more than the man had listened to him that day in his dank office years before.

The first time, his mother had paid the price.

The second, his uncle, his aunt and all three of their pure-white, Texas blue-blooded cousins, as well as Granddaddy himself, had paid. The only reason he'd agreed to listen to Kurt and step foot on that ranch again, much less accept it as his rightful, if decades-late, inheritance, was due to another man. A man who'd been as sincere and determined as the woman standing in front of him now. He could still hear Samuel Hatch's taunt. *"Dammit, son. Take the help. You've got nothing to lose except a strip of pride—and only if you let 'em take it."*

Hatch was right then.

Alex was right now.

He shrugged, leaving his boots and knives on the rug as he shuffled to the foot of the bed. He turned, barely suppressing a groan as he lowered his frame to the mattress. He couldn't prevent the next from escaping, however, as he stretched his leg out so she could remove his jeans. A second groan crawled up his throat and tumbled out as he tugged the rubber band from his hair, raking his fingers into his scalp for the first time in fourteen hours.

"Lie back and turn over. I'll be right back."

He was too tired to argue. Jared snagged the embroidered hem of one of the pillowcases, wedging his jaw smack into the middle of a feather pillow as he turned into the mattress. Lord, it felt good to lie down. The Demerol was beginning to take effect, too, the relief spreading across his hamstring, edging out the pain. He wasn't sure where Alex had gone, much less why, but he was halfway into his first dream by the time she returned. At least, he hoped he was dreaming. It wasn't the reality of the dip in the mattress or the warm compress that gently covered his gash that worried him, but the cool fingers that came with it. Especially when those cool fingers smoothed the rag across his hamstring before tucking the trailing edge snugly between his thighs. He tensed as her hands moved to his waist to peel his briefs down, baring his butt to the room and her kneading fingers.

"Just relax. Trust me."

God help him, he allowed the husk in her voice to rasp through him, and he did. He closed his eyes, swallowing another groan as she pushed and prodded at the charley horse in his rear, working the aching muscle over and over until, like the knot in his calf, this one too began to loosen and smooth out altogether. Damn, but she had *incredible* hands.

He could feel himself relaxing, drifting into a half dream, half hypnotic state, lured under by the Demerol and those deft, stroking fingers, as well as the exhaustion and light-headedness that'd been dogging him ever since he'd pulled that IV needle from his arm five hours ago. He didn't even argue as Alex finished kneading the cramp from his rear and pulled his briefs back up to his waist. Not even when she gently nudged him over onto his back. He stretched out willingly as she started in on the charley horse in his thigh, far enough gone to welcome the Demerol-induced fantasy that had somehow slipped into his increasingly fogged brain. By the time those amazingly agile fingers had finished massaging the final knot from his leg, he'd embraced the new ache that took over. Within moments, it consumed him.

There was no way he could resist it. Much less her.

Nor could he remember why he should.

Good Lord, she'd done it *again*.

Alex stared at the extra "leg" that was once again stiffening mere inches from her body, riveted by the force of the man's latest reaction. She couldn't help it. It was just so…intense. It was definitely her fault, too.

Maybe Jared was asleep.

In all honesty, that had been her only goal. All she'd wanted to do was take enough of the edge off the man's pain to help him relax so he could fall asleep until Orloff arrived with the antibiotics. But would Jared believe her?

Given their track record, probably not.

She dragged her gaze up to his face.

He wasn't asleep.

She flushed as that hot amber gaze not only captured hers, but held it. "I'm sorry. I swear, I wasn't trying to—"

"I know."

He reached down and covered her hands with his, carefully removing them from the proximity of his still-prominent erection. To her surprise, he didn't release her. Nor did he sever his heated stare. He cleared his throat. "I suppose my…interest…is rather obvious, isn't it?"

Her flush cooled, and another flame took its place. Desire.

He really did want her. She was certain of it when his gaze dropped to her mouth. The fire in his eyes burned hotter, until the amber practically glowed. She pulled her fingers from his and reached out to slip them through the loose strands of his hair. She half expected him to reach out and stop her. He didn't. But his gaze returned to hers. The glow in his eyes deepened as she slid the fingers of her right hand from that inky silk and dragged them across the late—evening whiskers that had sprouted along his jaw, not quite suppressing a shiver as the scruff rasped the pads of her fingers and then her entire palm. She was playing with fire and she knew it. Once more, she didn't care.

Dammit, she wanted to get burned.

She'd waited long enough for this man. If Janice didn't want him, she *did*.

He didn't have to know about the hearing aid. Until she'd told him, her ex-fiancé hadn't. She pushed Don from her memory and focused on the present, instead. On Jared. She reached out again, this time boldly smoothing her fingers across his lips. She sucked in her breath as Jared finally reached up and did the same. He trailed his fingers down her cheek and hooked his thumb beneath the curve of her jaw to draw her closer. Within seconds they were inches apart, staring directly into each other's eyes, breathing the same swirl of erotically charged air.

She refused to rush it. She refused to rush him.

Yes, she wanted him. More than she'd ever wanted another man. But she also needed Jared to be sure that he wanted her.

That he wanted *this*.

She waited until his fingers reached the center of her lips before she slipped the tip of her tongue out and slowly licked the pads of his fingers, telling him with her pace, her eyes and her smile just how far she wanted to go. Pleasure ignited within her as he groaned deeply. A split second later it exploded as he bit down on her fingers and sucked the tips.

Her entire body quivered.

That was all it took.

Before her eyes the man's iron control just snapped. One minute she was above him, slowly and deliberately teasing him, and the next she was trapped in a haze of scorching fire as he dragged her down to the bed, sealing the length of his body to hers as he rolled her beneath him in one smooth motion. He plowed his fingers into the curls at the base of her neck and used them to angle her mouth so he could finally delve deeply, completely, within.

To her utter satisfaction, his kiss didn't soothe.

And it sure as hell didn't sate.

It raged, consumed. She shuddered as he pulled her even closer, plunged deeper, his teeth scraping hers as he swallowed her moan. But it still wasn't enough. She wanted more. She wanted him.

Now.

She protested as he tore his mouth from hers—until he razed his lips down the side of her neck and bit gently but firmly into the curve at the base. A second moan ripped through her as she arched into the erotic sucking, pulling kiss that followed. She wrapped the fingers of her left hand into the inky strands of his hair and raked her right down his back to anchor his rigid erection to the juncture of her thighs. He growled into her neck as she rubbed against him and sucked harder. He stopped just below the cusp of pain and blew lightly across her flesh, then his tongue followed as he soothed the spot where his teeth and rasping stubble had been.

"*Please.* Don't stop."

He lifted his head and stared into her eyes, the golden glow in his confirming her deepest, darkest wish. He was just getting started. She shivered in anticipation as he dragged his fingers and his gaze down between them, staring at her chest as he pulled her sweater snuggly across her breasts. He knew as well as she did that she still had no bra.

The fact that she knew *he* knew made her hotter.

Wetter.

By the time he scraped the nubby sweater back and forth across her nipples, the flames had all but consumed her. Just when she thought she couldn't stand the rasping sensation a moment longer, he stopped. But then he leaned down to nip the now tender tips right through the fabric. A fresh wave of moisture flooded her core as he worried her nipples gently with his teeth. Just when she was sure she was going to come, right there, right then, with every stitch of clothing she donned that morning still plastered to her body, he released her nipples and raised his head—and smiled. *Damn him.* He knew exactly what he was doing. He was deliberately taking her to the edge and then backing off. He was trying to drive her insane. He was succeeding.

She returned his slow smile.

And lowered her hands.

Before he realized her intent, she'd slipped her fingers into the waist of his underwear and once again, began kneading his rear as she had earlier. But this time, she made no attempt to massage the muscles beneath his dusky skin. She stroked, soothed...and stoked.

The ridge cradled between her thighs grew thicker.

Harder.

By the time he lowered his trembling hands to her waist and hooked his thumbs beneath the edge of her sweater, she knew he was done teasing. He tugged the hem up and lowered his head, the silky length of his hair brushing her upper belly as she met him halfway. She moaned as he bathed each breast in turn with slow, hungry strokes, gasp-

ing as he ended each lingering caress with a slick, greedy
swirl around the base of each nub. He returned to her right
breast and covered her nipple with his entire mouth. Within
seconds she was suffocating in a maelstrom of sultry heat
and steady erotic suckling—until he ripped his mouth away
from her completely and cursed.

In German.

A split second later reality punched through the haze.
Jared didn't speak German. Not that well. Nor should that
curse have come from behind him. Way behind him.

They had company.

Alex didn't even bother yanking her sweater down as
Jared rolled to the right, his hand automatically reaching
for the backup piece in the holster at his ankle as she rolled
to the left to grab her leather bag—and her pistol—from
the edge of the mattress. They came up together, 9 mm and
.32 drawn as they vaulted off the bed, leveling both barrels
directly at the intruder's chest.

Orloff blinked.

A second later the man swallowed firmly, dragging his
dark gaze from Jared's .32, to her 9 mm, before whipping
it back to Jared as all three of them realized simultaneously
that her sweater was still snagged somewhere up above her
naked breasts. To her eternal gratitude, Orloff kept his stare
focused solely on Jared as he cleared his throat.

"I am sorry. I did not mean to…interrupt."

The apology hung between them. Hell, the piercing intimacy of what the man had just seen hung between them.
All of them. Alex lifted her free hand and pulled her
sweater down over her breasts as casually as she could.

It didn't help.

Orloff was still staring at Jared and, while Jared had finally turned his head to look at her, from the lingering
horror in his gaze she knew damned well he'd rather be
looking at someone else. Anyone else. The man might have
been interested moments ago, but he was definitely having
second thoughts now. She slid her gaze across the stifling

room, relieved when Orloff finally met hers—until she realized that not only had the doctor managed to get over his embarrassment first, but from the roguish glint in those dark-brown eyes, Roman had obviously decided to seek out the humor in the situation.

Damned if she could find it.

He held up a prescription vial in his hand, as well as a worn velvet box, as she slipped her pistol into her bag.

"Is your fiancé allergic to tetracycline?"

Orloff knew bloody well she and Jared were nothing more than partners. The moment he'd closed the door to his office, he'd cut straight to the chase, stunning her with his grasp of their situation. As well as the true nature of their job. She hadn't been surprised. After all, Orloff knew better than even the man beside her, calmly leaning down in his sweater and underwear to reholster his weapon, how truly elaborate her disguise had been. The fact that the doctor had kept his mouth shut—twice—was enough for her. While Jared hadn't been pleased to discover she'd confirmed Orloff's conclusions without his prior input, he'd understood.

Or so he'd said.

Right about now she'd give anything for Jared to say something. He finally did.

"The tet should work fine." He held up his hand as Roman tossed the plastic vial across the room, cracking the remaining tension with a lopsided grin as he snagged the antibiotics in midair. "Her fiancé thanks you."

He and Orloff were right. They were all adults. They should be able to get past the awkwardness of the moment without any lingering fallout contaminating their professional relationship. She'd worry about the fallout between her and her *fiancé* later.

Orloff stunned them both by shaking his head. "You are not engaged. Not any longer. Tonight, you marry."

Jared stiffened along with her.

Orloff nodded. "I have thought about this the whole way

home. If you are to stay with me, we must adjust your story.
As you both have already noticed, I have but one guest
room. I also have a maid. Though I cannot prove it, I have
long suspected the woman of spying on me for DeBruzkya.
I have toyed with the idea of firing her before now, but
lately—'' he used the velvet box to point to his battered,
but healing face ''—I have come to believe that might not
prove wise.''

A definite understatement.

But still, what did their marital status have to do with
some maid? Her confusion must have shown because Jared
nodded.

''You're hoping she informs DeBruzkya of your
guests.''

Orloff smiled grimly. ''Precisely. Should Herta do so,
the general may become curious. Unfortunately in this
country a wedding ring is one of the few protections a
woman has left.'' He captured her gaze. ''You would be
wise to submit to it.''

Alex searched the determination in his gaze. She had the
distinct feeling he was leaving something out.

Orloff severed his stare and returned his attention to
Jared. ''DeBruzkya and his men have been known to fre-
quent the hospital upon occasion. Despite my repeated as-
surances, I believe he fears I may abandon my countrymen
and cross our border to set up practice within one of the
refugee camps.''

''Why don't you?''

Like Orloff's earlier apology, Jared's question hung between the men. They stared at each other for a good ten
seconds. But while neither man moved nor spoke, she
swore they were communicating. How, she had no idea.

That was frustrating in and of itself. After all, she'd
gained a pretty good handle on man-speak over the past six
years. Evidently she'd missed something, because Orloff
finally nodded beneath that sharp amber stare.

The amber softened. ''What was her name?''

Orloff's answering smile was bittersweet. "Galena. We met in your country while we were attending Stanford. Despite the upheaval in my country, she came here to visit me. Galena was German-American, very bright and very beautiful. She was also very stubborn. She preferred to remain…independent."

"DeBruzkya."

Orloff sighed heavily, the light fading from his eyes as he nodded. "As I said, she was very bright. Galena was able to escape. Despite her injuries, as well as the misplaced shame and disorientation they caused, she managed to return to my home. But she hemorrhaged during the night. There was nothing I could do." His mouth opened again, but no sound came out. He finally closed it and settled on a terse shrug.

That shallow motion said it all.

The man turned, finally including Alex in his solemn stare. Tears burned at the corners of her eyes as he held up the scuffed, velvet box. She suspected the glitter in his own gaze was due to tears, too, as he studied the box. He finally broke his gaze and tossed the box to her. She caught it instinctively.

She opened the box slowly and gasped.

"They're beautiful!"

They truly were. Fashioned from white gold, the matching antique wedding rings were simple, yet elegant. A trio of slender vines had been intricately twisted and braided about each other until they formed a complete circle, stopping every few millimeters to sprout a tiny ruby. Though the gems weren't large or terribly expensive, they were bloodred and perfectly cut. The rings captured the faint light from the single bulb on the ceiling, refracting it until the rubies sparkled.

These rings were meant to be worn in love.

"I can't."

"You must. Please." He pushed forth another shrug. "Do not worry. Should you meet, DeBruzkya will not recognize the rings. If anything, the stones may draw his attention in the way you wish if, as you say, he is not done collecting gems. As I mentioned in my office, DeBruzkya is wont to wander our halls once a week at least, ostensibly to visit his wounded soldiers.'' His lips twisted bitterly. ''Though everyone knows his real intent is to comb firsthand for spies and assure himself of my staff's loyalty as well as my own. However, he has not been by in eight days. Hence, he should show soon. Perhaps tomorrow.''

When she didn't answer, he nodded toward the rings once more. ''Please. I would be honored if you wore them. To know that in some small way they had protected you.'' Orloff deliberately included Jared in his stiff nod before he turned to leave the room, gently closing the door behind him. Alex dropped her gaze to the rings as the latch clicked, nearly jumping out of her skin as Jared touched her arm. With his boots off, she hadn't even heard him move. She had to get her hands on that new hearing aid. Soon.

''Alex?'' The muffled name grated across her deaf ear.

She didn't dare shift position. The mood she was in, it wouldn't have been smooth. She kept her stare fused to the rings, instead, too tired and too raw to face his regret. She had enough regret of her own burning through her. Yes, Jared had finally been interested. But that didn't mean he'd forgotten about Janice. Making love to a woman and loving her were two different things. Even if he was free to care about her, how long would his interest have lasted? Given the fierce and very tactile way Jared made love, if they hadn't been interrupted, his hands would have run into reality and his desire would have done a complete and immediate about-face. Her stomach bottomed out at the thought.

She shifted her grip on the box, determined to close the lid on the temptation within. Even if she was willing to risk it in the cold light of reason, Jared would never agree to the pretense of marriage. ''It's a nice gesture, but I don't think we'll need it.''

To her surprise, his hand covered hers.

"We might. You might."

She jerked her chin up, stunned when he nodded.

He plucked the smaller of the two rings from the velvet bed and held it out. "At least see if it fits."

She studied the ring again. It did appear large enough. Scientifically, the rubies were fairly insignificant. Still, Orloff was right. From the robbery profile the first two ARIES agents had compiled, the gems weren't so small that they'd automatically escape DeBruzkya's voracious interest. The ring could be a plus.

She nodded, allowing Jared to take the box from her left hand and place the ring into the palm of her right. The ring slid up her third finger easily...until the band reached her knuckle. She tugged firmly.

Damn.

"What's wrong?"

She cursed the flush heating her cheeks. "It's stuck." So much for Galena matching her proportions.

"Let me—"

"That's okay." She jerked away from those dangerous hands. Hands that had been all over her on that bed. On her lips, on her breasts, in her hair. She tugged the ring again, this time adding a vicious twist. She nearly dislocated her knuckle, but the ring didn't budge. Desperate, she licked the fingertips of her right hand and used them to moisten the skin surrounding the ring before she gave it a third yank.

Nothing.

Jared tucked the jewelry box in the front pocket of his jeans and snagged her hand. She clamped down on the catch in her breath as he lifted her hand and slipped her ring finger into his mouth. Her gaze bumped into his and froze as his mouth slid over the ring, as his tongue slid around her.

Hot. Wet.

Just like that, they were back on that bed in her mind,

whirling toward the very edge of heaven on earth—together. She might not have been able to hear the catch in his own breath as he bit gently down behind the ring and slowly slid her damp, naked finger out of his mouth, but she damned sure felt it. She stood there, seared to the spot as he retrieved the velvet box and opened it. She watched him replace the first ring and retrieve the second. She was still seared into place, powerless to move as he slid the larger ring onto her finger.

It fit.

He fit.

After the passion they'd just shared—hell, after the day and the week they'd just shared—couldn't he see that?

Or was she the one who couldn't see clearly? The one who didn't want to. Was she half-blind, as well as deaf? He wasn't Don. Hadn't she watched Jared give his own blood to save a mangled child? A child who might still die by morning? Maybe he could handle the truth. If she gave him a chance. God knew she wanted to. She even knew where to start. She took a deep breath and voiced the one question she should have voiced three months before.

"Who's Janice?"

Chapter 8

His heart stopped.

For a split second, Jared was afraid—hell, he even hoped—he'd finally succumbed to the loss of blood. But when his heart restarted, when his lungs insisted on drawing the next blistering breath of air, when the deafening roar pounding through his head didn't cease, he knew he hadn't. He was still alive. And Alex was still standing six inches away from him, staring into his eyes, expecting an answer. An answer to the one question he'd have willingly shaved a year off his already numbered days *not* to answer. Not to her. Not after this past week.

Hell, not after this past day.

But if there was any hope left in his brain that he was still caught up in some Demerol-induced dream, that name on this woman's lips shattered it. This was no dream.

It was a nightmare.

Even as he replayed the conversation that had taken place in that guest room three months before, he knew Alex might not have heard everything, but she had heard enough.

Enough to form the wrong impression, that is. Judging by the pain in her eyes, Alex had clearly misinterpreted his relationship with Janice. Unfortunately she also clearly believed that because of that steamy necking session on the bed, she was entitled to an explanation. She was right.

He stared at the scarlet proof at the base of her neck, taunting him as it peeked out from beneath the collar of her sweater as she leaned down to snag his jeans from the floor. The last time he'd left a mark like that, he'd been a fifteen-year-old boy fumbling around on the porch with a girl.

For the third time in thirty minutes, he'd allowed Alex to gain the upper hand without even realizing it until it was too late. First the gate, then the syringe. And now, his pants. Though her fingers were carefully smoothing the wrinkles from his jeans, there was no doubt in his mind those fingers would dig in the moment he reached for his pants.

"Well? Are you going to answer me?"

He was tempted. Lord, was he tempted.

At least then one of them would be able to fight the smoldering desire that still threatened to consume him. Hatch was right about one thing. Alex was a damned good agent. Downright ingenious at times. Given the convoluted signals his brain, his mouth and his body had been sending all week, she'd go snooping. Frankly he was surprised she hadn't already. He wouldn't even have to tell her everything. All he had to do was give her enough rope to hang himself. By the time they completed their mission and she discovered how tightly the noose fit, he'd be back on that ranch. A world away from the one woman who'd actually made him pray for a miracle.

Unfortunately miracles didn't exist.

Reality did.

The inescapable reality of being teamed up with a partner—however intoxicating she might be—who still didn't even trust him enough to share her real name. The reality of having a boss who'd never before withheld vital information about a case, but now had. Then there was the harshest reality of all—knowing that he agreed with both of their decisions, however separately they'd been arrived at.

It didn't matter. The result was the same.

He didn't need any more classified information in his head than was absolutely necessary for him to complete this final mission. Because while he'd never spill a word of it willingly, eventually—as Janice had so succinctly put it—he'd no longer have the choice.

No, there was no way he could tell Alex the truth, not even to save his soul.

He forced himself to stare into her eyes. "I'm sorry, Alex. But this, us, it can't be. We can't be. It's not that I'm not interested." He ignored the fire searing up his own neck as he dragged his gaze to the scarlet brand on hers. "Hell, we both know by now I'm very interested. But I can't act on it. I won't. I shouldn't have even allowed tonight to happen—and before you ask, no, I don't want to talk about it. Please forgive me. I'm asking as a fellow agent and, I hope, as a friend. Accept my decision."

She didn't speak.

Nor could he find anything to add.

This time, the silence seemed to drag out forever.

He wasn't surprised. Nor was he surprised when she reached out to carefully settle his jeans into his hands. He wasn't even surprised when her fingers shook as she withdrew them and then turned to retrieve the expended Demerol syringe from the desk and carry it with her to the door. After all, his fingers were trembling, too. He wasn't even surprised when she opened the door and murmured something about stretching out on the couch, assuring him she'd wake long before the maid arrived. He wasn't even surprised when the door shut. But he was hurt.

So was she.

He reminded himself that it was for the best. For her, for him, for their mission. If Orloff was right, they'd be bumping into Bruno DeBruzkya soon. Perhaps even luring the man closer with that antique ring. If and when that happened, he'd need more than his wits about him. He'd need her complete trust. If Alex ever discovered who Janice was, she'd never be able to give it. If watching his mother fade away day by day while he was growing up had taught him anything at all, it was that.

He was right not to tell her.

Jared glanced at the fluid level in the second bag of packed red blood cells, willing them to drain more quickly though the thin loop of IV tubing and into his antecubital vein before he jerked his gaze back across the triage bay. He frowned as it settled on Alex. He'd spent half the night dreaming about his decision to withhold information from Alex, only to discover on waking that Alex was definitely holding out on him, as well. The first peg of proof had been her conspicuous absence this morning. Not only had Alex left for the hospital without bothering to nudge him, but according to the nurse who'd greeted him at six a.m., Alex had arrived at five, before even Orloff and half his staff had checked in.

At first he'd chalked up the abandonment to a desire to get away from the awkwardness that had been hanging between them since that session on the bed, maybe even a lingering desire to make sure he got enough rest. But then he'd reached the main triage bay and discovered that not only had Alex arrived before sunrise, so had the medical supplies she'd ordered less than twelve hours before.

FedEx did not deliver before the crack of dawn. Especially to a country that had been all but catapulted back into the Dark Ages.

And then there was the main packing slip for the mountain of supplies. He'd been inches from scanning the cover sheet when Alex had snatched up the manifest and shoved it into her pocket. Before he could blink, she'd grabbed four units of packed red blood cells—B negative—from the cold box that had arrived, as well, and immediately ordered him to pump the first two into himself, the others into the kid.

Yes, they needed them, but that didn't explain why she and Orloff had both downright demanded that he lie in this particular cot on the far side of the room, fifteen beds from the kid and twenty from that mesmerizing pile of overflowing boxes. Not when there was a vacant, albeit slightly stained, cot two feet from Alex and Orloff's overworked hands.

Almost everyone had been roped into service, racing against the early-morning clock to stow the sudden embarrassment of riches in the triage bay's cupboards and makeshift shelving before the armed receptionist and crowd-control stooges arrived to allow the line of patients inside the hospital's main doors.

Or worse, before DeBruzkya arrived.

Jared focused his attention on Alex as she and one of the nurses turned to shoulder matching stacks of blankets through the staff milling about. She and the nurse stopped to deposit a blanket at the foot of each cot, adding a potential, desperately needed layer to each existing threadbare sheet. Fortunately or unfortunately, he wasn't sure which, the nurse had inadvertently selected the opposite side of the bay, leaving Alex to service his.

Damned if his blood didn't begin to simmer as she gradually made her way to the foot of his cot.

What would she say?

What would he?

Roman had reintroduced them to his staff upon his arrival, blaming language differences as he shrugged off what he'd claimed was his mistake. Last night Orloff discovered that "Alice" and "Jeff" were in fact, married, not engaged. Due to the continuous stream of as yet unboxed supplies, not to mention Alex and Orloff's subsequent order that he receive his two units of packed red blood cells immediately, "Jeff" and "Alice" had not had a chance to speak to each other since.

Jared was beginning to suspect it was deliberate on her part.

She surprised him by briefly meeting his gaze as she reached the cot housing the soldier he and Orloff had operated on last night. Since the soldier was still unconscious and, unlike most patients, without a relative in attendance, she took the time to spread a blanket over a sheet that already needed changing. She dropped off thermal blankets at the base of three more cots before reaching the child who'd received two units of his blood. He'd long since rigged two more units from the supply Alex had somehow scrounged up. Jared stared at the thick swaths of gauze now covering the stumps where Mikhail's right leg and hand had been as Alex approached the grandmother, dozing lightly in the chair beside him. To his surprise, she tapped the woman's shoulder, leaning down and smiling gently as the woman woke.

He was even more surprised when Alex tucked her free hand beneath the hem of her sweater and pulled a tiny square of paper from the pocket of her jeans. He stiffened as she slipped the square of paper into the main fold of the blanket, murmuring something to the grandmother as she passed both blanket and paper to her. The woman nodded, then carefully tucked the latter beneath the collar of her rather drab, but generous dress into what he imagined was an equally generous bra.

There appeared to be no end to Alex Morrow and her secrets, did there?

He shifted his gaze as Alex turned, waiting until she'd reached the foot of his cot before he met it again.

"Morning."

Mindful of their audience, he managed to match his "wife's" tentative smile as she laid one of the two remaining blankets at his feet—until he spotted the mark he'd left at the base of her neck peeking out from beneath her collar. She followed his gaze as she rose, the sudden flush staining her cheeks now rivaling the scarlet evidence of their passion.

Of his passion.

He opened his mouth. To say what, he had no idea, but she turned before he could find his voice. She escaped him in favor of the slumbering patient in the final cot.

The woman's elderly husband rose from the wooden chair at the head of the makeshift hospital bed and met her at the foot. "I can get it." Speculation slipped into the rheumy blue of his eyes. The man smiled and reached out, patting her smooth hands with his gnarled ones, as he retrieved the thermal blanket. "Go ahead, assist your husband."

Jared couldn't help it, he grinned.

Not so much at her as at them.

Judging from the flush now bleeding from her face, Alex evidently had had no idea the man spoke English. A slow and somewhat stilted English, yes, but it was a heck of a lot better than his German—even hers. His smile faded as the man turned to spread the blanket over the sheet molded to his wife's emaciated legs before pulling the edge up to tuck it beneath her chin. The old man kissed her cheek gently and retrieved her liver-spotted hand once more as he reclaimed his chair.

Jared averted his eyes as the bitter irony of being chained to this particular cot beside this particular couple seared into him yet again. Unfortunately in avoiding his painful past, he'd run smack into his agonizing present. Into her. He clenched his jaw as Alex stared at the couple, clenching even harder as that soft gaze began to mist in earnest.

Christ, no. Don't let her cry.

Somehow he knew it would kill him more quickly than the pity.

He cleared his throat, breathing easier as she turned to him, despite the fact that she reached for the blanket.

"That's okay. I'm fine."

She shook her head, glancing at the old man's now drifting eyelids as she spread the silver fabric over Jared. He forced his lungs to draw another breath as she tucked the edges of the thermal blanket beneath his thighs. There was no doubt in his mind. Last night hadn't had a damned thing to do with the Demerol—or the exhaustion. Over one and one half units of packed red blood cells already inside him, and he was still suffering from dizziness around Alex. From the traitorous desire.

The collar of her dark blue sweater gaped as she leaned close to tuck the edges of the blanket about his waist. The scarlet mark taunted him from beneath. It looked angry, painful. He reached out without thinking, smoothing the tip of his finger over the stain.

"Does it hurt?"

He felt her breath catch beneath his finger. "No."

He traced his finger around the angry mark, over it. The flesh beneath was noticeably hotter than the surrounding ivory skin. Suddenly he wanted more than anything to cool the erotic brand his mouth had left, to erase it—and not yet.

He swallowed slowly, carefully. "I'm sorry."

She shrugged off his whispered apology. "I'm not."

Her pulse throbbed beneath his thumb as it slipped down to connect with the hollow at the base of her neck.

His pulse throbbed, too, along with something else. Just like that, the light-headedness returned.

Evidently the fresh blood he'd been pumping into his arm for the past thirty minutes had missed the "Welcome to My Body—Here's Where You Can Go and Where You Can't" anatomy lesson on the way in. Half of the lesson, anyway. His cache of new cells might be latching on to oxygen in his lungs with a vengeance, but they'd completely missed the turn that would take them due north, abandoning his brain altogether as the blood headed down en masse to pool low.

Very low.

He cleared his throat again and pulled his hand away.

The fog cleared as she straightened. Chained to the cot by the damned IV line and dangerous desire to keep her at his side, he snagged her wrist and glanced toward the center of the triage bay. "What was on the paper you gave the old woman?"

She stilled beneath his hand, but her pulse thundered.

He probed her gaze slowly, deliberately shifting his fingers, sliding them directly over the pulse point as he continued to stare, letting her know by his own steady gaze, as well as the gentle but firm pressure directly over her wrist, that he was gauging her every reaction, her every emotion. Her every word.

"Well?"

It was last night all over again and she knew it. Only now he held the gate, the syringe and his jeans.

"A phone number."

He pressed his fingertips ever-so-slightly deeper into her flesh. Into her pulse. "Whose?"

"Harold Blaine."

ARIES's own master of disguise. Their prosthetics expert. The man who'd crafted her face, her jaw, her chest.

"Are you sure that's wise?"

"Yes."

The fierce light in her eyes startled him, as well as that flash of intense, almost bottomless pain.

He loosened his grip without thinking.

Before he could stop her, she'd tugged her wrist from his hand and turned to flee. He tracked her with his gaze as she headed for the gradually dwindling mountain of supplies at the far end of the triage bay, assuring himself he was studying a fellow agent as she moved, attempting to ascertain whether or not she was lying or telling the truth. Whether or not she was using him for her own bizarre end. He was not lying here, chained to this damned cot, willing her to come back so that he could pull her close and soothe that inexplicable, but absolutely genuine pain from those green eyes.

By the time she returned to Orloff's side, she'd managed
to mask whatever it was that he'd seen. He was certain
when the man shifted his attention from the manifest in his
hands to her. She returned Orloff's smile easily.

Too easily.

She sure as hell had never smiled at him like that.

Dammit, he was not jealous. He was *not*.

He sighed heavily.

"Have no fear. He will not encroach."

Jared swung his gaze to the cot beside him, up to the
speculation swimming within those still sleepy and still
rheumy, but also very sharp, blue eyes. The old man nodded and patted his slumbering wife's hand, tucking it beneath the blanket once more before he turned to face Jared
full on.

Jared opted for obtuse. "Who?"

But those rheumy eyes saw right through him. The old
man smiled. "I think you know. You would be wise to
keep an eye on your wife, *Doktor*. You are both young,
prone to the doubts and insecurities that befall the young.
Trust me when I say there will be many men in the years
to come who will see the jewel you see in her. Though I
do not believe *Doktor* Orloff would try to woo her from
you, there are those who would. Worse, those who would
simply take."

Jewel?

No, it had to be a coincidence.

Still, two warnings in two days. From two different men.
Though motivated by two separately perceived reasons, it
was more than enough for him to take note.

While he doubted the latter half of this second warning
pertained to DeBruzkya and his men, he'd be a fool to rule
them out. Jared dropped his stare to the old man's wife, to
the thin strands of white that had been carefully combed
during the night. He knew full well by whom. He didn't
need to draw on his memory to know that the old woman
was beyond even the most basic of personal hygiene min-

istrations. Proof enough that, given the nature of his wife's dual illnesses, the old man had probably run into De-Bruzkya during the general's weekly visits more than he'd cared to.

Jared nodded slowly and formed his response even more quietly, in case any of the other patients surrounding them spoke English, as well as the old man did. "Are you referring to someone…high up?"

The speculation smoothed into respect.

Jared knew then his instincts were right about more than Alex. Despite the man's eighty-odd years, he suffered none of the symptoms of his wife's underlying illness. The man's brain was still as sharp as his tongue—in several languages. But was he brave enough to use it?

"DeBruzkya?"

To his surprise, the man didn't nod his snowy head, he shook it. "But you are…not far off."

"How far?"

To his irritation, the man shrugged and fell silent.

Now what? The old man knew something. Something big. But for some reason, he'd decided to clam up.

Guilt settled in as that gnarled hand slipped back to the cot, back beneath the blanket and threadbare sheet. Jared knew exactly why the man wouldn't finish. His wife was in this cot by the grace of DeBruzkya's thugs. They had let him in those double doors week after week, month after month. Given the woman's deteriorated mental state, they'd been letting him in for several years. He should know; he'd seen the old man corralling the woman in line for hours the morning before.

Were anyone but Orloff chief of staff, full-blown cancer or not, Jared sincerely doubted that a woman suffering from the latter stages of dementia would ever have been given a bed in Rajalla's remaining hospital. Not with all but one clinic gone, as well. Resigned, he met the man's rheumy gaze. "You're lucky to have such a capable neurosurgeon available."

Again, the man shrugged.

Jared knew the feeling.

But when that faded blue gaze connected with his again, they both searched, studied, recognized. This time, the old man sighed. "You must understand, I am careful not because I fear him for myself. I fear for others. Just know when you meet him that he will never understand what you did. He will only see what is before him. What cannot be fixed. This makes him more dangerous than you can ever know. Fear him."

What the devil was he talking about? *Who* was he talking about?

The boy? The transfusion?

Jared pushed his stare past the next four cots and shifted it to the opposite side of the triage bay to study the boy he'd hooked up to the second bag of packed red blood cells. The boy's grandmother was snoring lightly in the wooden chair beside the kid's cot. Other than the old woman, no one had been in to see the boy.

He turned back to the old man. Unfortunately he was done talking. At least for the time being. A vigilant night spent on death watch had finally done the old man in. Those rheumy eyes had drifted shut. A not-so-soft rhythmic snore escaped the man's lips as his chin dropped to his chest. Jared snapped out his free arm to steady the man as he swayed against the back of his chair.

Jared glanced at the unit of packed RBCs.

All but a few milliliters had been drained into his arm. He released the old man long enough to disconnect the IV line and tape a wad of cotton over the seeping puncture site on his forearm, rising easily for the first time in days as the fresh supply of red blood cells sucked up enough oxygen to feed his body, as well as his brain, succeeding in rejuvenating him where even a ten-hour stretch of sleep and rear end full of Demerol hadn't. He glanced at his watch: 0736.

Except for emergencies, the hospital doors wouldn't

open for another two and a half hours. Long enough for a nap—and time enough to cull a few answers on his own. Jared scooped the old man up and gently laid him on the canvas cot he'd just vacated, three feet from his snoring, seventy-something wife. Then Jared turned, his gaze automatically seeking out his own much younger "wife."

She wasn't there.

Jared spotted the back of Orloff's head as well as the fluttering tail of his lab coat as the man stepped out through double doors of the triage bay. Jared headed across the bay after him, drawing on every one of his new red blood cells, pushing them to the limit as he pushed his stride to catch up as quickly, yet inconspicuously as he could.

He left the triage bay and turned down the still-vacant, dimly lit main corridor, consciously working to keep the heels of his cowboy boots below a scuff as he rounded the turn at the end. He immediately whipped back around the corner as Orloff stopped at the base of the chipped granite stairs that led to the second floor—and his office.

Alex was with him.

He watched as Orloff retrieved a small brown box from the side pocket of his lab coat and tucked it neatly and discreetly into her waiting hands. Jared whipped his head back from the corner a split second before Alex's gaze swept the dank hallway.

What the hell was *that* about?

The exchange had happened so quickly, so smoothly, he'd almost missed it. But he'd definitely witnessed an exchange. That morning came slamming back. The doubts. He snatched another glimpse, confirming the worst. Something was going on, all right. He didn't care if every one of his marbles were cracked clean through, his instincts weren't. Nor were his eyes. The woman heading up those granite steps as Orloff headed down the far end of the corridor had an honest-to-God hidden agenda, an agenda he was not privy to.

But Orloff was.

God bless Harold Blaine.

Alex clutched the twine-knotted cardboard box in one hand, the key to Orloff's private office—more importantly, the man's very private mirror—in the other as she sent another round of praise heavenward. She didn't know how she'd find a way to thank Harold for responding to her SOS on such short notice, but she'd manage. Somehow. For now, she concentrated on watching her back as she reached the top of the granite staircase. A third and final glance over her shoulder assured that her nerves were simply working overtime. Jared was not following her.

She swung to the left, high-tailing it down the remainder of the darkened corridor—hoping to get into the office, get it done and get back downstairs to the main triage bay before anyone, especially Jared, realized she'd left. She reached the door to Orloff's locked office only to curse her slick fingers as she fumbled the key.

Relax!

Great. Bad enough that she'd had Jared's slight, but toe-curling Texas drawl in her good ear for days; now she had him in her head. She ordered the man out and her nerves back into line as she regained her grip on the key and made short work of the lock. Relief burned through her as she twisted the brass knob and pushed the door open. She stepped into the shadowy room and immediately pulled the door shut, relocking it firmly behind her before she dared to step far enough into the heavily paneled office to reach for the chain hanging from the pewter lamp on Orloff's desk.

She drew a deep breath and switched the lamp on. Light flooded the room, illuminating a scarred walnut desk, a pair of worn leather armchairs, as well as several rows of hap-hazard bookshelves, each filled to the brim. She skirted the desk quickly, setting the box in the middle of the leather blotter, then pulled the slim, center drawer of the desk open and retrieved a pair of scissors. She clipped the stiff twine tied around the length and width of the box, then moved

on to slit the label marked *"Doktor Orloff—Personliche!"*
and the strip of reinforced tape beneath. Her breath seared
out as she opened the box and stared at the priceless contents.

Priceless to her, anyway.

Her new hearing aid.

Hell, she was alone, behind a locked door. She could be
honest. The contents of this box might be priceless, but this
was far more than just her new hearing aid. It was her entire
right ear, right down the synthetic cartilage that made up
the outer auricle cup and the softer lobe beneath.

Her fingers shook as she reached inside the box to carefully slide the prosthetic ear from the familiar bed of
molded, cushioning foam. Harold had included the addi-
tional remote volume control she'd requested, too. Jared
wanted to know what else she'd done during those fifty-
eight minutes she and Orloff had spent inside this office?
Too damned bad. She didn't regret concealing this from
him for a second.

Okay, perhaps one. Maybe even two.

But that was before the man had coolly informed her that
while he was definitely interested in her, he'd never lower
himself to act on that interest. She retrieved the vial of
adhesive from the box as well and slapped it on the blotter
before sliding the upper right drawer of the desk open to
search for the mirror Orloff had promised would be waiting.
There it was, tucked beneath a yellowing prescription pad.

She was about to shift the pad when she recognized several of the words scrawled down it, as well as the penman-
ship. It was Jared's. "Quad infection. No Cipro; Reminyl."

His leg. The blood loss.

Dammit, she was not going to start feeling sorry for the
man, let alone feel something else. He was fantasy fodder,
nothing more. *Wrong.* He wasn't even that anymore. Not
after last night.

She shoved the allergy reminder aside and retrieved the
smudged mirror beneath. Using the empty box, she propped

the mirror up onto the blotter, staring at her reflection as she raised her right hand, staring at the illusion Harold and his genius had enabled her to maintain ever since Sam had contacted him on her behalf seventeen years earlier. She lowered her hand, this time staring into reality. A very cold, very lopsided reality.

One that did not include Jared. No matter how much she might want it to.

The Jared Sullivan in her dreams was just that. A dream. Like her ear, he was an illusion she'd held tight to so that she could pretend she had a normal life. So she could pretend she was a normal person. Well, she wasn't. She'd figured that out in grad school.

She'd suspected it throughout high school and college, but the prosthetic had enabled her to hide from the truth. Leave it to Don to drive the iron spike home. She still couldn't believe she'd loved him. But she had. So much so she'd decided to tell him the truth. To show him. Why not? Love could withstand anything, couldn't it?

It hadn't.

Oh, Don had tried. He'd managed to withhold his horror for a few days, anyway. Seven to be exact. It was then that she'd realized she'd left a sheaf of notes in his apartment. She'd shown up unexpectedly to retrieve them—and caught him in bed with another woman. A whole woman. To this day, Alex had no idea what she looked like. All she knew was that like Don, and unlike her, the woman had been absolutely, perfectly, balanced. Two legs, two arms, two breasts, two eyes. And, of course, two ears.

Alex drew a deep breath and retrieved the vial, twisting off the gold cap so she could apply Harold's magic adhesive to his even more magical creation, then she fitted the prosthetic into place with an ease honed through years of practice.

The illusion was complete.

Alex Morrow, the woman, was back.

It was a hell of a lot better than being Alexis Hatch

Warner. A hell of a lot safer, too. Personally, as well as professionally. Alex secreted the empty box, mirror and scissors in the bottom drawer of Orloff's desk and tucked the key to his office door, as well as the vial of adhesive, into the pocket of her jeans. The bulk of the evidence concealed, she snagged the remote control off the blotter and switched it on, deftly adjusting the volume.

Relief flooded her as recognizable sound slammed into her right eardrum for the first time in days.

Two and a half seconds later, she stiffened.

Footsteps.

No, *boot* steps.

On the other side of the door. The still-locked side of the door. Very soft, but definitely there. She held her breath as she waited. Sure enough, he tried the knob. Her nerves hadn't been working overtime. If anything, the damaged prosthetic had forced her unusually heightened hearing to work undertime. Jared had followed her—and now she was trapped.

How the devil was she going to get out of here?

Out of this?

The man was supposed to be her partner. How could she possibly explain her presence in Roman Orloff's locked office—without his knowledge? She ran through the possibilities, however remote, and latched on to the most believable one. She shoved the hearing aid remote deep into her brown leather bag and slung the bag over her shoulder as she stood.

Might as well get it over with. She rounded the desk in Orloff's office and twisted the doorknob before she lost her nerve, opening the door and plowing squarely into the chest she'd been sealed against on that bed in Orloff's house eleven hours before.

"Oh! Sorry," she said. "I didn't realize Orloff sent you."

"He didn't." He allowed her to insert six inches of desperately needed air between them, but retained the hold he'd acquired on her arms as the suspicion within those amber eyes deepened. "What are you doing up here?"

In the end, she blessed his proximity.

That piercing gaze.

The first succeeded in torching her neck with just the right amount of necessary heat, and the second prompted the perfect amount of evasion in her own gaze. "Um, it's that time of the month. Orloff gave me his key so I could use his private bathroom." She bit down on the satisfaction she felt. There wasn't a man alive who'd question that one.

Except him.

Those damned brooding brows lifted. "Really? Where did you get the tampon, honey? Or does Orloff keep a box of—"

He stiffened along with her.

Unfortunately she could tell he wasn't buying her sudden urgency any more than he'd bought her original story, as she grabbed at the sleeve of his sweater and attempted to haul the collection of muscles beneath, as well as the rest of his massive body, into the office. "Hurry! Someone's coming."

He vaulted into the room, dragging her with him as he closed the door behind them. "Are you sure? Your hearing's been off these past few days. Maybe you—"

"My hearing is just fine, thank you."

Though she hadn't yet had a chance to calibrate the new remote, she swore she'd heard voices at the base of those granite stairs. She ignored the suspicion still swirling in Jared's eyes as she pressed her index finger to her lips, straining to capture the sound waves beyond the thick slab of wood. Five seconds later she caught it again.

Them.

Orloff had reached the top of those steps. Though he was the only one speaking, judging from the number of footfalls that accompanied his, Orloff had several other men in tow. At least one of them was someone she and Agent Sullivan had come a long way to meet. Five more seconds passed before she was certain Jared had caught Orloff's voice, too. The subtle warning in the doctor's carefully phrased, almost painfully slow Rebelian words. They no longer needed to worry whether or not General Bruno DeBruzkya would show up at the hospital.

He just had.

Chapter 9

They had to get out of here.

Now.

Jared grabbed Alex's arm with his right hand and latched on to the knob of the doorknob with his left. Having never seen the woman in action, he had no idea how she preferred to arrange her confrontations, but his preferences did not include closed-in spaces with barely enough room to maneuver. Especially not when he was outnumbered by at least three to one. He wasted precious seconds as he strained to double check that herd of footfalls. He twisted the knob, putting his lips to her ear as she balked.

"Trust me."

He opened the door to the office and tugged her out into the corridor before she could argue.

"Ah, there you are!"

Jared loosened his grip, using Alex's elbow to spin her around with him as he turned toward Orloff's voice. His footfall estimation had been off. The squat Rebelian dictator had five armed camouflaged thugs in tow, not three, and unlike the prepubescent packs that roved the streets of Rajalla, these men had been shaving for ten years at least. DeBruzkya barked a series of orders, causing the squad to break off and fall into line at attention halfway down the corridor.

Orloff and the general continued on. The hallway was too dim for him to make out even Orloff's familiar features just yet. From the tension radiating off Alex, he suspected she couldn't make them out, either. He brushed his lips over the short curls at her ear, disguising the motion as a brief but loving kiss as he murmured, "Relax."

"Easy for you to say. He didn't have *your* head bashed in."

True. But there was no time for even a whispered come-back, much less outright reassurance, as Orloff and Bruno DeBruzkya closed the remaining distance. Jared settled for sliding his arm about Alex's waist and risked a quick squeeze as the men came into view. It worked. She relaxed.

Visibly, anyway.

He could still feel the tension radiating from her back into the muscles of his arm. He left his arm about her waist as long as he could, withdrawing it only when Orloff stretched out his right hand and clapped it into his as if they were old friends. The gleam in those dark eyes confirmed that was indeed the game.

Orloff's grin widened. "I see you've located your lovely wife. Good. General, may I present Dr. Jeff Coleman and his wife, Alice." The physician deferred briefly to the balding general, allowing Jared and Alex the opportunity to study the notorious Bruno DeBruzkya up close for the first time. The assessment Jared had formed while reading the man's dossier on the transatlantic flight was dead on.

General or not, DeBruzkya hadn't seen a gym in years. At five-nine, the man was nearly as round as he was tall. Definitely more brute pudge than brawn. And definitely interested in Alex.

Salivating.

Even as Jared looped his arm back about her waist, he told himself he was doing it to protect their cover. That was all. This woman—his *partner*—could handle herself. So why had his arm tightened instinctively as the man drooled on her boots?

Unfortunately DeBruzkya wasn't stupid. He picked up on the subtle motion and grinned. The man's fleshy lips parted a moment later, but Orloff beat him to sound.

"Feeling better, Alice?" He turned to DeBruzkya before she could answer. "Jeff and I met while attending university in the United States. Alice, however, is new to their marriage, as well as hospital work. She became queasy." His conspiratorial smile spread. "I believe she may be presenting a special gift to my friend this Christmas." He capped the grin with a sigh. "But so far, she has refused to allow either of us to run the necessary tests."

Jared had to give Orloff credit. Whatever Orloff and Alex were hiding, the doctor was doing his best to look out for her. Unfortunately the fact that DeBruzkya had been willing to use Lily Scott's own son against her weeks earlier to coerce her into submitting to the general's perverse will suggested the man wouldn't give a damn about a hypothetical pregnancy.

The moment that dank-brown gaze slid down Alex's curves, Jared knew he was right. Barely suppressed fury crawled through his gut and straight up into his heart as the general's gaze finally rose. It intensified as DeBruzkya's gaze stopped to study a particular set of curves he had no right studying.

So much for DeBruzkya's undying devotion to Lily.

The general finally managed to drag his gaze above her neck. A smarmy smile followed. "Congratulations, Alice. My sister is pregnant, too. Though she is—" His gaze slid low once again. "Much further along. In fact, that is why I stopped by this morning. To arrange for a specialist to come to my home to examine her. I'm afraid her usual *doktor* recently met with a most unfortunate…accident— much like my son.''

Alex blinked. "You have a son?"

DeBruzkya nodded. "A recent acquisition. From what Dr. Orloff tells me, I believe you have met.'' The general finally included Jared in his gaze. "As have you, Dr. Coleman. In fact, Orloff tells me your blood flows through the boy.''

This time, Alex stiffened. "Mikhail is your son?"
Orloff stepped forward, covering for them before Jared could. "Yes. Our benevolent general has just been to visit the patients in our main hospital bay. He was so taken by the child's plight, he has decided to adopt the boy. There will be press conference this afternoon to announce the wonderful news.'' By the time Orloff finished speaking, Alex had recovered.

Her smile even looked sincere. "Congratulations, General. And I'm sure your sister will be thrilled to discover a readymade cousin for her own child—especially if she has a son. Mikhail is such a brave boy. He'll be a great role model.''

DeBruzkya frowned. "My sister carries a girl.'' He shrugged. "No matter, I will still have my heir.''

Christ. Nothing like a little perspective on life. Then again, Jared knew firsthand there were men who managed to treasure one child, while finding another eminently dismissible. However, he could still feel this particular child's mangled flesh in his hands as he'd worked to staunch that unending flow of blood. And to know this bastard was indirectly responsible? Despite the bile scalding up his throat, Jared managed to join Alex and Orloff in a passingly polite nod.

DeBruzkya's smile returned. The revolting gleam came with it. "So…you must join me in a celebration.''

A party? Now?

Their collective shock must have shown.

The man appeared impervious as he nodded. "Of course.

We must toast the foreigner who came to the aid of my son.'' If the man had been looking at the foreigner who'd provided the blood, Jared might have bought the sentiment. As it was, DeBruzkya was still focused on Alex. He finally turned to include Jared and Orloff in his gaze. ''You must all come to dinner. Two nights hence. We shall dine at nine o'clock. My aides have arranged a small celebration at my private compound for my most trusted supporters to observe the anniversary of my reign. The fete shall now be twofold. Tell me you can attend.''

It was not a request.

Jared almost laughed at the irony of it.

Just like that he and Alex had managed to finagle their way back into that castle, back to that cache of gems—with Orloff in tow, no less. Jared studied DeBruzkya as the man openly studied Alex. They had an invitation, all right. A gilded one. But at what cost?

Orloff nodded first. ''I would be honored.''

Jared forced himself to add his own brief, stiff nod. ''As would I…and my wife.''

DeBruzkya ignored the subtle stress he'd placed on the word *wife* as he hooked his meaty fingers into Alex's slender ones. The dim light flickering throughout the corridor glinted off the general's naked scalp as he lowered his mouth, intent on pressing his fleshy lips to the back of her hand. The man spotted the ring and paused. ''Beautiful.''

''Thank you.''

His head rose a fraction of an inch. His gaze shifted to Jared's, his interest locked in.

''An antique?''

Much as he was suddenly loath to fan this man's interest regarding anything even remotely connected to Alex, Jared nodded. ''I purchased it in Bosnia.''

''Really?''

Yup, interest had definitely been fanned.

''When was that?''

''Couple of years ago, during the war. I bought it off an

impoverished officer's wife.'' He gave a light, easy shrug. "She needed the money. I figured I'd eventually need a wife.'' Relief seared into him as the general finally released Alex's hand and stepped away.

"It's set, then. Dinner at nine. You will meet my pilot at the helicopter pad on the roof here at the hospital at eight.''

"We'll be there.''

"Excellent. I'll let you get back to your duties. I understand the doors open soon.'' DeBruzkya turned, then stopped as if he'd suddenly remembered something. From the speculation gleaming in his eyes as he turned back, he had. "You attended Stanford University with Dr. Orloff?''

Jared bit down on his curse.

Orloff had improvised without warning him. While it wasn't impossible, it would take the information techs at ARIES an hour or two to insert the evidence to support the change. But if DeBruzkya's thugs got on the horn quickly enough…

He nodded, anyway. "I did. I was premed at the time. Roman was already in his specialty.''

DeBruzkya nodded. "I don't suppose either of you met a man by the name of Krazner? Doctor Gregory Krazner?''

Jared waited until Orloff shook his head, before adding a quick shake of his own. "Not that I recall.''

DeBruzkya stared at Jared for a moment, then shrugged. The speculation gone from his eyes, he turned and headed down the corridor. Back to his squad of idle thugs. Jared waited until the general and his goons and reached the granite stairs and stepped down onto them before he turned to follow Alex and Orloff into the doctor's office. He closed the door behind himself.

"Do you know a Krazner?''

Again, Orloff shook his head.

"I do.''

They spun together to face Alex.

She nodded. "Unless DeBruzkya was referring to someone else, Greg Krazner is a colleague of mine. A geologist. Greg did his graduate work at the Colorado School of Mines, but he could have completed his undergrad stint at Stanford. I'll check. Also, unless I'm mistaken, Greg has a more than a passing interest in—''

All three froze as a frantic knock reverberated through the tiny room. Since it was his office, Orloff stepped to the door and opened it. His nurse stood on the other side, her apron already stained with the first blood of the day. So were the sleeves covering her frantically waving arms.

''Doktor Orloff, Doktor Coleman. Come, come!''

Orloff tore out of the office before the woman could finish. Alex shoved him out after them. ''Go. I'll make the call. Find out if they're one and the same. If so, I'll have them create an emergency that'll get Greg out of harm's way until we can figure if he's my replacement—and why.''

''…man.''

Alex paused in the middle of shaking out the thermal blanket and glanced down at the man sitting beside his slumbering wife. The same man Jared had been lying beside earlier this morning as he'd pumped two units of packed red blood cells into his arm. Abel Braun and his devoted wife, Elsa. She knew because she'd stopped to chat with him earlier this afternoon after she'd caught him staring at her. The old man was on a deathwatch and desperate for distraction.

She offered it once again, along with another smile.

''I'm sorry. I'm afraid I wasn't paying attention.''

The old man's eyes twinkled, clearing the rheumy blue for a moment. ''I said your husband is a good man. But I think you know this, since you have been thinking of him all day.''

She flushed.

Damned if Abel Braun wasn't right. She had been standing here daydreaming about Jared, trying to figure out what the heck was going on with him. Because after that conversation or, rather, lack of conversation she'd had with her uncle regarding Jared earlier this morning, she was convinced something was wrong. Alex finished shaking out the thermal blanket and settled it over Abel's wife, leaving the old man to tuck it in around her as she headed across the triage bay for the tiny cup of pills Orloff's assistant had prescribed.

She could still hear the shock in her uncle's voice as she finished her business query regarding Greg Krazner, then launched one last rushed question before she lost her nerve. She couldn't believe she'd done it. She'd actually grilled Sam about an ARIES agent's personal life. About her partner's personal life.

She'd asked about Janice.

While she'd been tempted to abuse her relationship with Sam once or twice through the years, she'd never actually done it. Until today. But that wasn't the worst of it. The worst part was Sam had refused to answer. Why? It wasn't as if her uncle hadn't let a personal comment or two slip over the years. He had. She'd just made a point to let them go. She'd certainly never, ever picked up on one and used it to probe further. She hadn't had to probe this time, either. Sam's terse silence had said it all.

Janice must have worked for ARIES. Maybe still did.

Alex reached the nurses' desk at the far end of the overburdened triage bay and requested the medicine cup for bed 20A. She thanked the nurse for the two pills and water in German and headed back down the center aisle. Ironically it was DeBruzkya who'd initially planted the idea. If Greg Krazner could have bumped into Orloff at Stanford, why couldn't Jared have met Janice through ARIES?

So she'd run her check on Greg *and* Janice.

Both names had popped. Greg had gone to Stanford and he was a geologist. Unfortunately there were two Janices.

Since Janice Errington was a scientist in her late fifties, as well as a recent transfer from another agency, she'd placed her money on Janice Angeline Grey. Janice Angeline was a twenty-eight-year-old, petite, blond-haired, blue-eyed, very curvaceous translator who specialized in Eastern European languages. Alex knew, because she'd viewed the woman's electronic photograph. Alex frowned as she reached the end of the triage bay. No wonder the man's accent stunk.

He'd been too busy honing his other skills.

"Danke."

She flushed as she spilled a third of the water over Abel's hand in her distraction. "I'm sorry. Please, let me—"

The old man tsked. But his eyes twinkled once again as he wiped his gnarled fingers on the edge of his wife's thermal blanket. "Still thinking of your husband, eh?" She couldn't help but respond to that weary, whiskered grin.

"How did you guess?"

He returned her genuine smile and patted the empty wooden chair beside his. "Because I think of my wife often, too."

Alex passed the plastic cup of pills to the old man, sighing as she slipped into the vacant chair. She could use the break. It was late, almost 9:00 p.m., and she was exhausted. Abel glanced at the antique ring Orloff had lent her.

"The rubies are small, but beautiful."

"You know gems?"

He shrugged. "It was a hobby of mine. I taught science and math here in Rajalla years ago." Though he lowered his voice to a near whisper, her new hearing aid had no trouble picking it up. "Before DeBruzkya's time."

Intrigued, she slipped the ring from her finger and passed it over, accepting the small cup of pills so that the old man could concentrate on angling the ring against the light shining from the line of flickering fluorescent bulbs running the length of the ceiling.

He smiled as he glanced back. "Small, yes. But as I said, very beautiful. Very dark. I have seen only one stone darker. But that one was as large as these are small."

"It must have been expensive, too."

He surprised her by shaking his head. "Free." He chuckled at her disbelief, clapping his hand and the ring against this chest as his laugh mutated into a hacking cough. She passed the cup of water back, waiting as he drained it. *"Danke."*

"You're welcome. Even if you are pulling my leg."

He swung his gaze, rheumy once again, to her work boots. "Pulling your—ah, a joke. But I am not teasing. It was enormous. Eighty-five and one-half carats." Abel paused his whispered confession long enough to wave her closer, waiting as she scooted her chair flush with his. His voice was beneath a whisper as he continued, "I found it in the Hartz forest two months ago, amid the rocks beside the river."

She couldn't help it, she smiled.

Either the man really was pulling her leg or one of the more debilitating effects of old age had unfortunately already set in. Rubies, as gorgeous as they were, were simply crystals formed from the mineral aluminum oxide. They owed their color to the presence of chromium. The more chromium in the aluminum oxide, the darker the red and, of course, the more precious the gem. If he'd taught science here in Rajalla, he would know that. He would also know that rubies had never been found in Rebelia. A ruby as blood-red as the one he'd described would have come from the metamorphosed limestones in Myanmar or the placer deposits in Sri Lanka. And none of those finds had ever produced quality crystals in excess of eighty carats.

"You don't believe me."

"It's not that I don't—"

"It was already cut."

She blinked. "Really."

That did change things. Perhaps. *If* he was telling the truth. "Someone misplaced a piece of jewelry that large?"

"A brooch. Antique. The ruby was oval and set in white gold, much like your wedding ring." He shrugged. "I was attempting to fish in the river, but my line landed on the opposite shore, catching a rock, instead. I waded across." He flashed his yellowing teeth. "It was my last hook."

It was a wonderful story. But it was still a whopper. "I'll bet you can afford as many hooks as you like now." She couldn't help but stare at the old man's meticulously darned sweater, the painfully thin shoulders beneath. He sure as heck couldn't afford adequate food or new clothing. For himself or his wife.

"It was stolen."

Alex froze as her stomach bottomed out. She forced herself to count to ten. Then slowly, carefully, she swept her gaze around the triage bay. Jared and Roman Orloff had returned from surgery and were now examining a patient at the far end of the room. She didn't dare alert them. She didn't dare breathe. All she could do was whisper one word. One name.

"DeBruzkya?"

"One of his men."

Sweet Mother in Heaven.

The dizziness from days past slammed back into her, but it had nothing to do with her coma or the whack she'd taken to her skull. It had to do with one-hundred-percent blinding excitement. The blistering rush of pure adrenaline flooding every square inch of her body. The thunder of blood pounding through her heart, hammering through her head, coursing through every blessed one of her veins. She sucked in her breath and forced out the next whisper, the next prayer.

"Does this stone have…a name?"

He shifted his gaze across the bay. By the time he pulled it back, the rheumy blue was careful, wary. "Why would it?"

He hadn't said no. Hadn't denied it. If anything, he appeared to be waiting to see if *she* knew. She sucked in the next breath and pushed out the next plea. "Tell me what happened. Everything that happened."

He might be an old man marking the increasingly labored breathing of his dying wife, but he was a scientist. She didn't doubt that anymore. Not given the light now shining within those faded eyes. The blue seemed to deepen, darken before her very gaze as his shoulders straightened. His spine locked.

"I lied. The stone was not stolen from me. But it would have been. So I traded it." He glanced about the triage bay. His voice was still soft, but proud. Defiant. "By then, I knew what it was. Still, I traded it. I willingly exchanged it for this room and for this cot. For that cup of pills you hold in your hand. For the clean water I drank. For the right to replace that water so I can give it to my wife to aid those pills in their journey down her throat. In their journey to free her from the pain. It was the stone or her. I chose her."

She already knew the answers to her next questions. She asked, anyway. "Why are you telling me? Why now?"

"Because she is dying. My Elsa will last another day. Perhaps two. If I am very lucky, three. That is all. And then I will no longer care. Someone must know. I bequeath the knowledge to you and your husband."

"Why?"

Abel Braun glanced across the room, to the tiny cot that a woefully stitched-together Mikhail had already been transferred out of this afternoon. "Because you care."

"Dr. Orloff cares."

"He does. But he also has too many others to worry about. The knowledge must leave this place. He will not. The stone must be located and destroyed." He knitted the gnarled fingers of his right hand into those of her left and clamped down as he nodded. "It killed my wife. Yes, she would have died, anyway. But not so soon. Not so very painfully. And even though she was becoming little more than the shell of the woman I married, she was still my wife. I pinned the brooch to her sweater myself and within days she was ill, then dying. She wore it only *once*."

Alex gasped.

He squeezed harder. "Yes, I am dying, too. Do not concern yourself with me. I have nothing left. Instead, you must find the man who took it before he learns how to use it. I met him only twice. He accompanied DeBruzkya on one of his hospital tours. I knew he could help me help her. God forgive me, I offered it to him. Find the man, and then you find the stone."

She couldn't move. Hell, she couldn't think.

But she had to. Jared had finished with his post-op patients. A glance at her watch told her it was nearing 10 p.m. Well past time for them to head back to Orloff's for the night. There, she could safely fill Jared in on what she'd just learned. She should go, grab his attention. But she was also loath to leave Abel Braun beside his wife with nothing to do but time his heartbeats against her increasingly labored breaths.

The old man reached out and patted her hand. "Go. I shall be fine."

She nodded and traded the pill cup, now crushed, for the antique wedding band. "I'm so sorry."

Abel offered up another of those resigned shrugs, retrieving one of the pills from the squashed cup as she stood. "It does not matter. I will keep the morphine, but Elsa is past any assistance the Reminyl could have given. Please return the tablet to the desk and inform the nurse. Someone else may need it." He pushed the cup, the second pill still inside, into her hand before she could turn.

Reminyl?

She couldn't help it, she stepped back.

She shouldn't ask, dammit. She'd already asked too much of this man. Fate had already asked. Stolen. But when she sought out Jared's broad shoulders as she had so many times during the morning, afternoon and evening, and saw the utter weariness in them—the sobering futility in his eyes as he scanned cot upon cot filled with their fresh crop of mangled bodies and the constant, quietly weeping resignation beside them—when he finally met her gaze and struggled so hard to produce a simple smile, she knew she had to ask. She had to know.

"Abel, may I ask what was wrong with your wife? Before you gave her the stone? Why did she take the Reminyl?" She waited as the old man pulled his lingering gaze from his wife's slumbering face to smile sadly into hers. Prayed.

"The Reminyl was for her Alzheimer's."

Chapter 10

She knew. Jared swallowed the acid that had been slowly but surely eating away at the lining of his stomach and his throat for the past thirty minutes. Ever since the moment he'd glanced across that triage bay, desperately needing the solace those soft, green, eyes could provide, only to discover that blinding horror and gut-wrenching pity, had finally replaced it.

Alex *knew.*

Naturally he hadn't confronted her while they were in the triage bay. Nor did he when they reached the main doors of the hospital, as he settled her jacket on her shoulders and pulled her close—for their armed audience, of course—while they waited for their cab. Nor did he dare to broach the subject while in the rear of that cab, just stared straight ahead into the dark. Hell, he didn't even pause in front of Orloff's house, lock his hand to the top of that rusted, wrought-iron gate and demand she come clean. No, he waited until they opened the door, shut it firmly and carefully picked their way up those polished wooden steps to reach the cloying privacy of the cramped guest room at the end of the hall. The moment she closed the door behind her, he spoke.

"He told you."

She didn't deny it. He hadn't expected her to. But neither did she have the decency to face him. She stood at the door with her back to him, instead, dragging that gray jacket down her arms. She went on to waste another fifteen agonizing seconds as she zipped up the jacket and shook out the sleeves before folding one over the other. Only then did she pull herself up to her full height and turn.

"Of course he told me. Why shouldn't he? I asked."

Maybe it was the lingering horror, the pity. The complete calm. The quiet determination in her face. He didn't know. All he knew was that he just snapped.

"Why shouldn't he? Because I asked him not to tell anyone, that's why! Christ, I damned near begged. I still can't believe I trusted him—again—but that's my problem, not yours. I just want to know one thing. How the hell did you get it out of him when he swore on his wife's grave he'd never tell? Hell, maybe you are screwing the man. Maybe you just decided it was prudent to lie about it. God knows you're lying about everything else."

When she didn't answer, when she just stood there, as if rocked to her core with that damned phony innocence locking in to every single bloodless inch of her face, he threw up his hands and stalked across the room, stopping when he reached the narrow, shuttered window between the nightstand and the bed. He spun around in time to catch the silent working of her throat. He watched, still seething, as those full lips parted, quivered, then pressed back together.

Several moments passed before they parted again. A shallow breath bled out. *"Sam knows?"*

Oh, she was good. Better than good.

He tore the zipper to his jacket open and yanked the sleeves down his arms. Unlike her, he balled up the coat and flung it at the foot of the bed. "Give it up, lady. Why else does the man have you skulking around behind my back?"

Her throat worked again, this time not quite silently. "Wh-what are you talking about?"

"This morning? The mysterious package handoff? Orloff's office? The locked door?" He shoved his hands beneath his bloodstained sweater as he stalked across the room to her. When she held her ground, he hauled the crumpled sheet of paper from the pocket of his jeans and slammed it up against the wall, six inches from the deceptively soft curls at her right ear. Satisfaction seared through him as she flinched.

But a moment later she was back to cool. Composed.

"What's that?"

"Take a look."

She refused to release his gaze long enough to glance at anything. The mood he was in, he didn't blame her.

"It's the goddamn manifest."

Another swallow. Again, not quite silent. She followed it with another quick working of that slender throat. "How…how did you get that?"

"How else, *Agent* Morrow? I lifted it. From your bag."

"It's not what you think."

The hell it wasn't. He flattened the sheet against the wall and jerked his chin toward the top. "Take a good look at the header block, honey. You told me you got that blood and those supplies from a friend. I sensed then you were lying. But stupid, doubting me, I chalked up the instinct to the Alzheimer's. Figured maybe I needed to up the Reminyl level in my blood so it could rack my neuroconnections in tighter and stop up the slowly leaking sieve I've got for a brain. But you didn't get that blood from a friend, or the supplies. This manifest proves it. Want to know why?"

Nothing. Not even the quiet working of her throat. Just that damned deceptive mist in her eyes.

Determined to ignore it, he flicked his gaze to the manifest. To the string of words that'd been branded into his memory from the moment he spotted them. "It says here the supplies were donated by Endlich Medical, Inc. Perhaps you'd care to tell me how you're friends with a company that doesn't even exist—except on paper? Endlich Medical is a goddamned phony shell, Dr. Morrow. Much like that rubber chest I cracked open out in the middle of the Hartz forest. A *dummy* corporation. Or am I the dummy? Am I just having another charming *senior moment* courtesy of my blisteringly premature case of early-onset Alzheimer's?"

She finally opened her mouth.

He heard the air pull down into her lungs, felt her soft, shallow exhale. Smelled the tantalizingly sweet scent of her warm breath as it swirled up between them. He promptly purged each and every one of the unwelcome memories from his brain.

"The man who set Endlich Medical up is—"

"ARIES director Samuel Hatch. You know, our boss? That guy you're not sleeping with? The same guy who didn't tell you about the Alzheimer's. The guy who doesn't have you slinking around behind my back, making sure the marbles in my head don't drop out one by one and roll into the gutter before I can stoop over and scoop them up, much less finish my final mission. The same guy who's—"

"My uncle."

He tore his gaze from the crumpled manifest and plunged it straight into her tortured stare. She was telling the truth. He didn't need another four milligrams of Reminyl to prop up his gradually disintegrating brain. He didn't need forty. He could see it in her eyes.

Just like that his fury evaporated. He searched for it vainly, desperate to grab on to so much as a trailing wisp. To have something to hold on to as he tried to acclimate himself to this sudden spinning sensation in his head. To the absolutely incredible knowledge. Samuel Hatch was her uncle?

She nodded slowly. "Yes, he's my uncle. And he never told me about you, I swear. I did call him today. To fill him in on the information I'd unearthed about Greg Krazner. I was lying to myself. I really called to ask about another name I ran a check on. A woman by the name of Janice. Sam didn't say a word. Hell, he practically hung up on me for the first time in my life. I'm guessing now that you were never involved with a twenty-eight-year-old, curvaceous translator who specializes in Russian."

He blinked.

She shrugged. "Thought not. Then I'm also guessing that the woman I overheard you speaking to three months ago is a fifty-six-year-old scientist by the name of Janice Errington. And I'm betting Janice is a bit more than your run-of-the-mill scientist, too. Maybe even a doctor?"

"Geneticist."

She nodded. "Makes sense. Now. So does that phone call I overheard in my uncle's guest room. While we're on the subject, let me make it clear one more time. Sam told me *nothing*. I ran across a note in Orloff's office listing your infection, Cipro, and another drug called Reminyl. I'm guessing now that Orloff was checking drug interactions for you. I may never have connected the Reminyl if it hadn't been for Abel."

She seemed to think he knew what she was referring to. Christ. Had he forgotten something critical already? Maybe he did need to increase his dosage, because he had no idea.

"Abel Braun? Elsa?"

He shook his head. Her stomach roiled.

"The couple you lay next to for over an hour in that cot this morning while red blood cells drained into your arm?"

Relief flooded him. He flushed. "I didn't catch their names."

He hadn't even asked. The social lapse had been deliberate, too. Why ask for someone's name when you were just going to end up forgetting it? Forgetting them. Only, once the old man had dropped his cryptic warning, he'd realized he was going to have to let the guy in. At least far enough to get the rest of the story out. But the old man had nodded off before he could ask. And then he'd spotted Orloff leaving. With that package.

"What was in the box?"

The second her throat began to work, however subtly, silently, he knew it was coming.

The lie.

"Jared, that box was private. Personal."

Yeah, that's what he'd thought. He pushed off the wall and stepped back. Away from her. The contents of that box were personal, all right. He didn't doubt her for a second. Sam had probably mailed her a personal bar of soap so she could have it on hand in case she needed to clean up after his very private, very dirty laundry.

She grabbed his arm. "Wait—"

He held up his hands. "It's okay. You keep your secrets. It's a good move. A smart one, too. It's not like I wouldn't have a fifty-fifty shot at blabbing your business all over the world before I forgot it, anyway, whether I meant to or not."

He never should have said it. Much less let her know he felt it. Because here came the pity.

Jesus, Mary and Joseph.

He'd pulled some pretty ballsy stunts in his career. Pulled off some damned daring missions. Gone in to rescue folks his buddies had told him could never be rescued— and brought them out alive. He'd stared death itself in the eye more times than he cared to remember and had always come out the winner. But right now he knew that deep down, he was nothing more than a goddam, sniveling coward.

He proved it to the both of them as he turned away, slinking across that all-too-tiny room. He didn't stop until he was staring directly into a set of wooden slats, trapped on the wrong side of that suffocatingly narrow window.

He heard her cross the room, as well, felt her stop behind

him. He knew exactly what she wanted. More. She'd begged him to open up in that cabin. Well, he just had. He'd said more in the past five minutes than he'd said in days, than he'd said in years, and they both knew it. He also knew he had nothing left to give. Not to her. He couldn't risk it.

"Jared?"

He flinched. A moment later he was forced to close his eyes as those strong, capable hands reached out and tentatively cupped his taut shoulders. The same hands that had spread blankets, distributed pills, changed bedpans, mopped puddles of blood and far, far worse from the floor today. Hands that'd worked beside him and then with him to keep the life from seeping out of yet another child and then been willing to learn how to stitch the gaping wound left behind because there were no more pairs of hands left around to help.

Those same hands threaded into his hair, smoothed it, their subtle caress causing his breath to hitch somewhere in the middle of his throat, then stop up his lungs altogether. He cursed his decision to pull the ponytail out in the cab. Aching scalp be damned. Anything would have been preferable to the heightened sensation the loose hairs were picking up on and then magnifying before shooting down into his groin.

Lord, was he a bastard of the first degree. That he could even think about sex right now.

But the truth of it was, he'd thought about it a lot lately. Mostly about how much he missed it. About how much he wanted to have it…with her. Hell, he wasn't kidding anyone. He didn't want to have sex with the woman standing six inches behind him. He wanted to make love to her.

All night long. Over and over again.

He wanted to memorize every inch of that long, lean body. Every dip, every curve. He wanted to memorize her scent and her taste. The sensation of those agile fingers as they slid over him. He wanted to soak up the sounds she uttered as he kissed her. Every moan, every gasp, every sigh. He wanted to stare into those soft green eyes and watch as the passion slowly clouded into the mist. And then he wanted to watch her as she came apart in his arms.

He'd give anything to remember it. To remember her.

Hell, he still wasn't even sure how it had happened, much less why. He just knew it had. He knew in his heart and in his soul that he'd sacrifice every word he'd ever read, every memory he'd ever formed, if he could just guarantee that he'd remember the woman standing quietly behind him now. But he couldn't.

And eventually he wouldn't.

Alex stared at the man's back as the last of the fantasy came crashing down around her. Jared Sullivan was dying all right, but it wasn't from Alzheimer's. At least, not just yet. Right now he was dying from the most insidious disease of all. Loneliness. She should know. She recognized the symptoms all too well. Even as she waited for him to turn, she knew he'd never do it on his own. She'd have to force him. Maybe even beg. She didn't care. All she cared about was figuring out a way to staunch his pain. She sucked up her pride and did it.

"Please."

To her surprise, he actually turned.

She almost wished he hadn't. The anger and accusations had been bad enough, but she'd understood them. She also refused to let them get to her, to let him get to her. But how could she ignore the agony? The absolute devastation?

His eyes.

They were dark, almost black with pain and self-doubt and, yes, even fear. To see that in this man, knowing what he'd done in his life, knowing what he'd done for *her*—

Oh, God. She couldn't even finish the thought. All she could do was feel.

She reached up and cupped her hand to his face, smoothing the fingers of her right hand across his cheek, catching the single tear that had slipped free, soothing it from his skin before it could bleed down into the dark shadow covering his jaw. She sucked in her breath as he closed his eyes and turned his face into her palm. His lips were as warm and as smooth as they'd been in this very room twenty-four hours before.

Except now they trembled. He trembled. And it wasn't from passion.

Before she realized what she was doing, she'd already stretched up into him, the agonizing band on her own heart easing as he turned down into her, catching her own tears with his still-warm, still-smooth, still-trembling lips. And then they weren't. She didn't even flinch when his hands came up to frame the sides of her face, directly over her ears, as he tilted her head to gain instant, scorching access to her mouth. She simply answered his driving, needy kiss. His groan rasped through her, stoking the desire.

Within seconds she'd plowed her fingers into that glorious hair and used it to drag him closer. He groaned again, shifted again, sealing the length of her body to his—but then he froze. A split second later, he tore his mouth from hers, leaving her confused and bereft as he dug his fingers into her shoulders and shoved her to arm's length.

"No."

"But—"

"Dammit, I will not be a charity case. And I sure as hell won't be a pity f—"

"Don't! Don't you dare say it. Don't even *think* it." She knew he was hurting, but, by God, he was not going there. She sucked in a lungful of blistering air, using it to purge herself of the fury. "You're wrong. You are not and will never be a—"

"Oh, yeah? What am I supposed to believe? That you're in it for love? That you care? That you're hot for my body? Or are you looking for a baby to go along with the picket fence and the rest of that mythical forever-after crap. Sorry, can't help you there, either. Had a vasectomy when I was eighteen, compliments of the U.S. Army, just in case. Or maybe it's the photographic brain that turns you on? Well, I've got news for you, sweetheart. It won't last. None of it will. *I* won't last. Take my advice and get out now. While you've still got the chance.''

''No.''

He slammed his hands down on the desk. ''Jesus, woman! What is it with you? You think this is some kind of game? It's not. It's ugly and it sucks, but it's life. *My* life. And trust me when I tell you the first time you end up having to hold my hand so I can cross the street or wipe the drool off my chin—or, worse, wipe my goddamn naked ass—it's gonna get old. Very, very, old. Pretty soon, you'll wish to hell it was just plain over.'' He stood there, his arms locked over that desk, his shoulders still shaking with the rage of it. With the desolation and the shame, the fruitlessness. The guilt.

His mom.

She was certain when he finally broke his tortured gaze from hers and turned to sink onto the edge of the bed. The absolute resignation as he stared off at that shuttered window. Lost in the past. In the pain.

I got the memory from her.

She didn't need a geneticist to know Jared had gotten something else from his mother. From the file she'd read today, she knew he hadn't gotten a thing from the rest of his father's family until it was too late. He truly believed he was alone in this. Like his mom, he wouldn't have a spouse to share the coming burdens with, and unlike his mom, he wouldn't even have a child.

She ached for him. For the boy who'd dropped out of junior high so he could be there for his mother.

Thirteen. Nowhere near a man but no longer a boy, either.

Just a son. A son desperate to form enough memories for the both of them. Determined that at least *he* would remember. But in the end, he wouldn't even have that. And he sure as heck didn't believe that someone could love him enough to stick around and do the same for him, especially if she knew about the Alzheimer's going in.

He was wrong.

She hadn't even realized it herself until that moment. He might be pushing her away, hell, shoving her, but she wasn't going anywhere. Not without him. She was right to tell Jared about Sam, even though Sam would be furious with her. But she was also right not to tell Jared about her hearing aid.

Her ear.

Sure, she could pull it off. One quick twist of her wrist and she could prove to him that no one made it through life unscathed. But if she did, if she showed him what was really in that box—and what she was really like without it—would he believe she truly loved him for himself and not because she thought she was too flawed to get someone else?

She didn't have the answer. She could only hope she'd be able to figure it out before it was too late. Not for him. For them.

He finally pulled that dark amber gaze back to hers and sighed. "I meant what I said. I can't do it. I won't."

She didn't answer. She couldn't.

He wasn't ready for the truth, and she refused to lie. So she did the only thing she could. She turned and walked slowly to the door. There, she leaned down and scooped up her bag as well as the jacket she'd dropped on the floor. She laid the jacket on the desk and retrieved the micro computer data disk she'd secreted within her bag and flipped it to him.

He caught the tiny CD neatly. "What is it?"

"While you were poking through my bag today, I was in Orloff's office banging away on that wireless laptop we snuck in with us, poking through Greg Krazner's life."

Even as his brows rose, she noted the relief that had slipped into his eyes. Relief that she'd let it drop.

She had. For now.

"What did you find out?"

"You sure you wouldn't rather just read it?" They both knew it would be quicker in the long run.

Hope blossomed in her heart as he shook his head. Though he refused to say it—hell, though he'd refused *her*—it was obvious he didn't want her to leave him alone.

It was a start.

She turned slightly and leaned back against the edge of the desk, hoping to ease the tension in her body before she locked up for good. "I was right. The Greg Krazner I know is the same man DeBruzkya mentioned. Like me, he did his doctoral work in rocks—but it gets better. Not only does Greg have a Ph.D. in geology, that degree he picked up at Stanford?"

"Let me guess. Like you, chemistry."

"Bingo."

He dropped his stare to the disk in his hands and ran his fingertips around the edge of it.

"We share the same hobby, too."

His gaze shot up. "Lapidary?"

She nodded. Granted, cutting gems was a common hobby among geologists. Still, "He's supposed to be good."

"Like you."

She shrugged. "Depends on the stone. You have to work with what's there. I've been lucky."

"Anything else?"

"Yeah. His papers."

"Scientific papers?"

"I haven't had a chance to read them all. But judging from the titles, we share another interest. One a bit more unusual."

"Environmental causes?"

"Out-of-the-box chemistry."

He frowned.

She couldn't help it. He looked so bemused with her favorite chem prof's label, she grinned. "Greg and I tend to favor the rarer elements of the periodic table. The ones you don't see every day, if ever. I haven't been able to detect any specific patterns yet, pull out any common elements. I'll need to read the actual papers for that.''

He tossed the micro disk several inches into the air, then caught it. ''DeBruzkya steals gems from all over the globe for almost a year, his fascination with an old Rebelian legend regarding a specific gem, and now an interest in out-of-the-box chemistry? It's odd. Damned odd. It's beginning to sound like Karl was right.''

''He was—or is.''

Those brooding brows shot up. ''Which is it?''

''Both. I believe there *was* proof. Karl just never intended to show it to me. Not until they got me wherever it was they'd originally intended to take me.''

''Veisweimar, most likely.''

''Agreed. If we're lucky, we'll find out for sure tomorrow night. Or better yet, we'll find the ruby, itself.''

His fingers closed over the disk. ''Ruby? Karl didn't mention anything about a ruby. Are you telling me you finally remember the rest of that meeting?''

''No. I still have no idea what Karl was trying to tell me. He could have been trying to classify the stone for me at the last minute—warn me that it *was* a ruby. I don't know. Like you, I'm beginning to wonder if the blasted memory's not gone forever.'' The moment he tensed, it hit her.

What she'd said hit her.

Sweet Mercy. Talk about a faux pas. First the unintentional slam in the forest regarding his GED, and now this. Only this was much, much worse. As God was her witness, she'd been referring to his initial medical evaluation of *her*. She swallowed softly. ''Jared, I'm sorry. I did not mean that how it sounded, I swear—''

''I know.''

Silence locked in.

Just when she thought they'd never get past it, he slid over the key. "The ruby?"

She nodded slowly, gratefully. "Abel Braun. Before we discussed his wife's Alzheimer's, we discussed the stone. It's a ruby all right, and DeBruzkya has it."

"How can you be sure?"

"Because Abel found it."

Once again the silence returned. They both knew it had nothing to do with Abel or the ruby.

It had to do with them.

Jared dropped his stare and traced his fingers around the disk. "If we play this right, it could all be over tomorrow."

"I know."

"If that happens...*when* that happens..."

Her heart began to throb painfully as he trailed off. She ignored it, concentrated on praying, instead. He finally sighed heavily and dragged his gorgeous amber eyes up to hers. Only, the glow was gone now, snuffed out. Completely.

"Since you haven't discussed me with Sam, you probably don't know. I'm not in ARIES anymore. I'm no longer an agent. I've been out since that call." He shrugged. "I'd decided it wasn't worth the risk. But your uncle, he's a persistent man."

She actually managed a smile. "I know. I'm glad."

He nodded. "Me, too. But I'm also serious. The moment this mission is over, so is our partnership. When you and I leave Rebelia, I'll be leaving ARIES...and you. For good."

Chapter 11

"Ah...the hero of the hour."

Jared forced himself to step forward in the black leather shoes and tuxedo trousers Marty had been able to scrounge up on short notice, and clap his hand into DeBruzkya's fleshy palm. He even managed not to give in to the intense urge to shift his body exactly eighteen inches to the right, just far enough so the man's smarmy, speculative gaze would no longer be connecting with the woman on his arm.

"I am so pleased you could make it, Dr. Coleman."

"The pleasure is all mine, General." Or it would be. Sooner than later, too, if the Rebelian bastard didn't find somewhere else to fuse that stare. At the moment it was gleefully plunging down the V at the front of Alex's sea-green sheath. The one that reached damned near all the way down to her navel. When Alex had tried the clingy scrap of fabric on two hours ago at Orloff's house and discovered it was two sizes too small, she'd sworn vengeance on their mission's erstwhile Man Friday. Jared didn't bother adding that he'd taken one look at her when she stepped out of the guest room and decided to take Marty out himself. But for now, they were facing dinner across from those greedy eyes.

DeBruzkya finally managed to tear his gaze away. It shifted to the left, beyond Alex, to Roman Orloff and the intimate army of uniformed colonels, majors and pompous statesmen milling about behind them. "Ah, Dr. Orloff, it is good to see you, as well. In fact, my sister would like to see you later." The man finally included Jared in his gaze. "The both of you. She would like to thank you personally."

"She won't be attending the celebration?" Alex asked.

DeBruzkya seized the opportunity to turn back. To stare once more. "I am afraid not. She is tired tonight."

Jared kept a tight rein on his reflexes as DeBruzkya latched on to Alex's left bare arm and stepped out of the makeshift receiving line, doggedly drawing her with him.

"And how is Mikhail, General? Is he…staying here, too?"

"For the moment. I wanted him near. And since we have an excellent medical room within the castle, I thought the boy could convalesce along with my sister during these last months of her confinement." Jared clamped down on another wave of fury as those meaty fingers slid up Alex's arm. "And you, my dear. How are you feeling this evening? Perhaps you are feeling faint and need to lie down?"

"Not at all, General. Impending motherhood seems to suit me quite well."

"You have taken the necessary tests, then?"

"Just this morning."

Pity.

Though the man didn't say it, they all heard it. Just as they all knew Bruno DeBruzkya wouldn't wait around to rectify the situation should the desire strike him. But at least he'd relinquished Alex's arm. "I must see to my remaining guests. I shall return shortly. Perhaps we may take a walk after dinner and I will show you my castle, yes?"

"I'd like that."

Jared knew what she was doing.

He also knew it was necessary. If Orloff couldn't manage to create a distraction for them, Alex would be their backup plan. But that didn't mean he had to like it. And it sure as hell didn't mean he wasn't going to do everything—and he did mean everything—in his power to make sure Alex and DeBruzkya didn't spend sixty seconds alone together tonight, much less long enough for a private tour of the castle.

The buffoon's triple row of medals clattered as he took Alex's hand and bowed stiffly. Jared immediately stepped up as DeBruzkya stepped away, claiming Alex's arm before the general could change his mind. He shifted his gaze quickly to avoid her eyes as she turned to him to adjust the black tie on his tux. It was a mistake.

His gaze instinctively followed the exact same path DeBruzkya's had taken minutes earlier—and immediately discovered something new. That V didn't dip damned near to her navel, it dipped past it. At least from this angle.

He was going to kill Marty Lyons.

He tore his gaze away. "Let's get some air."

Her eyes widened. "So soon? You think it's wise?"

No. But he needed to clear his head. He shot a glance across half-a-dozen uniforms and caught Orloff's attention.

The neurosurgeon nodded discreetly.

"We're covered. Let's go."

He didn't give her a chance to argue, slipping his arm about her shoulders as they stepped under the stone archway leading to the massive French double doors and the second-floor balcony beyond. He glared at the set of camouflaged guards they passed, both armed with Romanian Kalashnikovs, daring either punk to stop them. The taller of the two read his mood and stepped aside.

Wise kid.

Jared shoved the doors open and nudged Alex through.

"You're drawing attention to us with that scowl," she murmured.

"Honey, that dress is drawing enough for both of us."

"Well, don't blame me. I didn't pick it out." She grimaced down into the V. "If I had, I sure as heck would have picked something a bit more flattering. It's not like I want the world knowing I haven't got enough topside to anchor a feather in a lazy breeze."

"Yeah, well, you know what they say." He reached the stone baluster and turned around just in time to watch those smooth honey brows arch.

"Really? What do they say?"

Mistake number two. He didn't even need the Alzheimer's to screw up tonight. He was doing beautifully on his own. He opted to bluster his way out. He didn't have much of a choice. "Hell, you posed as a guy. I'm sure you heard it."

"Heard what?"

He flushed. Fortunately it was dark but for the flickering wrought-iron sconces hanging from the castle wall. "Less than a handful's not enough, more is just a waste."

They both knew she fit in his hands perfectly. Absolutely perfectly.

She stepped forward, directly into his personal space.

"Don't—"

She smoothed her fingertips across his lips, pressed lightly. "Shh. Relax. Isn't that what you're always telling me?"

It was. But how could he relax with that dress six inches away? With her six inches away? With that soft green gaze growing softer before him? With those honey curls catching the unusually warm spring night and brushing lightly against her cheeks? With that endless, creamy neck—and that distinctly erotic mark he'd left behind. He stared down at it, mesmerized by it. By her.

Every man here knew how that mark had gotten there, DeBruzkya included. They'd all stared at it. All he wanted to do was cover it with his hands, smooth it away. Erase it.

And then lean down and give her another.

He closed his eyes and felt her fingers in his hair, slipping through the strands she'd asked him to leave free just before he'd dressed. "I did some extra research today."

He froze. Opened his eyes. "Extra?"

She nodded. "Care to know what I learned?"

Yes. No. God help him.

"I learned that early-onset simply means the disease manifests before age sixty-five. Your mother's onset was extreme. Not unheard of, but very extreme."

"She was my mother. My biological mother. I was tested specifically for early-onset. Late-onset doesn't carry markers, but early-onset does. I have them."

"I know. But that doesn't mean it's carved in stone. Not the timing, anyway, just the final result. You have your father's genes, as well. They may temper the rate."

"Don't you think I—"

Her finger found his lips again. "Shh. Someone might hear." He knew then why she'd chosen tonight. Here. He might have picked the spot for their mission's sake, but she'd had this balcony, this moment, in mind all day—for her personal agenda. It was the gate, the syringe, the jeans all over again. The woman was too damned clever for her own good. Definitely for his.

"As I was saying, the timing's not carved in stone. You could have twenty more years, perhaps even thirty. If things work out between us and *we* decide to make a go of it, we could have twenty years, even thirty. That's more than my mother and my father had. More than Sam and my aunt Rita. More than your mom and dad. More than a lot of people have."

Yeah, but what would the majority of those years be like? For her. "Alex, please…don't do this."

"Then you do something for me. Tell me, if your mom had it to do all over again, if she'd known before your father left for Vietnam that he'd never be coming home, would she have stopped loving him? Or would she have insisted on marrying him before he left, instead? With or without your grandfather's approval.''

He refused to answer, because he knew what it would be.

"Jared?" Her voice was so low he could barely hear it. He leaned forward instinctively.

"What?"

Her breath caressed his ear. "Have you considered that I might die first?"

He slammed his eyes shut against the thought. His mind and his heart followed. He would not consider that. He could not.

"I'm right and you know it. You of all men know what I do for a living. Even if I didn't, there are no guarantees in life. Absolutely none. So if I'm willing to run the risk, if I'm willing to take the chance, who are you to tell me no?"

He forced his eyes open, then his mouth.

But her fingers had returned to his lips. "Just think about it. Okay?"

He stood there, counting his heartbeats, running the first five volumes of the *Encyclopedia Britannica* though his brain as he tried *not* to think about it. He failed. He finally nodded. There wasn't anything else he could do. "I'll think about it."

"Thank you."

With that, she rose onto her tiptoes and kissed him. He sucked in his breath as her lips caressed his. As the tip of her tongue trailed lightly across his bottom lip, then dipped gently into the corner. It would have been so easy to shift his head, to pull away, to break it off. But he couldn't. He simply stood there and savored the slow, bittersweet taste of her mouth, knowing that given where they were tonight, what they were about to do, this was as far as it would go. In a way, it was all the sweeter for it.

It was over far too soon. She pulled away and slowly turned around.

Until then, he hadn't even realized Orloff was standing on the far side of the double doors, patiently waiting. At least, the man appeared to be waiting patiently. But from the way he'd loosened the side of his threadbare tie, as if accidentally, Jared knew, Orloff wasn't waiting patiently at all.

And it was time.

"You have the plans?"

"In my head."

Alex winced as Orloff stiffened. If a neurologist could react like that, God only knew what Jared had faced growing up with his mother. Fortunately Orloff was a good neurosurgeon, because he didn't say it.

Unfortunately he didn't say anything.

She stepped away from the balcony into the silence. Before it grew worse. "Jared is fine. He has a photographic memory." She refused to add anything else. Whether or not Orloff was helping them, whether or not he'd covered for her, that was all the man was going to get. "How long do we have?"

"Fifteen, twenty minutes. Perhaps longer."

She blinked. "What did you do, knock them all out?"

He shrugged. "I did not have to drug anyone. We were interrupted by one of DeBruzkya's men. There has been an emergency, a skirmish near the Delmonican border. A group of freedom fighters surprised DeBruzkya's men and have gained ground. DeBruzkya and the soldiers left, saying only they would return soon."

She swung her gaze to Jared's and caught his nod.

"Let's do it."

He was right. It was the best they could hope for.

She slipped her heels off and twisted the right three-inch wedge around and around until the heel unscrewed completely. She carefully removed the vial of sedatives from the compartment within, then twisted the left heel off to remove the miniature blowgun. By the time she'd finished reattaching both heels, Jared had retrieved the darts, his lock-pick kit and three of his ever-present throwing knives. The dart and picks had been in his heel compartments. Without his boots, she didn't want to know where he'd hidden those knives.

Orloff stepped up to the balcony doors and opened them, deftly obscuring the view as Jared vaulted over the side of the stone baluster, landing lightly on the slight rise in the lawn beneath. He held up his hands as she turned her back to Orloff, grunting softly as she dropped neatly to his arms.

"Sorry."

"I'm fine—and so's your dress. Let's go."

He didn't have to tell her twice. She shadowed him as he turned and led the way, slipping into the mature pine trees surrounding the castle, using the thick trunks to conceal their forward, zigzagging progress as they drew closer and closer to their objective—the outer door Jared had blown off its hinges the week before. Within minutes they were there.

As close as they could get, anyway.

Still a good twenty feet. And all of it wide-open, moonlit clearing. She raised her hands to her lips and cooed softly into the night, mimicking a very-early-rising mourning dove. Two soldiers, both armed, stepped into the clearing.

Dumb.

Jared rewarded each with a swift dart from the miniature blowgun, tipped in a quick-acting sedative compliments of Orloff.

The boys fell like bricks.

She and Jared raced forward. He snagged the Kalashnikovs while she removed the darts. He retrieved his kit and hunkered down in front of the lock of the brand-spanking-new door.

The seconds dragged out unmercifully, punctuated by the magnified scraps and clicks of metal against metal within her right ear as Jared continued to calmly work the lock.

"Hurry."

"I am." His words were little more than a murmur. "You want faster results, give me a stick of C-4 and a blasting cap."

"What I want is to not feel so bloody exposed."

His head came up, three inches from her naked navel and the inner curves of her braless breasts. A half smile crooked his lips. "I've got news for you, sweetheart. You are exposed. And this time I had nothing to do with it."

She smacked the back of his head as he returned to the lock. "Jerk." Three seconds later she caught the blessed click as the padlock's internal mechanism gave way and breathed out her relief. "Thank God."

He glanced at her in surprise.

Great. She probably should have waited until he'd actually opened the damn thing before she'd said something. Fortunately Jared didn't have time wait around and question her. He eased the door open and they were off again.

As before, he knew the route, so he took the lead.

Three more guards and three more knockout darts later, they arrived at the inner door Jared was supposed to have stopped at on the way out of the castle the week before, but hadn't in his quest to save her hide. She closed her eyes, blocking out the scuff of Jared's shoes, the magnified scrapes and clicks, as he hunkered down to work on this lock, too.

The room beyond the door was silent. Empty.

The mechanism gave way. He tucked his left hand inside the right cuff of his tux, deftly trading the pick for one of the deadlier pieces of his cutlery collection.

She nudged the razor-sharp knife back up his sleeve. "We're good to go."

"How can you possibly know—" Before he could finish, Alex twisted the knob and slipped inside, flipping on the light. "One of these days, you're going to have to explain that."

One day, she would. But not now. Right now, she gaped. They both gaped. Though they'd discussed this end of the operation in detail, neither of them had been sure what to expect. It sure as hell wasn't this. DeBruzkya wasn't merely filthy rich. The man was Midas incarnate.

A waist-high worktable had been set up along one side of the lab. A spectrometer, an electron microscope and gem scale flanked the sides of the black table. But the focal point was not the array of scientific equipment, but the large wooden chest in the center. It was filled with gems. Every blessed variety on the planet.

Diamonds, rubies, emeralds, sapphires, garnets, topaz, amethysts and every crystal formation in between. Fluorescent light from the ceiling reflected off the sparkling stones, igniting a thousand, miniature shimmering rainbows within the room. The jewels themselves ranged from less than a carat to more than fifty. The only thing each gem in the blinding cache had in common was that each and every one had been removed from its original gold, silver or platinum setting. She knew, because the skeletal rings, necklace pendants and brooch settings were still piled haphazardly within two open crates that'd been shoved beneath the table. Crates that also flanked a safe.

A completely closed and securely locked safe.

"Christ."

She glanced up.

"I don't do safes. Not without an explosive. Never quite got the hang of them."

She stepped forward. "Help me get it on the table."

"Why? You got a stethoscope in those ears, too?" But he stepped forward along with her, dragging the safe out from under the table and hefting it up on top by himself.

"Thanks." She tucked the loose curls behind her right ear and got straight to work. By the time she'd clicked through all three stages of the tumbler and jerked the lever up to swing the steel door open, his confusion had mutated into awe. She flushed. "I wear a hearing aid. It's... sensitive."

"I guess so. It also explains a lot."

She swung back to the safe, uncomfortable with the admiration within his eyes, amber eyes that glowed more fiercely and more beautifully than all the gems beside her combined. If he knew the rest, there was a good chance it wouldn't be there. He might not react as Don had, but she doubted he'd be thrilled. She could only pray he'd still be...interested.

"It's not here."

He was right. Other than the notebook resting on the bottom shelf, the molded bed of velvet on the upper shelf, the safe was completely empty. She snagged the book and flipped through several pages of heavy Delmonican scrawl.

Eureka! Her excitement must have shown.

"What is it?"

"These are Karl's notes. Records of several scientific tests he conducted on a particular ruby. I'll need time, but I should be able to translate them." The devil with time, what she really needed was a—

"Camera?" The man had gotten way too good at reading her mind.

She nodded. His crooked smiled hooked directly into her stomach as he held out his hand. She passed him the notebook and forced out her breath as she moved back to the door to stand guard. By the time she turned, he was flipping through the fifty-plus pages with a speed that completely floored her. He'd pause ever so slightly at each chemical formula and diagram, but other than that the scorching gaze never even slowed down.

That was when it hit her.

Hit, hell, the realization slammed into her so hard she nearly gasped. This was about more than losing his memory. Even about more than losing his mother. Like most loving sons, like most Alzheimer's patients themselves, Jared might have been able to come to terms with both those blows eventually, but to lose the very core of his identity? What then? Did he wonder if there would be anything left?

All this man had ever had that was truly his own was his brain. His insatiable thirst for knowledge. A thirst that not even a missing high-school and college education had been able to dampen. He'd just gone out and gotten it on his own. She didn't have to ask how deeply he'd delved into his local library's stacks growing up. She already knew it was deeper than she'd get in her entire lifetime.

But the same gift that had forged this man's rigid backbone and fierce pride had also set him up for thrice the blow. One he might decide he wouldn't recover from, despite her plea tonight.

"Done."

She blinked. "Already?"

He flushed. *Welcome to the freak show.*

What else had he been called growing up? She didn't want to know. She smiled softly, instead. "I'm right beside you."

And she was.

Between the two of them, they had the notebook back inside the safe, the safe securely tucked beneath the table, the light off and door locked behind them. Three still-slumbering guards later, and Jared was relocking the outer door, as well. The two outer guards were precisely where they'd been left, too, snuggled up beside the bushes. Given the peach fuzz on the jaws of all five soldiers, the young men would be too terrified to admit to DeBruzkya that some mythical intruder had either gotten the drop on them or they'd fallen asleep on watch. Soldier shortage notwithstanding, they had to know by now that to displease the general was to earn a one-way ticket to a cold, bugle-less funeral. She didn't argue when Jared grabbed her hand and spun her around, half dragging her with him as he headed for the trees.

She wasn't interested in a Rebelian funeral, either. Hers or his.

She was fairly confident they could avoid both, right up until they reached the base of the stone balcony. It wasn't the height of the granite wall that daunted her. She and Jared could scale those massive, uneven blocks blindfolded. It was the voices. Orloff's—and another man's. A man she didn't recognize. And not only were they speaking Rebelian, they were rounding the far side of the balcony—at ground level.

Jared caught the swift cock of Alex's head and knew something was wrong. Very wrong. "Someone's coming?"

"Yes."

Blast it to hell. They were almost *there*. He lowered his whisper to match hers. "How close?"

"Very."

There was only one solution then.

He pulled Alex close. He caught her swift gasp and swallowed it as he nudged the back of that clingy, shimmering sheath into the hewn stones behind her, a split second later he was forced to swallow his own gasp as he pressed right up against the sheath's nonexistent front. Right up against her. Harold Blaine's genius aside, he much preferred this warm, soft chest to that cold, rubber one. So did his body. His hands. So much so, the darn things actually quaked in anticipation as he dragged them up the side of that clingy sheath and delved them straight into the V, greedily cupping the curves beneath. He meant what he'd said.

An absolutely perfect handful.

The next gasp he consumed was low and husky and filled with enough raw passion to match the desire now raging through his body, as well as his mind and heart. By the time those voices rounded the corner, he couldn't be sure if the next gasp had come from Alex or himself. Either way, it did the trick.

The crude chuckle behind them confirmed it.

He didn't have to feign reluctance as he turned to face an older soldier he'd yet to meet, much less peg from the photo array that made up the agency's collection of De-Bruzkya's advisers. The man must indeed be important to the general's plans to have remained unphotographed by

Marty for five years. Judging from the Rebelian ranking insignia stitched to the ends of the man's camouflaged fatigues, he was a colonel. But did he have a voice?

"You must be Dr. Coleman."

Evidently so. And a piercing stare to go with it.

Jared stuck out his right hand, careful to keep Alex behind him as she finished restoring the precarious fit to that scrap of fabric Marty called a dress. "Jeff. It's a pleasure to meet you, Colonel…?"

Orloff stepped forward. "Sokolov. I just met the colonel myself ten minutes ago. Apparently the dastardly rebels have advanced farther than was originally reported. Colonel Sokolov and his men must leave to do what they do best. As must we."

Sokolov nodded. But that stare was still piercing. Still suspicious.

Orloff attempted to cover the moment with a knowing grin. "As you can see, Colonel, I was right. Dr. Coleman and his lovely wife, Alice, were merely enjoying an evening…walk."

The stare flicked past his left shoulder, to Alex. The suspicion finally ebbed. A thin smile replaced it. "So I see. And did you? Did you enjoy yourself, Frau Coleman?"

"I did, Colonel. The grounds are lovely. And it's very warm tonight." Even with Alex behind his back, Jared could feel the slow flush, the calculated, but seemingly natural awkwardness in her voice. But there was something else, too. Something he couldn't quite place.

But he couldn't risk turning around. In Rebelia, women were second-class citizens. With the colonel suspicious, it would only hurt both their covers to defer to her now.

Sokolov nodded, then promptly ignored her. "Dr. Orloff is right. The skirmish has—how do you say it?—gotten out of hand. And so, you must leave. The party is over. This way, please. The helicopter awaits." The colonel, however, didn't.

Orloff turned to follow Sokolov back around the corner

The Impossible Alliance

of the balcony, leaving him and Alex to bring up the rear. But when Jared turned and finally caught a glimpse of her face, he wasn't sure she could move, much less speak. It was as if she was frozen, trying to absorb a shock to her system. A damned powerful one, too. He was right, something was wrong.

"What is it?" He slipped his hand behind her neck and used his thumb to tilt her chin up. "Honey?"

Her shiver unnerved him. "Did you see the pockmark on his face? That's the man who killed Karl. The man who kidnapped me."

Chapter 12

She was dreaming again.

Jared lifted the laptop from his thighs, a moment from leaning over and setting it on the nightstand beside the bed in Orloff's guest room, when the tension locking Alex's limbs finally eased. His own tension eased as the furrow between her brows smoothed and her breathing evened out.

She was resting peacefully again.

He returned the computer to his thighs so he could finish. Finish, hell, he'd barely started. Two hours had passed and he'd entered all of thirteen pitiful pages onto the laptop's hard drive. Memorizing was easy. But typing? Now that was hard. Took too blasted long, too.

He hit the return key and settled back against the bed's headboard, determined to ignore the smooth curves splayed out beside him as he continued to tap out word after word in a language he didn't even understand onto the keys and then the screen. At first he'd been relieved when he'd noticed Alex succumbing to exhaustion. Knowing her soft, yet sharp gaze was taking in his every movement as he worked, that that bionic ear registered his every sound right down to his studied breaths, had been disconcerting, to say the least.

The moment the chopper had landed on top of the hospital's dilapidated helicopter pad, Orloff had been called away. Yes, Alex had been able to peg Sokolov as the man who struck her. But that was all. The lack of case-specific answers during the cab ride home had led to silence. To that question she'd asked him out on that balcony. *"If I'm willing to run the risk, if I'm willing to take the chance, who are you to tell me no?"*

But it was his right, wasn't it?

Dammit, two weeks ago he'd known exactly where he stood. Exactly what the grim reaper had in store for him and exactly how ugly it would get before it was all over. He'd even come to terms with it. Probably because he'd always known that this was how it was going to play out. Only now, he wasn't so sure.

Lord, was it tempting. Taunting.

Consuming.

Could she handle it? Would she? Or would she end up hating him at the end? That, he knew he couldn't handle.

Jared swallowed a sigh as he continued to peck at the keys. Three sentences later he stiffened. Because Alex had stiffened. And then she whimpered. The sound ripped into him. The hell with this. He dumped the laptop on the nightstand and then tugged the blanket he'd added to that clingy dress up to her chin, smoothing the honey curls from her temple. It didn't help. She whimpered again. Flinched.

"Alex?"

Her horrified gasp ripped though him as she bolted upright on the bed. He reached out automatically, pulling her close, steadying her. "Hey, it's me."

She blinked. The confusion cleared. But the anguish lingered. "Jared?"

"Yeah." He managed a half grin, hoping to ease the

remaining horror at what he was pretty sure she'd been reliving. Karl Weiss's death. "You gonna hit me?"

That worked. "Depends."

He notched a brow. "On what?"

"On you. You going to deserve it?"

Despite the moment—hell, despite the night—his grin spread. "Depends."

The horror faded. "That's what I—" She tensed as it slammed back in. "That's it! I remember now. All of it. I know what Karl was trying to tell me. Or at least, the part he managed to get out before that bastard slit his throat."

"What did he say?"

Something entwined within the pain had him wondering if he really wanted to know. "'Beware the enemy from within.' Karl was trying to tell me that someone within the agency sold me out. But who? I can list on one hand the number of agents who know about me, and they include you, Aiden and my uncle." She shoved the blanket to her waist and swung her legs to the opposite side of the bed. "I've got to e-mail Sam. He was right. Someone is after him. And Karl may have known who."

Someone was gunning for Samuel Hatch and had used Alex to pull it off? Jared grabbed her arm and hauled her back down to the mattress. "Try that again, and this time start from the beginning."

"Dammit, Jared, I don't have—"

"Please. And you do have time. Hours. While you were sleeping I e-mailed Sam a situation report regarding to-night. I received an automated response. Something's come up at his end. He didn't say what. Just that he'll be out of communications range for the next four hours. You can send an update then."

She finally sat, turned. He almost wished she hadn't. Alex had been so exhausted earlier, she'd fallen asleep without changing. And now he was staring straight into that V.

Samuel Hatch's niece. Christ, who'd have thought?

"What makes you think Karl wasn't just screwing with you from the grave? Hell, why connect it to Sam at all?"

"Because Sam has enemies."

Jared nodded. It wasn't exactly an earthshattering disclosure. After all, the man was the director of ARIES. You didn't get to that level and not rack up at least a dozen enemies along the way, whether or not their hatred was deserved. His thoughts must have shown.

She sighed. "I know. It's a normal agent fear. *Protect thy family.* Only, Sam learned firsthand it's not always possible. I'm not saying this is connected to Sam. Just that it's possible. Years ago my uncle had an affair with another agent by the name of Eugenie Williams—Agent Ethan Williams's aunt. It was before Sam married my aunt Rita. Anyway, a couple of years later Eugenie's family was targeted because she got too close to something. Sam never told me what it was. Only that he's always feared his family would be next—and that he's still after the guy who murdered Eugenie's family."

"That's why you created *Alexander* Morrow."

She nodded. "I got my first taste of ARIES in grad school. It came at a time when I really needed the distraction. Sam asked me to investigate a physics professor I knew on campus. He was suspected of passing scientific information to someone he had no business sharing it with. Aiden Swift had been assigned to the man, but even Aiden couldn't get close enough to take the professor down. That's when Sam brought me in—mainly because I was already *in.* He warned me up front it could blow up in my face. But he was also desperate. My own dad died in a training accident when I was two. He was a jet jock for the Navy. Maybe because I don't remember much about him, Sam's been more of a father to me than an uncle. I'd have done anything for him."

"You accepted the job."

She smiled. "By the time it was over, I was hooked. But when I told Sam I wanted in for the long haul, he freaked.

Refused to consider the idea. So Aiden decided to help and Alexander Morrow was born. By the time I made it through the interview—with my own unsuspecting uncle on the panel—Sam realized I was serious. He caved in, but under one condition. I had to keep the alternate identity. Naturally we've refined it over the years.''

"Naturally." Jared knew he should say something more, but he was reluctant. Maybe because once he did ask, she'd realize how very badly he wanted to know. He slid his gaze to the laptop and stared at the words he'd typed but couldn't understand, stunned that he could be so unnerved by the most basic question of all.

"Yes, it is."

He jerked his gaze back to hers.

She nodded. "My name really is Alex. Well, Alexis. Alexis Hatch Warner." She raised her hand and held it out. "It's been a pleasure getting to know you, Agent Sullivan."

He met her hand, folding those agile fingers in his as he nodded. "Jared. And trust me, the pleasure's been all mine."

She smiled softly. "I'm glad."

He sat there for a moment, enjoying the warmth. The connection. The knowledge. He retrieved his hand reluctantly and stared down at his now empty palm. He needed to think. "You may be right about the mole." The fact that Karl chose those specific words when he clearly understood they would be his last said a heck of a lot. But not enough.

"So, what now, partner?"

"We tell your uncle. But since we have the time, why don't I finish typing Karl's notes first? See if we can come up with something new to add to what we both already learned tonight."

She glanced at the laptop. "Mind if I take a look?"

Normally he hated anyone looking over his shoulder while he was spitting out information from his brain, but this was Alex. He leaned forward to snag the corner of the computer casing, pulling the laptop onto his thighs as they settled side by side against the cramped headboard. "You want me to keep going, or would you rather start from the beginning?"

"Keep going. From what little I saw, the notes appeared to be in chronological order. The first part should be mostly standard scientific housekeeping. Measurements, basic tests and the like. Then the hypotheses. Let's skip to the conclusions."

He picked up where he left off. She didn't say anything for a few minutes, then, "How *do* you do that?"

He shrugged…and kept typing.

"You have no idea what that says?"

"Nope. It's just a picture in my head. I just focus at the top of the frame and scroll down."

Several more moments past.

"Okay, I admit it. I'm jealous as hell."

"Don't be."

"Oh, *please.*"

He glanced up. "No, really. Trust me, there are *some* things you never want to see again."

"Name one."

He grinned, determined to keep it light. "Army-enlistment contracts, bills, Dear John letters." His grin faded before he could stop it. "Test results, death certificates."

"Oh."

Though it wasn't necessary, he jerked his stare to the computer and fused it to the screen as he forced his tiring fingers to pick up the pace.

Another minute passed.

Alex leaned forward. "What the—? No way. No blessed *way.*"

He jerked his gaze to hers. "What's wrong?"

"Scroll back a few pages."

"How many?"

She shook her head. "I don't know, three or four. To that huge column of numbers."

He knew exactly what she was referring to. Two and a half pages later, he ceased scrolling.

Confusion furrowed her brows. "This has to be a mistake."

He shrugged. "Could be, but it's not mine."

"Are you sure you haven't forgotten—" She killed the rest immediately. He shook his head before the flush finished slamming into her cheeks.

"Don't worry. I know what you meant. To answer your question, no. I can still see the pages clearly. If those numbers are wrong, the error's Karl's, not mine."

"Did the notes have a picture to go with them? A graph? Maybe even a diagram?"

"Several. Got 'em right here." He passed the laptop into her hands and reached for the spiral notebook he'd left on the nightstand. "I like to do the diagrams and pictures first. Reproducing them can be tricky." He shrugged as she flipped the cover open. "Use your imagination. I'm a lousy artist."

She chuckled as she turned the page. "It's all in the hands, partner. All in the hands." Another flush stole across her skin. He knew exactly what she was thinking. What she was remembering. Because he was remembering it, too.

Two nights ago. Her hands, on him.

Tonight. Beneath that balcony. His hands. On her.

They exhaled together.

She flipped the page—and cursed. "Oh my God."

"What?"

"Keep typing."

He took one look at the sheer terror blazing on her face and performed exactly as ordered. What the hell *was* he writing?

"We're in trouble. Big trouble."

He kept typing. "Why?"

She kept reading. "That second column of numbers you

typed a page back? Those are radioactive-decay rates for a little-known element called astatine. There's less than one gram of astatine on the planet."

"Out-of-the-box chemistry?"

She kept her gaze fused to the screen. "In its most incredible form. But in this case we've got a guy named Bruno DeBruzkya tossed into the mix."

"Hell."

"You got it." Her fingers bit into his arm. "Keep typing."

He did.

She grabbed his right biceps, digging her fingers into the cut that hadn't quite finished healing as she followed up the next page with an even darker curse. It took another page before her fingers loosened their grip. "You can stop for now."

"You sure?" Her hand might have fallen away, the overwhelming urgency faded from her eyes, but the new light burning within scared the ever-lovin' bejesus out of him.

"Yeah. Karl's just repeating experiments now. Verifying results. Remember that hokey-sounding ancient myth?"

"He who owns the stone owns the world?"

"That's the one. It is ancient, but it's not hokey. That stone—that ruby—is older than our entire planet, than our entire solar system. And all those mysterious deaths that were attributed to the jewel? They're not so mysterious anymore."

"Alex, what are you saying?"

"According to Karl's hypothesis, the original, uncut crystal was found several hundred years ago smack-dab in the middle of the Hartz forest. In a very large, still steaming crater."

"A meteorite?"

She nodded. "The crystal was inside it."

"Crystal? You mean the ruby?"

"It's not a ruby per se. Not given our frame of reference. It's more. The stone is comprised mostly of corundum—

aluminum oxide—and it does contain enough chromium that its color has got to be blood-red.''

He could hear the *but*. "You mentioned a radioactive element called astatine, something about there being less than a gram on the entire planet? Are you saying there's astatine in there, too?''

"Yes, but I was wrong about the amount. So is modern science. There's at least another gram in that stone. I also forgot to mention that astatine is the most radioactive element known to science. Our science. But there's something else besides the astatine in that crystal. Trace elements that don't match anything I've seen before. There's at least one new chemical element in that crystal, perhaps two. Karl wasn't sure and neither am I. I'd have to examine the stone. But I do know that the presence of those particular elements are allowing the astatine to bind with the chromium and corundum in unusual ways—very unusual ways. *Jared?*''

Something in the way she whispered his name drilled straight up his spine. "Yeah?''

"Do you know what a 'flash lamp pumped laser' is?''

He flipped through his memory, dragged the corresponding file to the fore. According to a spread *American Scientist* did five years ago, a flash lamp pumped laser was simply a laser that used ruby rods as its operating medium. But also according to the magazine, ruby lasers weren't very powerful.

Until now?

"Alex, are you saying what I think you're saying?''

"That depends on what you think I'm saying.''

"That this particular ruby, with that particular combination of extra elements, will be able to power one hell of a laser?''

She nodded slowly.

His air bled out. "But that's not what you were saying.''

She shook her head.

"Spell it out, sweetheart. You're out of my league.''

She took a deep breath and turned to the next page in

the spiral notebook. To the last diagram he'd sketched. She tapped the center with the tip of her finger. "A ruby laser fueled by rods made from this particular crystal will be powerful enough to take out satellites in outer space. General DeBruzkya will have his very own, very private, deadly effective star wars."

She closed the notebook and leaned back against the headboard, staring across the room.

The overhead light flickered as if on cue. Underscoring the sudden precariousness of their mission, of the entire blasted world order. A new world order. The likes of which had never been seen, much less contemplated before. Not by men with a conscience. With that much power at his disposal, Bruno DeBruzkya would see that the ancient legend come to pass. He would truly own the world. And then it hit Jared. What had already hit Alex.

Karl Weiss hadn't sold her out. The man had been hoping like hell his friend, his connection, would be able to figure out a way to get him and that gem out of Rebelia for good.

But there was more.

The relatively lax security at Veisweimar castle, Sokolov's willingness to kill Karl before the laser had even made it past the sketch stage in a scientist's notebook, the fact that Karl himself had supposedly lured her into the deadly trap and then tried to warn her with his very last breath.

"DeBruzkya doesn't know what he's really got, does he?"

Her eyes glistened as she shook her head. "Nope."

The notes were written in two different languages DeBruzkya and his thugs didn't speak. Delmonican and chemical. DeBruzkya's ignorance was easy to understand. Jared didn't speak the languages, either. But at the moment, the second scientist who'd been invited into that makeshift lab, however unwillingly and unknowingly—Alex is Hatch

Warner, aka Alex Morrow—was speaking a language he did understand. In fact, she was screaming it.

Silently.

The piercing agony of losing someone she'd truly cared about. The all-consuming fear of not knowing if that person had realized before it was too late that, in the end, she had understood. She had forgiven.

Jared closed the file he'd created and shut down the computer. When the screen went blank, he leaned forward and set the laptop on the nightstand. He carefully loosened the spiral notebook from Alex's pale arms, stopping to unhook the crimped end of the wire as it snagged at the V of the sea-green sheath still clinging to her curves. He ignored the brief glimpse of perfection itself as he dropped the notebook to the floor and leaned forward again, this time to smooth the tears from her cheeks. "It's okay, honey. He knows." Oh, God, those eyes.

"Does he?"

He tucked her curls behind her ears. "Sure he does. Karl was your friend, Alex. He knew you."

"No, he didn't. Karl didn't know me at all." Her shrug was almost helpless, the soft twist to her lips beyond sad as her shimmering, reddened stare met his square on. "Neither do you."

What on earth was she talking about? Of course he knew her. And she knew him. Better than anyone did. He didn't care how many days they'd spent together. She knew him better than Sam Hatch or his own mother had known him. But when she shook her head, the fear slipped in. The almost blinding panic. She had concealed something. But what?

"Alex…what are you trying to tell me?"

The fear locked in as the silence dragged out. Her throat began to work. He glanced down at her hands. She'd bunched the stretchy fabric into her hands so tightly, her knuckles were stark white against the green. He might be afraid, but she was absolutely terrified.

"Sweetheart?"

For some reason that seemed to help. She managed to draw a deep breath, even managed to loosen her fingers slightly. "I need to tell you some—" Another breath, this one achingly shallow. "Well, it's, ah, not something I can say. Or, well, something I seem to be able to say, so I'm…just going to show you. Okay?"

He forced himself to sit there. To not reach out and grab her and haul her close. To let her do whatever it was she seemed determined to do—while he prayed.

"Sure."

She sucked in another breath. Unlike her last, this one seemed to reach all the way to her toes. Then she slowly raised her hand. At the base of her neck, she skirted her hand to the side. There she reached up and fingered the lobe of her right ear. Funny, until that moment he hadn't realized they weren't pierced. He shoved the observation aside as her fingers lingered, as the terror in her hands finally locked into her eyes.

The hell with this. He reached out—

But her hand was gone, and…so was her ear.

Completely.

Cleanly.

The side of her face wasn't marred in any other way, or in any way at all. Her entire right ear was simply *gone*. It was as if the cartilage had been neatly trimmed down until its edge was almost flush with the smooth skin of her face. He dragged his gaze to hers as he struggled to absorb the sight.

The naked shock.

She simply shrugged. "Welcome to the real freak show. Front row, center seat."

Chapter 13

The second that word came out of her mouth, Jared snapped out of it. A millisecond after that, he realized what was really going on. Alex wasn't terrified. And she sure as hell wasn't waiting, calmly or otherwise. She was dying. And it was his silence that was killing her.

So he said the only thing he could. The truth.

"I want my money back." He anticipated her flinch, whipping his own hand up and grabbing hers before she could raise it again, before she could return what had to be Harold Blaine's most amazing masterpiece yet. He leaned close. Close enough so she couldn't escape. Close enough so there would be absolutely no mistake. "I want my money back because I don't see a freak."

She didn't say a word.

But the tears had returned. With a vengeance. His hands still locked to hers, he leaned forward, this time, smoothing the silent rivulets with his lips.

She stiffened. Almost imperceptibly, but it still tore through him, through his heart. Especially as she pulled away to slip her hand into the leather bag she'd tucked at the side of the bed before she'd fallen asleep earlier. The one he now knew why she never seemed to be far away from. It wasn't the bag. It was the gold vial she withdrew from within. That's what the adhesive he'd noticed when he'd located the manifest was for. What that box had been for.

Her on-again, off-again, on-again hypersensitive hearing made sense now. Perfect sense. Given just how powerful her hearing was, he'd lay odds the entire outer ear was a cleverly disguised microphone array. Harold Blaine was truly brilliant.

And Alex was absolutely beautiful.

He closed his hand over hers before she could open the vial and apply it. "It's not necessary. You don't have to wear it." While they were on the job, yes. But not here. Not now.

Not while they were alone.

"Yeah, I do." She shrugged. "Harold designed it for Sam—for me—when I was a kid. I've been wearing it so long I guess it's become a part of me." He waited for her to open the gold vial and apply the adhesive, then waited as she reattached the prosthetic and turned to slip the vial back in her bag. The moment she finished, he slipped his fingers into hers, knitting their hands securely, intimately. Then he leaned forward, closer than he had before.

"Alex?"

"Yes?"

"I want to become part of you, too."

He anticipated the smile, had even prayed for it. But not the impish gleam in her eye. "You sure I'm not just a charity—"

"Don't even say it."

Her smiled grew. "Good."

It was. And it was about to get better. He had no idea what tomorrow would bring and he refused to waste another second on what he knew lay beyond. Not tonight.

Tonight was for her and for him. For them. He smiled into her grin, determined to keep it light. At least one of them was going to walk away from this bed with one hell of a memory. He owed her that much.

He loved her even more.

"Wait right here. Don't move a single muscle."

Her smile broadened. "Okay."

"You moved." Jared rose from the bed and turned his back on that playful tongue sticking out at him. He'd get even soon enough. For now, he had a mission. And that mission started with a locked door—because nothing and no one, host included, would interrupt them this time. He pulled the bedroom door shut and threw the lock.

Loudly.

She laughed as he turned around. He tugged the shirt to his tuxedo out of his pants and released the remaining studs one by one as he returned to the bed. Alex mirrored his eager preparations, pushing the blanket off those long, gorgeous legs and swinging her bare feet to the floor.

"You moved again."

She shrugged. "Some men can't draw. I can't follow orders. Bad, bad agent." She disobeyed a third time, stretching as she stood, causing him to fumble the final stud on his shirt.

"Do that again."

"Do what?" She caught his stare and followed it to her own body, down to the exact spot that had captured his attention.

The V.

The edges of the dress had parted far enough during her stretch to expose nearly all of her left breast to his greedy gaze. Hell, he could see the base of her nipple as it puckered beneath his stare. He tried very hard not to groan—and failed.

She grinned. "I get it. I mean, most men are pretty visual. I managed to pick that up even before I became one myself. But something tells me that a man who can freeze-frame any sight he wants is probably a bit more sensitive to whatever's currently in front of the naked eye...."

He didn't respond. He couldn't. He swallowed another groan, instead.

The tempting witch knew exactly what she was talking about. And she definitely knew exactly what she was doing. He stood there, frozen, four feet from that bed, four feet from *her,* as Alex lifted her hands and hooked her fingers beneath the shoulders of that clingy fabric. His next groan tumbled out in perfect time with the excruciatingly slow peel that followed. Soon he was staring at the creamy upper curves of those amazing and achingly feminine breasts.

But there, she stopped.

He held his breath in anticipation as she pulled her hands away, waiting for the fabric to fall down on its own accord, nearly cursing in frustration as that blasted clingy fabric did what it did best. Clung. In all honesty, the dress might have ceded to his fervent desire if her nipples hadn't hardened beneath his gaze, thrusting up just enough to snag and hold the edge of the silky right *there.* He swallowed firmly.

"Like what you see?"

Oh, yeah.

She grinned. "Cat got your tongue?"

No, something else had latched on to it and refused to let go. But he still had command of his feet. He used it, closing the distance. Bringing his aching body, his aching palms within inches of that fabric and what puckered beneath.

She stepped back.

His hands shot out instinctively, closing about her arms before she could take another step. "Not so fast, sweetheart."

"I was just going to finish the show."

"I appreciate the consideration. Truly, I do." He lowered his mouth to her ear, the one he knew would be able to pick up the raw anticipation he couldn't quite keep from his voice. "But we're partners, honey. A team. And, as

someone once told me, partners work together. Now, I also
hope you enjoyed the show as much as I did, because it's
time to get ready for act two.'' He dipped his head lower
and bathed her lips with the red-hot desire burning through
him. That lush, bottom curve, the top, the intoxicating seam
in between, over and over until they finally parted on a
husky moan.

Still he waited.

He drew a lazy circle between her soft lips and her hard,
slick teeth. It was his turn to chuckle softly as she tangled
her fingers in his hair and used the strands to pull him close
and hold him there. He relented for a few sizzling seconds
and then withdrew again, sliding his mouth down the endless column of her throat until the heady, salty sheen drove
him back up. He nipped the throbbing pulse beneath her
jaw, then dragged his mouth down to the scarlet mark he'd
left behind two days before in this very room. He traced
the outer edge with the tip of his tongue, then soothed it
with the flat. By the time he returned to her lips, her shaky
breath mingled with his.

This time Alex didn't wait for him.

She invaded his mouth, sliding her tongue along the
length of his, enticing him into her own mouth on a dec-
adent promise.

He followed. Delving deeper and deeper, until he could
think of nothing but tearing off that damned dress and sinking onto the mattress behind them, sinking into her. Her
nimble fingers returned to the waist of his trousers and
deftly unhooked the catch. The soft rasp of his zipper
hauled him back to his senses. He closed his hands over
hers a split second before she tugged his pants down. ''Uh-
uh. It's still my turn.''

He pulled away just far enough to hook his fingers into
the sea-green fabric that was surprisingly still clinging to
the curves of her breasts. Then again, not so surprising.
There was more than enough to hold it there. He trailed his

fingertips across her skin, tracing the curves, mesmerized by the sight of her creamy skin against his darker skin.

"Hurry," she begged, "before I faint."

He chuckled. "Oh, darlin'. My memory's not so far gone I can't remember basic first aid. Then again, we should probably make sure." He stared at the shock in her eyes that he could joke about it. It amazed him, too. But not as much as his determination to live in the moment. He'd spent his whole blasted life dreading the future. Right now, he intended on glorying in the moment. In her.

He slid a finger across her bottom lip. "I vote we start here, with mouth-to-mouth." He dipped his head before she could argue and plundered at will, stealing her breath and giving it back within a slow, drugging kiss. He captured her hands as they inched back to his waist. "You know, I bet I can still take a pulse, too." He grazed his lips over her wrist, dampening the flesh, then drying it with a puff of air. He reveled in the shiver that spread up her arm as he bent his head again.

"Not bad," she conceded, her breath coming in soft and shallow.

Jared chuckled. She was definitely getting into the spirit of it. She was holding up remarkably well, too. His own restraint was dwindling rapidly. Careful to keep his gaze locked on hers, he trapped her hands behind her back with one hand and tugged one side of that annoyingly resilient fabric past her left breast, the other past her right. He released her arms just long enough to peel the fabric past her wrists, then trapped her hands again. "I still remember my pressure points, too." He peeled the fabric over her flat belly and trailed a finger across her inner thigh. "In fact, there's one right about here."

He made the mistake of looking at her body then, at all that long, lean, sinfully smooth flesh enhanced by a single wispy triangle of cloth. His first thought was that he'd have to kill Marty for even knowing it existed. His second was that he thoroughly approved. Mint-green and unadorned the panties shimmered in the light flickering from the ceiling, catching it and highlighting her curves, setting him aflame.

Unable to stop himself, he skimmed his palms over the silky mound. She arched into his hands, drawing him back to the game at hand. Anticipation fired his blood as he knelt before her. He slipped his fingers between her thighs, rasping them higher and higher until he reached her panties. She moaned as he dipped his head and latched onto the inner seam with his teeth, tugging it aside and branding a kiss in its place.

"How am I doing so far, Doc?"

Alex struggled for air as Jared grinned up at her. To hell with renewing his medic's certificate. If the man kept this pace up, she'd have to award him the whole damn medical degree. She took another shaky breath. "Your technique is truly amazing, *Dr.* Coleman."

Jared's grin was downright lecherous as he rose to his feet and trailed a finger from the hollow at the base of her neck to the valley between her breasts. "Oh, darlin', just wait'll you catch a glimpse of my bedside manner."

Liquid heat poured through her as he finally released her hands to slide both of his beneath her breasts, cradling them in his palms as if savoring their weight. Starting at the tops, he traced his fingers around the swells with incredible slowness. All the while she knew what he was doing. Knew that those amber eyes were taking picture after picture, freezing them, hoarding them in his brain so he could drag them out later. Finally, mercifully, his hands were underneath. He cupped her breasts again, this time pushing them up and together as he dipped his head. She sucked in her breath as he drew a line of wet fire back and forth between the tips, over and over until she was certain she was going insane.

She pressed herself into his mouth, silently pleading with him to fulfill the fantasy she'd been obsessed with since that night they'd first run into each other in her uncle's home. A shudder escaped her as he finally latched onto a nub and worried it between his teeth. Within seconds the fantasy had been seared away, allowing a magnificent, glorious reality to consume her.

She moaned. Unable to bear the sweet pain a moment longer, she reached out for his trousers again, determined to rip them from him in shreds if she had to. She peeled the zippered edges down, sucking in her breath as he sprang forth. His sharp inhalation echoed her own as she reached out and slid a finger down his thick, jutting shaft. Mesmerized, she drew it slowly up, savoring the hoarse catch in his breath as it grated through her right ear. The blunt tip jerked up as she caressed his smooth skin. She wanted— no, needed—to hold him in her hands, to squeeze him.

She gave in.

He captured her gaze then, and they both knew the time for teasing and gentleness had passed. Seconds after she grasped him, he sucked in his breath and jerked back to shuck his pants. A deep growl rumbled in his chest as he tossed them after her underwear. Two seconds later she was flat on her back, wrapped in his arms, reveling in the rock-hard muscle covering every inch of him as he pressed kiss after kiss on her mouth, her chin, her neck, her breasts and everywhere in between.

Desperate to finish her quest, she reached down between them and closed a hand around him, forging steel beneath her fingers as she slid them up and down his length. His hot breath and hoarse grunt carved out a hole in the pit of her stomach, causing her to clutch him tighter and quicken her pace. He grabbed her bottom and sealed her against him, rubbing his shaft over her, again and again. Just when she thought she was going to die from frustration, he reared up and cupped his hands beneath her bottom, parting her legs and tilting her hips just enough to receive him. A split second later he was deep inside her, buried farther than she'd ever thought possible, staring directly into her eyes as he touched her soul.

They gasped together.

And then he moved.

He shuddered as he bent over her, nipping and sucking her neck as his hips took up a grinding rhythm she prayed would never cease. Her own moans combined with his erotic suckling, fanning the fire between them until it burned even hotter and brighter. She grabbed on to the gold medallion jabbing into her breasts with one hand, clutching it as she dug the nails of her other into his massive arms, desperately trying to anchor herself to him as the blistering wave inside her gathered in strength, wrenching her along with it. Harder and harder, faster and tighter, he pummeled into her, swirling her senses together in a dizzying inferno of sound and touch until all that existed was Jared's ragged panting, his taut muscles and their driving hot, wet need. She climbed higher and higher as he chanted her name, pleading with her, until his hoarse, ''Please, Alex. Now!'' catapulted her over the edge, seconds before him.

They hung there together, suspended, for a few glorious moments, before she drifted back down into his arms—drained, secure and loved.

''Wow.'' His muffled voice tickled her neck.

Laughing softly, she tried to push at him, but he was too heavy and she was too exhausted.

He took the hint and slowly shoved himself to his elbows, brushing the unruly curls from her forehead and twisting them about his fingers. ''Go ahead and laugh, woman, you're not breathing so well yourself.'' He looped his arms beneath her, gathering her close as he rolled onto his back.

Alex propped herself on his chest and smoothed a palm over the sheen covering his dusky skin. He groaned, closing his eyes as she swirled her fingers around his nipples before fingering the medallion, wondering if the gold coin had left as many marks on her chest as she'd left on his. Not that Jared seemed to mind. His deep sigh echoed the contentment radiating through her as she twisted the chain about her fingers.

"You almost killed your partner, you know that?"

She tugged the chain as she leaned down and whispered in his ear, "That's okay, I know first aid, too."

"Darlin', I'm surprised you haven't been nominated for the Nobel prize."

She smiled, wondering if he knew that spent passion magnified his subtle drawl, much less what the result did to her still-pulsing insides. "You never know what'll happen now that I've found a research partner to work with. Though in all fairness, I should post notice for the position before I make my final decision."

His lips twisted wryly as he opened those gorgeous amber eyes. "Sweetheart, I'd kill any man who dared to apply."

The second the words came out, he regretted them. She could tell by the way the heat in his gaze immediately lost ten degrees. The way the air surrounding them cooled. Froze.

She waited for him to take them back.

He didn't. But he did reach up to smooth the damp wisps of hair from the side of her cheek. "I'm sorry. I had no right to make such a proprietary statement."

Yes, he did, dammit. Not only had she clearly given it to him, from the longing hovering at the outer edges of the amber, he desperately wanted it. But right now voicing it wouldn't solve anything. She concentrated on unraveling and withdrawing her fingers from the gold chain as she smiled. "No problem."

It helped. It did allow him to ease out from under her body and then up from the bed entirely. It even allowed him to snag the blanket that had fallen to the floor during their lovemaking and carefully cover her with that, instead. It even allowed him to turn and withdraw the pair of jeans he'd left folded inside the armoire and don them. But it didn't staunch the pain. In her, or in him.

She was certain when he retrieved the laptop and the spiral notebook. Especially when he faced her.

Oh, God, he was leaving.

"Do you, ah…have a plan?" She plowed ahead, desperate to get his attention back on the mission and off them, desperate to get him anywhere but out that door. "Veisweimar, DeBruzkya, the ruby. We have to go back. Tomorrow. We both know it. The only question left is how we're going to manage it."

He relented, at least for the moment, setting the laptop and notebook onto the mattress between them as he lowered his frame to the edge of what was now an extremely rumpled bed. A bed that also smelled of her and him.

Of them.

She forced herself to wrap the blanket above her breasts and tuck the ends beneath her arms as if nothing had happened, then scooted up to the headboard to brace her shoulders against it. Frankly, she needed the support. Especially when he met her gaze. How could he look at her and not look *at* her?

When his glance fled, however briefly, she saw through the illusion. Somehow, that made it worse. As did the slight, but unmistakable, strain in his voice when he spoke. "We'll need to find a way in that will buy us at least half an hour. My guess is the ruby is still in the lab. Remember the boxes stacked on the opposite side of the room from the gems and the safe?"

She forced herself to concentrate on his words. "Not really." She'd been too busy trying to locate the ruby amid all the other jewels. "Why, did you see something?"

"A metal box. Given the rest of the boxes surrounding it, I'd assumed it was just another crate for all that equipment."

"And now you don't?"

"This one was a dull, almost lifeless gray, scratched up in quite a few spots, a corner crushed in where it had obviously been dropped. The metal was definitely soft."

226   *The Impossible Alliance*

"Lead."

He nodded. "I think so."

"How big?"

"Roughly two and a half by three feet, another two deep."

She did a rough calculation in her head. Large enough to shield the next scientist from the radioactive decay within.

Thank you, Karl.

But how to get back in and get it? And how the hell did they get it out without DeBruzkya and his thugs figuring out what they were up to? A lead box that size would weigh roughly two hundred pounds. She slid her gaze down Jared's still-naked chest and arms, pushing the memory of how those arms had made her feel minutes earlier as she studied them analytically. He'd hefted the safe, yes. Her, too. But could how far could he carry an oversize slab of deadweight?

"Maybe Orloff can help us again?"

Jared nodded. "He did a good job with those darts. Didn't leave more than a drop of blood between them."

Blood?

She snapped her gaze back to Jared's arm. To the biceps that hadn't quite healed. To the one she'd tried hard not to grab when they— Stop! Don't think about it.

She voiced the solution instead. "Packed red blood cells."

"Mikhail."

Relief spread through her as they breathed the name, the connection, simultaneously. At least they were still in sync on something. For all his visits to the hospital, DeBruzkya had no idea which supplies were in current stock and which supplies weren't. No one had told him about the packed red blood cells. If they played this right, Orloff and Jared's blood supply would become their ticket back in to Veisweimar—and if necessary, the boy could become their ticket out.

"It could work."

"You know it will." She saw the regret biting into his gaze, felt it mirrored in herself. "Jared, we don't have a choice. Mikhail will be fine. He'll probably get a kick out of the helicopter ride. DeBruzkya won't even care enough to follow him." In the end they both knew it was a risk they had to take. If they failed and DeBruzkya succeeded, Mikhail's future would be grim indeed. At least this way, the boy had a chance.

"Agreed."

Silence filled the room. With the mission set, it seemed they'd run out of things to discuss. Things they could discuss, anyway. Unable to bear the tension any longer, she pulled the blanket tight and turned to scoot off the opposite side of the bed.

His hand snagged her arm, stopping her. "I don't want you to come."

She turned back, stared into those gorgeous eyes. The burning concern. The desperation.

"Jared, I—"

"Please. It's dangerous. There's a good chance we won't make it out."

She nodded. "I know."

"Is there…anything I can say to change your mind?"

"Is there anything I can say to change yours?"

They weren't talking about the mission anymore. He didn't pretend they were. She almost wished he had. Maybe then she wouldn't have gotten that agonizingly slow shake of his head.

"I thought not." She sucked up her pride. "I love you."

She'd have given anything to hear those three words come back to her, even whispered from his heart.

But she didn't.

Nor did he acknowledge hers. He stood, instead. "I…need to finish typing Karl's notes. I'll e-mail the file to Hatch, along with the information about the potential mole when I'm done. In the meantime, get some rest. I'll work downstairs so I won't disturb you.''

The distance already disturbed her and he hadn't even left yet. Unfortunately calling him on it wouldn't help.

Somehow she managed a nod. ''I'll be fine.''

But as Jared reached the door, unlocked and opened it, as he stepped through, relocking the knob just before he nudged the slab of wood shut once again, she knew. She wasn't fine.

Nor was she sure she ever would be again.

He was nervous.

At first Alex had chalked it up to her imagination. But when Jared had insisted on grilling her on the layout of the castle for the third time and then tried to force a blueprint he'd sketched on her she was certain. The one man her uncle swore never got nervous was definitely on edge.

And that terrified her.

Even now, with her hearing aid turned off because of the rhythmic thumping of the rotor blades atop this rickety bird, she swore she could hear the man's equally rhythmic, far too studied breathing. She glanced across the belly of the Vietnam-era Huey that DeBruzkya had claimed as his following the assassination of the Rebelian royal family years before. Like her, Orloff was beyond nervous. The good doctor was also pissed off.

For all their meticulous plans, DeBruzkya wouldn't even be home. Colonel Sokolov, either. Hell, DeBruzkya's sister hadn't even answered their phony, but frantic offer to double-check Mikhail's red blood cell count or their subsequent offer to transfuse the child on site if need be. It had taken a second phone call and a separate request to speak to the boy's natural grandmother, Helga, before the main guard had released the chopper. She was the one who would be standing by.

Maybe Jared was right. Maybe they shouldn't risk tangling the boy up in all this. She hated the idea that an innocent child could lose his life for their mission. Jared must have read her mind, because he reached out and squeezed her hand. Alex clamped down on her nerves as she stared into her lap. Until that moment, she hadn't realized how much she needed the strength of those big, dusky hands. How much she needed him. She met Jared's gaze as the pilot's thick German filled their headsets.

"Eine minute!" One minute.

She squeezed Jared's hand back, once again silently agreeing to the lie: everything would be fine.

She would be fine.

The minute reprieve was over much too quickly. The dense pines of the Hartz forest parted to reveal the massive granite walls and stone turrets in the rapidly closing distance. Soon the razor-sharp coils of concertina wire were in view, then the explosion of a million blinding, fractured rainbows as a blanket of embedded glass shards captured the glint of the early-morning sun. The Huey thumped onto the roof seconds later, and they were out.

Like the night before, she was two steps behind Jared, with Orloff two steps behind her, all three clenching the first-aid cases they'd packed thirty minutes before, though the majority of the supplies fell neatly within DeBruzkya's world, rather than that of emergency medicine.

"This way!"

They followed the guard's terse shout as well as his buddy's frantic wave, bypassing the southern facade of the castle and the direct vertical drop Jared had taken the week before to clamber down the winding stairs in the darkened corner turret. In the end it wouldn't matter. Both routes led to the makeshift hospital room in the basement—and that cache of priceless gems a corridor and a half away.

The guards were breathing heavier than her, Jared and Orloff combined when they reached the bottom step and exited the turret. Jared coughed loudly as they reached the first turn in the musty corridor beyond, distracting both guards long enough for her to slip her hand into her first-aid bag and turn on her hearing aid.

She blinked thrice as they reached the hospital cell. She could hear the boy, his grandmother and someone else inside. From the tenor of the voice, an older man.

She flicked her gaze to the left.

Jared returned her nod, his barely there whisper filling her ear. "I'll take the blonde and whoever's in the room."

She nodded again.

Seconds later, the first guard stepped into the room with Jared inches behind. The moment she heard the first knife clear his boot, she spun about, slamming the heel of her palm straight up into the second guard's nose. He grabbed at the shattered, bloody cartilage as he flailed backward. The exact moment his skull smashed into the granite wall behind him, Mikhail's grandmother let out a bloodcurdling scream from inside the room. Alex spun around again, leaving the dazed guard to the mercy of Orloff's needles as he hit the floor, vaulting into the room, instead, to back up her partner, her lover.

He didn't need it.

"Get his boots."

She grabbed the man's feet as Jared took the hairy arms. Together they dragged the inert body, complete with Jared's favorite knife protruding from his chest, the final two feet into the room so they could close the door. One of Jared's spare knives was lodged directly between a grizzled guard's wide-open eyes, two feet from the farthest gurney. The gurney she'd spent three weeks of her life on. A steady rivulet of blood flowed down the side of the man's whiskered face, soaking into the portable hospital curtain that had once shielded her view.

Helga appeared fine now. She still clutched Mikhail's body to her bosom, the boy's gauze-bound limbs clutching her neck and torso just as tightly. Orloff hurried in to assure the woman her grandson was fine. To their surprise, Helga became agitated when he admitted they wouldn't be taking the boy with them, after all.

"No, no, you take. You *take*. Please!"

Jared snagged her arm as Alex struggled to make out the frantic jumble of Rebelian that followed.

"What's wrong?"

"I don't know. I don't think Orloff knows, either. She's too hysterical." But something was wrong. The woman kept clutching the boy's head to her breast as she wailed over his head.

Jared ripped open his first-aid kit and pulled out the empty rucksack he'd stashed beneath the cover supplies before stooping down to retrieve both his knives. "You stay with Orloff, protect his back. At this rate, I'll grab the gem and be back before you figure what the hell she's saying."

She didn't like it, but he was right. They had an obligation to the three innocent bystanders they'd embroiled in their plans.

"Hurry." Before she realized what she was doing, she grabbed his arm, hard. *"Be careful."* Her heart lurched as he wasted precious seconds lifting his hand to her face.

He brushed her cheek. "I always am."

And then he was gone.

Orloff vaulted over the grizzled guard's body as the door closed. "We have to take them with us."

"Why?"

"Helga overheard DeBruzkya and Sokolov talking. It seems the general has already tired of fatherhood. Once DeBruzkya has reaped the benefits of his recent press coverage, they plan to murder the boy. They hope to gain even more sympathy by claiming a rebel soldier killed the child during a fabricated attempt on DeBruzkya's life."

Alex sucked in her breath. Given both men's track records, she didn't doubt they'd do it, too.

Orloff's brows shot up, underscoring her gut assessment. He didn't bother flicking his own gaze about the clammy hospital cell, the cell he, too, had been dumped in after his brutal beating.

"Let's go." She'd worry about the political fallout later, as well as the ass-chewing the director of the CIA would probably end up delivering personally. For now, she led the way down the hall to the cache of jewels as Orloff dragged Helga and her grandson behind them. Before they hit the first turn, she knew they were in trouble.

Boots. Running...toward them.

Before she could open her mouth to warn him, Jared stepped out from the doorway, the fully loaded rucksack already on his back. She could tell from his stride as he raced toward them that the box was lighter than they'd both expected. She could only hope the shielding was enough as she grabbed his arm. "Hurry!"

"What's wrong?"

"I hear several contacts coming around the corner, still silent—"

Jared slammed her into the wall in the nick of time. The spray of bullets chewed up the granite two feet from her head. Before she could raise her 9 mm, his MP-5 was up, his answering spray chipping the corner of the wall at the end of the corridor. Helga and Mikhail screamed as Orloff pushed them into the wall and covered their bodies with his own.

Jared slid the ruck from his shoulders and shoved it at her, helping her to don the straps before Alex could argue. She'd been wrong. The box was a hell of a lot heavier than it looked. She had to square her feet to stay standing. Jared tucked his 9 mm in her hands. "You may need the extra ammo. Take the gem and the others. Get them to the chopper. I'll hold them off as long as I can."

"What about—"

"I'll be right behind you." He slipped his hand behind her neck and pulled her close, sealing his lips to her right ear. Even with the hearing aid, she barely caught his murmured "I love you, too." Before she could blink, much less draw her next breath, he was gone, turning away to raise his MP-5. The blistering spray from the room broom afforded her enough cover to retrieve the others and advance down the hall.

She took it.

She had to. Jared's ammo supply wasn't endless. She refused to waste a single round of it. By the time they reached the turret, her back was screaming, but Orloff, the old woman and kid were holding their own. A damned good thing, because when two guards slammed out from the turret door four feet in front of them, they didn't freak out. She took down the first guard without thinking, but by the time she shifted the barrel of her 9 mm for the second, he was gone.

Lying at her feet.

Bemused, she met Orloff's stunned gaze as she shoved Helga and the child through the doorway of the turret.

"I shot him," he said flatly.

She grabbed Orloff's arm and pulled him in, as well. "You had to." Still, she knew what was going though his head. He was a doctor. He'd just killed a man with a—

She jerked her gaze to the still-smoking Colt .32.

"Where did you get that?" But she already knew.

"Your partner."

Jared had given the man his backup piece? But why? He'd already given her his 9 mm. Why cull his weapons to supplement theirs? Unless…the terror slammed in. *He'd told her he loved her.* Something he had no intention of ever doing. Why do it now? The dead weight on her back evaporated as she grabbed Orloff's arm and practically shoved him up against the moldy turret wall before she could stop herself. "Did he give you anything else?" Please God, not the knives. Anything but the knives.

"Yes. But it was earlier. Before we left."

What on earth was he talking about. "Before?"

Orloff nodded. "A gold coin. On a chain. He asked me to give it to you should this—"

She didn't wait for the rest. She spun around. "Take this, and get the hell out of here! Wait for us as long as you can. But if you have to go, then go. Contact the medical company I got the supplies from. They'll know what to do." She shoved her 9 mm into Helga's hands as Orloff adjusted the ruck onto his back, then ruffled Mikhail's hair, earning a quick, terrified peek from those huge brown eyes.

Jared was right. There were some memories you didn't need.

But she was keeping *him*.

Whether he wanted her to or not.

"Good luck." She shoved Jared's Colt back into Orloff's hands and vaulted out of the tower as he turned to urge Helga up the stairs. She didn't even hear the door slam behind her—she was too busy following the next spray of gunfire as the sound waves ricocheted down the corridor and straight up her spine.

She didn't need a blueprint to follow.

Her heart was doing just fine on its own—until she rounded the corner and her heart jammed up her throat.

Jared. He was trapped in front of the far wall, pinned in place by the barrels of no less than six Kalashnikovs. His expended MP-5 lay at his boots. Where the hell had all those soldiers come from? DeBruzkya, Sokolov—good God, had they come back?

If they had, she had no time to lose.

She only had three rounds left, but they would have to do. She waved her right hand and caught Jared's gaze. She held up three fingers, then pointed to herself, then to the right. He'd retrieved his first two knives. He should still have three. But would her gunfire distract the remaining three soldiers long enough for him to retrieve them?

There was only one way to find out.

She held up three fingers again, dropping them one by one as Jared tipped his chin ever so slightly.

Three, two, one. Now!

She picked off her quarry in rapid succession. The ex-

plosions in her ear prevented her from hearing the knives
leave his boots, but she did see the glints from the first two
blades as their victims fell atop the others, then a glint from
the third as Jared sliced his hand up and across the remaining soldier's throat, slitting it from end to end.

Only, that *wasn't* the final soldier.

For some bizarre reason she never even heard the shot.
Maybe because she was too busy screaming as her brain
registered the fact that although Jared turned, he couldn't
quite lift his arm far or fast enough to release his final blade
as he fell.

He'd been shot.

"No!"

Pure, blinding terror ripped through her as she raced
down the remaining nine feet of hallway to slam onto her
knees inches from that dark, gorgeous head. His amber gaze
glowed up at her as he smiled or, rather, as he tried.

"You're right, you don't follow orders."

"Shut up." She tore off her sweater, bunched it up into
the pocket of his right arm, directly over the raw, seeping
hole in his shirt. In his flesh. "Hold this." She shoved the
hem of her remaining T-shirt out of the way and reached
for her belt next, desperately hoping it would be long
enough to hold the sweater against his wound. She froze
as she caught the deliberate scuff of boots closing in. She
knew that pace. She'd heard it before—in a hotel room in
Holzberg.

"Sokolov."

Confusion tinged the pockmarked face above the rock-
steady hand holding a pistol, a Makarov she'd also seen
before, this time sans silencer. "I was right. You do seem
to know me. How?"

"You murdered a friend of mine."

The confusion actually ebbed. "Hmm. It's possible. But
I confess, I have killed many men. Who was your friend?"

Why not? It just might give her the distraction she
needed.

"Alice, don't—"

"I said shut up." She ignored the thick brown brows that shot up as she yelled at her "husband." She ignored her husband's hand, as well. The one that was crushing the feeling from her own as he silently ordered her to look down and meet his gaze.

Why? She'd just have to ignore that, too.

"Karl Weiss."

Sokolov blinked. Unfortunately the hold on his Makarov also tightened. But then he smiled. Chuckled. "You must be mistaken. I had him watched. Karl had no friends who looked like you."

"Alice."

Despite the fact that the warning in his voice had weakened, that the grip on her hand had weakened, she smiled. "I went by another name at the time. Perhaps you remember it—and me. Morrow. Dr. Alexander Morrow."

Another blink, this one rife with disbelief. "What? You lie. I met Dr. Morrow. We stood as close as you and I stand now. As close as you and I stood last night. He was a man."

"You mean, he didn't have these?" She whipped her T-shirt straight up, offering the murdering doubting Thomas an eyeful.

It was the last thing Sokolov ever saw.

She flinched as the blade speared the colonel directly between the eyes. Like the grizzled soldier in the hospital cell, Sokolov never had a chance. By the time she spun around, Jared had staggered halfway to his feet. She scooped up two of the Kalashnikovs and hooked her shoulder under his left arm, leaving him to hold her sweater against the pocket of his right as they made their way down the hall at a modified, shuffle-run.

"Told you I'd have to kill the man who tried that."

"The hell you did. You didn't intend on coming back at all, you jerk. I should kill you myself. Now shut up and save your strength. You're bleeding all over the damned place.'' But most of her fury evaporated as his exhausted grunt filled her ear. By the time they reached the base of the turret, she was beyond worried. Full-fledged panic set in at the top. He could barely move as they reached the door. She dragged him out onto the roof. Orloff was there and, miraculously, the idling chopper was still standing by.

Then again, it wasn't so miraculous, after all.

It was a sixty-five-year-old grandmother named Helga with a 9 mm pistol crammed up against a Rebelian Army pilot's skull. From the steely glint in those faded gray eyes, even Alex wouldn't have messed with her. The old woman shouted something and the blades began to rotate. Within seconds the vibrations were pounding though her skull.

Unfortunately her remote was down in the dungeon.

There was no way in hell she was going back for it. She managed to help Orloff heft Jared into the belly of the bird and scramble in after them as the chopper took off. Alex tore though the remaining medical supplies they'd packed to make their cover look good. She laid them out for Orloff as he worked.

''There is no pain medication. Hold his hand.''

She knew then that she was in trouble. Her eyes were watering so badly from the agonizing noise she couldn't find Jared's chest, much less his hand. *The hell with it.* She tore off her ear and shoved it into her pocket.

Orloff didn't bat an eye.

And Jared was too far gone trying not to crush her hand as the doctor rooted around on the inside of the pocket of his shoulder with a pair of forceps.

''Christ.''

She leaned down, smoothed the hair from his face as she laid her cheek to his so she could talk directly into his ear. It was the only way she could beat the blades. ''It's okay. It'll be over soon. Just don't bleed to death on me, okay?''

''Depends.''

''On what?''

''On you. You gonna hit me?''

Damn him. She couldn't help it, she smiled. "Probably."
"Alex, I—"

"You are a class-A bastard, Jared Sullivan. And don't
even try to worm your way out, much less lie to me. You
might not have set out to kill yourself, but the thought sure
as hell crossed your mind that if you had to sacrifice yourself, it would all be over. You wouldn't have to face the
next twenty years. You wouldn't have to face me. You're
a coward, you know that?"

"Done." Orloff sat back. "And...I believe we have
landed."

They both ignored him.

She continued to stare into that dark, amber gaze that—
praise God—was still glowing with life as the chopper
powered down. Through no fault of his own. She waited
as Orloff retrieved the boy from the webbed seat at the rear
of the chopper where he and Helga had evidently stashed
him and then bailed out to link up with the grandmother,
as well as head off Marty Lyons and his men as they converged on the bird.

She stared down at Jared. "Well?"

Nothing.

"Damn you, Jared. I want my twenty years!"

Again, nothing.

She finally sighed. It was useless. He'd never give in.
She was about to remove her hand from his and straighten
when his fingers bit down harder than they did when Orloff
had been rooting around inside for the bullet. She gasped.

"What if I don't have twenty years before it gets bad?
What then? What if I only have ten or five? What if I have
one?"

She leaned in close, staring directly into those gorgeous
eyes. "*I'll take it.* And every other damned day I can get.
Don't you understand, you dense, boorish oaf? I'm not
leaving you. I don't care if I have to camp out on the front
lawn of that blasted Texas ranch for the rest of my life.
You're stuck with me."

"Alex—"

"Don't. Don't say a word unless you're ready to say what I want to hear. What I need to hear. So the ear doesn't bother you. Whoopee. You know what? I've learned these past few days that it just doesn't matter. I don't care if I have to walk around lopsided for the rest of my life. What I need to know is if I had something else—for example, if *I* had early-onset Alzheimer's—would you be able to walk away from me?"

The blades had finally stilled. She didn't need her missing hearing aid to know that Jared's breath was searing into his lungs. She could feel it. "Well? Are you going to answer me?"

"No."

She stiffened. "No?"

He shook his head slowly. "No. I couldn't abandon the woman I love any more than I was able to leave my mom." Her breath caught as his hands cupped her face and drew her closer, right down onto the floor of that blasted metal bird.

She didn't care.

"So...I guess what I'm saying is, you're stuck with me, Alex. For as long as you want me, for as long as we have." Her eyes began watering as he pulled her the rest of the way down to his kiss. But this time it wasn't the thunder in her ear that caused the tears, it was the thunder in her heart. Because she knew, as long as she had with this man, it would never be enough. But she'd take it.

Epilogue

Everything had gone exactly according to plan.

He hated that.

Something always went wrong. Hell, that was why the Army created fragmentary orders, so that once an operation commenced—and the Op Plan went promptly to hell— everyone had something to base the new, ever-changing plan on. But nothing had gone wrong today. Which, of course, meant they were in for a doozy.

"Relax. It's a wedding, not a mission."

"I am relaxed."

Jared ignored the disbelief in those soft green eyes as his wife slipped one of her amazingly agile hands in his. The left one. The one he'd slipped that antique ruby wedding band on for the second time—in front of 150 of their closest friends, relatives, neighbors and fellow agents. Well, mostly Alex's friends and relatives. Though surprisingly, quite a few agents he'd worked with over the past decade had shown up, as well.

"I know it's a wedding. I was there, remember?"

She took the teasing in stride. Though she wasn't fond of the jokes about his condition, she seemed to understand that he needed it. He still wasn't sure why. Maybe because he was still worried she'd have enough one day and walk away. But for now, the insidious fear ebbed as she tiptoed up into his arms, her fingers sliding about the collar of his tux to tangle in the hair she'd once again insisted he leave loose. He took the hint and slid his own hands down the lush curves currently encased in a body-hugging ivory sheath.

A sheath he couldn't wait to peel off.

He dipped his head and trailed his lips down the endless column of her neck, nipped the hollow at the base, then kissed his way back up. He lingered beneath her right ear, pouring out his suggestion at a thrumming volume meant for her only, even if they were alone in the foyer. "Let's go upstairs."

"We have guests. Lots of guests."

He sighed. "I know. Let them find their own beds."

She chuckled softly. "I think that's your job. You're the host." She matched his sigh. "But since I'm now married to the host, I suppose it's my job, too." She slipped out of his arms far too easily. "I'd like to greet our guests. Are you coming with me…or should I interview for another escort?"

They both already knew the answer to that one.

Hell, the whole blessed town of Greenlaurel knew. They'd all heard him in that church. Alex might put up with his references to the darker future that awaited them, but she was determined not to let him live in the past—much less, as she put it, in limbo. He still couldn't believe she'd gone to the blue-haired mavens of Greenlaurel the day after they'd returned from Rebelia with an offer. If The Belles of Texas Historical Society helped her put on the wedding of a lifetime in just three short weeks, Jared would foot the bill for the entire upcoming Bluebonnet Ball.

The Belles had been thrilled.

As for him, it had been worth it to see Alex smile.

He shoved the double doors open and shook his head at the massive tents for food, dancing and just plain mingling that had been erected out on his lawn beyond the circular drive. Every blessed one of them was full of smiling, laughing people, too. As operations went, he had a feeling The Belles could teach the Army, as well as ARIES, a thing or two. He gave in to the spirit of things, sliding his arm around his wife's bare shoulders as he guided her down the front steps.

As they reached the outer throng, damned near every adult they passed was still either talking about the town's upcoming Bluebonnet Ball or the World Bank Heist that had been pulled off days before.

"I read in the *Post* they stole fifty million dollars!"

"Well, I heard just this morning on CNN that they may have taken more than 150 million."

He steered Alex away from that particular group.

While personally he suspected neither figure came close to the dent the cyberthieves had placed in the World Bank's monetary reserves, he wasn't interested in tossing Alex into the middle of the discussion. She'd end up there soon enough. Several ARIES agents were already on the case. He just hoped to hell Alex wouldn't be added to the list until after the honeymoon. He still wasn't sure how he'd feel the next time she was called up. Or worse, how he'd feel if she refused.

Though with her cover blown and the knowledge out within the agency that the section director was her uncle, she was contemplating moving into another line of work, anyway. Or so she said. He just hoped to hell she wouldn't end up regretting it.

Or him.

"Jared? Are you okay?"

The moment he glanced down into that sea of green, he was.

"I'm fine." He tugged her close and pressed a kiss to

the honey curls at her temple, then nodded to their left. "Look, there's the private eye I told you about."

Jared returned Kurt Miller's wave, despite the fact the SOB was ultimately responsible for this entire swollen gathering. If the bloodhound hadn't tracked him down after his grandfather's death, he'd be holed up with Alex in a quiet hotel room somewhere right now on a bed, instead of dodging more wedding guests than a man should ever be cursed with—a hard, cramped bed that wouldn't allow him and his recovering arm nearly enough freedom to show his wife how much he loved her on their wedding night. The oversize bed Alex had delivered just yesterday, the one they'd yet to baptize, flashed before his mind's eye.

What the hell, maybe he'd thank Kurt, instead.

"Aiden!"

Jared took one look at the man five bodies to the right of Kurt and grinned, despite the fact that he promptly lost his bride. Alex rushed out of his arms to throw hers around her former mentor. A few inches taller than Alex, Aiden managed to get her feet to clear the ground as he spun her around in a hug.

Aiden grinned as he released her long enough to stick out his hand. "Sorry, buddy. I know she's yours, but it's not every day a gorgeous lady throws herself into these old arms."

Alex clipped his jaw. "Forty is *not* old. And if you can't get a date, you're not looking in the right spot, much less looking at all. Come to the Bluebonnet Ball next Saturday. I'm sure the local Belles can set you up."

Jared mimed slitting his throat.

That earned a deep chuckle from Aiden. Unfortunately Jared also earned his bride's renewed attention as she spun around. He dropped his hand in the nick of time. At least, he thought he had—until Alex smiled sweetly. Too sweetly.

"Just for that, we'll be going, too."

Aiden's chuckle died. "Wait a minute. I didn't do anything. How come I gotta go?"

The moment the gleam entered her eyes, Jared knew Aiden was doomed. Especially when Alex tsked softly. "You're right. You didn't do anything. The best man at the wedding and you didn't even bring a gift. I'd say that means you owe me one." She smiled as the noose tightened. "See you there, Aiden."

"Sorry, buddy."

"Yeah, right, *buddy*. See if I don't tell her now about that time in Tanzania when you and I—"

Jared swung his arm about Alex's shoulders before Aiden could finish and spun her around. He didn't need that story coming out. Not with his wedding night ahead and a bed he dearly hoped to be sleeping in and not beneath. Undaunted—and laughing—she simply stared up at him.

"Tanzania, huh?"

"Look, I see Sam."

She refused to bite.

A split second later, he *did* see Sam—and the man was headed straight for them. With an envelope in hand. A manila envelope large enough to contain new orders. A mission overview. Dammit. Couldn't he at least get in a honeymoon with the woman before she was torn from him?

"What's wrong?" But she was already following his gaze. "Sam!" He lost his bride for the second time, to the only other man he didn't mind losing her to. As long as she came back.

She did, her uncle in tow.

Old habits must die hard indeed, because Jared automatically eased the three of them from the crowd. "Good to see you, sir."

"Sir, my ass. It's Sam. Say it."

He nodded. "Sam."

"Good job, son." Hatch held out the envelope. "Here's your reward, hot off the fax machine."

He stared at the envelope.

"Go ahead. Take it."

"Sir—*Sam*—I'm out. You know that."

"It's not a mission brief."

Then what the devil was it? It sure as hell wasn't a wedding present. The his-and-hers Thoroughbreds were already stashed in one of the barns. And what the hell was it with that tone? He'd never seen Sam Hatch so guarded.

Jared glanced at his bride. "Alex, you read it."

"Are you sure?"

"Yeah." If he was getting another load of crappy news, he'd rather it came from her.

Alex had either picked up on her uncle's vibes or his, because she took it, though reluctantly. She whittled a year off what time he had left slowly breaking the seal on the envelope and carefully withdrawing the plain paper fax from within. Her brow furrowed as she skimmed the contents. He watched her gaze stop, shoot back to the top of the fax and begin again. By the time she finished, tears were rolling freely down her cheeks and he was damned near dead.

"What?" His voice was hoarse.

But so was hers. "Read it."

"Alex—"

"*Read it.* I want you to see the words. Forever."

Determined to get it over with, he took the sheet and ripped his gaze down the form...the medical form? Lab work? He didn't have any outstanding lab work. But the form was his. Like Alex, he shifted his gaze to the top and stared at the header block. Early Onset Alzheimer's Results.

Negative.

His gaze blurred. He blinked to clear it, but he couldn't. Worse, for the first time in his life, he couldn't pull the picture in front of his mind's eye just by thinking about it. He was dimly aware of Alex retrieving the paper and reaching up to slide her arms about his neck. Then her lips were merging with his, right along with their tears. He finally managed to drag his mouth to her ear. "Did I just read what I think I read?"

She pulled away slightly and nodded, and then all he saw was her blinding smile. But he heard Sam's cough.

They turned together.

"Sir…I…don't understand."

His old mentor shook his balding head. "Sam. And neither did I at first. But when Alex mentioned Karl Weiss's claim regarding a mole, I started to sift through some old information. Old suspicions. I also questioned Janice Errington at length. Yours wasn't the only genetics record Janice was ordered to falsify. If the man I suspect of murdering Eugenie William's family is involved, it even makes sense.

"*Who?*" He and Alex practically shouted in unison.

Hatch merely shook his head. "You're both too close. You have too much to lose. And I…I don't have enough proof. Not yet. Just the rambling of an old man. Or so I've been told."

"That's a load of bull."

"I know, son, I know. But it's the way it has to be for now. Promise me, both of you. You can't even confront Janice. She never met the man who blackmailed her. To expose her could ruin my one chance at nailing this bastard for crimes far, far worse than this. Agreed?" The sharp green gaze that resembled Alex's more than he'd ever realized stabbed her first, then him.

He looked at his wife and waited.

She finally nodded.

He turned to Hatch. "Agreed…and thank you."

Jared swore his old mentor's were watering, too. He was certain of it when the man nodded and turned abruptly, mumbling something about wedding cake as he strode off. Jared turned to his wife and gathered her close, wondering how the hell he could ask what he desperately wanted to ask.

He had no right.

"Don't worry. I'm already out of the business."

He stiffened.

She, however, laughed. "Oh, don't tell me you weren't thinking about it."

"I won't."

"Good." The sun caressed her shoulders as she snagged his hand to lead him between the tents and back toward the front steps to that once-cold mausoleum that was growing warmer and brighter by the minute. By some miracle, not a single soul stopped them.

"Alex, are you sure?"

She nodded. "It was supposed to be a wedding present for you and me. I was going to tell you tonight." She smiled. "And, no, knowing I'm going to be stuck with you for the next sixty years, instead of twenty, doesn't change anything." Her smile ebbed as she stopped at the top of the steps and glanced down on a sight he apparently wouldn't be forgetting, after all. "But, Jared, it does change one thing."

"What?" Damned if his voice hadn't grown hoarse again. This time with fear.

"I want kids."

Kids? But—he'd had a vasectomy. He wouldn't reverse it even if he could. He might not have Early-onset Alzheimer's, but it was still genetic. He still carried the gene.

"I know."

Something in her voice made him follow her gaze. To a little boy in a fancy, new high-tech wheelchair Sam had sent, along with the horses. The boy's grandmother, Helga, stood beside the wheelchair, along with Sam. The boy's new "Uncle Roman" knelt to show him how to work the controls. Alex was right. Orloff would be leaving to work in the refugee camps soon. Helga and Mikhail would need a home.

Mikhail would need a mother and a father.

Damned if his eyes didn't begin watering once more as he stepped behind his wife and drew her into his arms. Piercing joy and humbling relief burned through him as they gazed down together on another scene he never wanted to forget. Though he could now see the form in his mind, he still couldn't quite believe it. To know that he would be able to hold the memory of this perfect day, this perfect moment, this perfect woman, in his mind for the rest of his life was almost too much to grasp.

Until his wife turned in his arms.

"Hey, Soldier, I hear there's a virgin bed upstairs. Want to help me make a memory to last a lifetime?"

Everything inside him burst into his grin as he pulled his wife close. As close as he had on that bed three weeks before in Roman Orloff's house. Close enough so she couldn't escape. Close enough so there would be absolutely no mistake. "You bet I do."

And they did.

* * * * *

There are more secrets to uncover!
Look for
BROKEN SILENCE,

Three brand-new stories by reader favorites
Maggie Shayne, Eileen Wilks
and Anne Marie Winston

Coming in May 2002 to Silhouette Books

If you enjoyed what you just read,
then we've got an offer you can't resist!

Take 2 bestselling love stories FREE!

Plus get a FREE surprise gift!

Clip this page and mail it to Silhouette Reader Service™

IN U.S.A.
3010 Walden Ave.
P.O. Box 1867
Buffalo, N.Y. 14240-1867

IN CANADA
P.O. Box 609
Fort Erie, Ontario
L2A 5X3

YES! Please send me 2 free Silhouette Intimate Moments® novels and my free surprise gift. After receiving them, if I don't wish to receive anymore, I can return the shipping statement marked cancel. If I don't cancel, I will receive 6 brand-new novels every month, before they're available in stores! In the U.S.A., bill me at the bargain price of $3.99 plus 25¢ shipping and handling per book and applicable sales tax, if any*. In Canada, bill me at the bargain price of $4.74 plus 25¢ shipping and handling per book and applicable taxes**. That's the complete price and a savings of at least 10% off the cover prices—what a great deal! I understand that accepting the 2 free books and gift places me under no obligation ever to buy any books. I can always return a shipment and cancel at any time. Even if I never buy another book from Silhouette, the 2 free books and gift are mine to keep forever.

245 SDN DNUV
345 SDN DNUW

Name	(PLEASE PRINT)	
Address	Apt.#	
City	State/Prov.	Zip/Postal Code

* Terms and prices subject to change without notice. Sales tax applicable in N.Y.
** Canadian residents will be charged applicable provincial taxes and GST.
All orders subject to approval. Offer limited to one per household and not valid to current Silhouette Intimate Moments® subscribers.
® are registered trademarks of Harlequin Books S.A., used under license.

INMOM02   ©1998 Harlequin Enterprises Limited

**Don't miss the latest miniseries from
award-winning author Marie Ferrarella:**

Meet...

Sherry Campbell—ambitious newswoman who makes
headlines when a handsome billionaire arrives to sweep
her off her feet...and shepherd her new son into the world!
**A BILLIONAIRE AND A BABY, SE#1528,
available March 2003**

Joanna Prescott—Nine months after her visit to the
sperm bank, her old love rescues her from a burning
house—then delivers her baby....
**A BACHELOR AND A BABY, SD#1503,
available April 2003**

Chris "C.J." Jones—FBI agent, expectant mother and
always on the case. When the baby comes, will her
irresistible partner be by her side?
THE BABY MISSION, IM#1220, available May 2003

Lori O'Neill—A forbidden attraction blows down this
pregnant Lamaze teacher's tough-woman facade and
makes her consider the love of a lifetime!
**BEAUTY AND THE BABY, SR#1668,
available June 2003**

**The Mom Squad—these single mothers-to-be are
ready for labor...and true love!**

Silhouette®

COMING NEXT MONTH